EVERY GOOD DEED AND OTHER STORIES

Persephone Book Nº 118
Published by Persephone Books Ltd 2016

Every Good Deed (1944) was published by John Murray.
'Miss Pratt Disappears' appeared in *Argosy and Storyteller*
in 1931 and was published, as was 'Susan', and 'Bitter Sauce',
in the collection *On Approval* (1935). 'Exit' appeared in
Lilliput in April 1941; it was published, as was 'Boarding House'
and 'One Dark Night', in the collection *After Tea* (1941). 'Tea at the
Rectory' appeared in *Atlantic Monthly* in December 1945. 'The Swan'
and 'Sunday Morning' appeared in the collection *Wednesday* (1961).

Endpapers taken from a 1950s dress fabric
in a private collection

Typeset in ITC Baskerville by
Keystroke, Wolverhampton

Printed and bound in Germany by
GGP Media GmbH, Poessneck

978 1910 263 082

Persephone Books Ltd
59 Lamb's Conduit Street
London WC1N 3NB
020 7242 9292

www.persephonebooks.co.uk

EVERY GOOD DEED AND OTHER STORIES

by

DOROTHY WHIPPLE

❖❖❖

PERSEPHONE BOOKS
LONDON

CONTENTS

EVERY GOOD DEED

CHAPTER ONE

❖❖❖

The Miss Tophams lived tranquilly at The Willows, a pleasant house left to them, with an adequate income, by their parents. Miss Susan took no part in public affairs. She managed the house and had a great admiration for Emily, her senior by two years, because she sat on Committees. Emily, on her part, had a great admiration for Susan and all she did in the house and garden. They frequently exchanged compliments.

'Your speech is reported, Emily,' Susan would exclaim with excitement, opening the local paper. 'And it reads so well. I don't know how you do it, dear.'

'Your strawberry jam is delicious this year,' Emily would say at tea. 'It really tastes better than ever, Susan.'

Of all her public affairs, Miss Emily enjoyed most her connection with the Children's Home. Though the sisters had never had anything to do with children, they loved them. Their only brother, James, who lived in London where he owned a chemical works, was married and had a daughter. But he did not come to see them or invite them to come to see him. He had a smart wife who could not be bothered with his sisters, and after the Miss Tophams had overheard themselves referred to as 'mouldy' by James's wife, they were sensitive about forcing themselves upon James in any way. They wished they had been allowed to have some share in the little girl, Doreen, but it was not, they thought with resignation, to be. That was the way they usually accepted their disappointments. 'Well, dear, it was not to be,' one would say, and the other would agree that it evidently wasn't, and they would, like most of us, turn to something else and begin to hope about that.

The sisters were incurably benevolent. Miss Susan never turned a beggar from the door and Miss Emily was constantly finding jobs for people who mostly didn't want them. The sisters were frequently taken in, as Cook did not fail to point out. When they were taken in, they admitted it with dignity, but pointed out to Cook, in their turn, that it was better to be taken in occasionally than to fail in an opportunity to help when help was really needed.

'I think we do more good than harm,' Miss Emily would remark to Cook. 'I think the balance is on the right side.'

Whereupon Cook snorted, a habit Miss Susan found peculiarly exasperating. Cook had been with the Miss Tophams a long time. She was in her thirties and they were in their forties, but she felt they needed looking after for their own good and did not hesitate to advise and admonish them. Emily might have the infuriating ways of fellow members of committee to put up with, but Susan had Cook. She felt the balance was pretty even, and when Emily brought home some tale about committee, Susan could generally cap it with one about Cook. But for all that there was a strong bond of affection and mutual respect between the three women at The Willows, and they were, on the whole, very comfortable.

Miss Emily was glad when she was elected to the chairmanship of the Children's Home because at last, she said to Susan, she would be able to do something for children. Susan said that here was a chance for her to do something for them too, and to Cook's indignation set about inviting the orphans in parties of a dozen to tea in the garden during the summer months. Miss Emily kept in close touch with the Children's Home, knew almost all that went on there and came in time to feel that it was practically hers. She met with no opposition from Matron, who was glad to shelter behind Miss Emily. Matron was not so young as she had been, but Emily felt vigorous enough to protect Matron or indeed anybody at all. Between them they conspired to conceal from the Director of Education and the committee the fact that Matron was no longer quite up to her job. Matron's little weaknesses, dependencies and failures to manage only endeared her the more to Miss Emily.

Miss Emily very much enjoyed the meetings at the Home. She enjoyed sitting at the head of the table, with Matron beside her, discussing the Home business, at least most of it, with the committee, and she enjoyed it when, after the meeting, the other members dispersed, but she, by virtue of her position, went into Matron's room to have tea.

On a certain summer afternoon all had gone as usual, and Miss Emily was in Matron's room drinking tea and listening to several items of news that had not been brought up in committee.

'The Dobsons are back,' said Matron with a sigh. Her face above her stiff collar was red from the heat and the nervous strain of committee. The Dobsons seemed an additional burden in this weather. 'All five of them,' she added. 'The baby and all.'

'Ah,' said Miss Emily, pleased to be able to place the Dobsons so unerringly. 'So the mother has gone off again?'

'Yes, with another man. And yet if you were to see her, Miss Topham, you'd think butter wouldn't melt in her mouth. She's one of those *quietly* bad women,' said Matron. 'They're always the worst.'

Miss Emily, sitting by the open window in a flowered silk dress and mushroom hat wreathed with white roses, had no experience of bad women, quiet or otherwise, but she nodded as if she had plenty. Miss Emily cherished several delusions about herself. She imagined, for instance, that she knew all about the seamy side of life, all about children, that she was a woman of authority, very firm, a good manager of other people. The truth was that, like her sister, she was gentle and innocent, naïve and romantic.

Strange to say, she found the Children's Home romantic. Put up in the days when the authorities considered that any building intended for the use or education of children should be either punitive or ecclesiastical in appearance, the prison-like Home seemed romantic to Miss Emily. She felt a childlike, thrilling interest in the great bare rooms, stone floors, high barred windows, strong smell of carbolic, rows of hard beds covered with coarse red blankets, and above all in the fatherless, motherless or foundling children. She never admitted that she found it romantic, even to herself. Probably she didn't know. But her eyes, over the rim of her cup now, showed that the quiet badness of Mrs Dobson and the return of her five children at intervals to the Home seemed more like a story to Miss Emily than actual sordid fact. When evidences of evil were presented to her, as they constantly were, she exclaimed over them in amazement; then they slid away into the past and she went on devoting herself to doing good.

'That Gwen Dobson's more of a handful every time she comes in,' said Matron with another sigh. 'Thank goodness she's thirteen now. Next time, she'll be too big to come here. But I've got her on my hands for the present and she's making trouble already. Are you coming round today, Miss Topham?' she asked as Miss Emily put down her empty cup. 'Or is it too hot for you?'

'Dear me, no,' said Emily, rising, with a smile. 'It's never too hot for me to see the children.'

'Well, they're out in the playground just now,' said Matron. 'But of course there are always the babies.'

'Ah yes, the babies,' said Miss Emily. 'The best of all – the babies!'

Matron sighed as she led the way. It was well to be some people, she thought.

The babies were having their supper, seated in little chairs at very low tables. Several small faces were hideously blotched with bluish-purple paint. Impetigo, Miss Emily remembered, as she bent benevolently over them. Some were so shy they cried, others went on eating stolidly, until the nurses in charge made them all get up and sing a verse of some song about thanking God for everything, to show the Chairman that they could do it. Miss Emily stood smilingly by, but she wished the children had been allowed to get on with their supper. Everybody was relieved, including Miss Emily, when she went away.

All over the building, cleaners were busy getting the place ready for the next day. The sash windows were thrown up, chairs were piled on tables, floors were damp from scrubbing. The big rooms were empty except for one where a girl was standing by the high fireguard before the empty grate. When she saw Matron, she made a dart for the opposite door, but Matron, with a temporary recovery of her one-time stentorian tones, shouted: 'Gwen Dobson, you come here at once.'

Miss Emily, who deplored Matron's shout – no one should shout at children – watched the approaching girl with benevolent interest. Surely Matron must be wrong about Gwen Dobson. This was a nice child; a nice, fair, open face she had, with blue eyes. There couldn't be anything wrong about a child with a face like this. Faces never lie, thought Miss Emily, who had read it somewhere.

'Gwen Dobson, what are you doing in here?' asked Matron, with what Miss Emily considered undue harshness. To soften it, Miss Emily laid her hand on the girl's head.

Under the hand, Gwen Dobson's face, which had been mutinous as she came up, assumed a meek expression. Miss Emily noticed the change and was delighted. 'You see?' she mutely pointed out to an invisible audience. 'It's only a question of the right approach.'

'What are you doing in here?' repeated Matron.

'Nothing,' murmured the girl with downcast eyes.

'Why aren't you out in the playground with the others?' asked Matron.

The girl raised her blue eyes to Miss Emily's face. Gwen Dobson was said by unkind neighbours to be 'sharp', by the kind to be 'old-fashioned'. That is, when she wanted anything she knew how to get it. At the moment she wanted to get out of trouble and here was someone with more authority than Matron. The thing to do, evidently, was to appeal to her. So she raised the blue eyes to Miss Emily and said with a childish quaver: 'I were only thinking about my Mum.'

It was true too. At this time of the day her mother often gave her a penny to keep out of the way, and with it Gwen went to the chip shop. Her stomach had turned from the Orphanage tea and now yearned for the customary chips and the giver of the penny that secured them. The words were prompted by her stomach and not her heart, but Miss Emily at once put the most pathetic construction on them and was sure that, bad though the mother was, the child must love her. She drew the girl to her side.

'Poor child,' she said. 'Don't be cross with her this time, Matron. Run back to the others now, dear, and try to play and enjoy yourself. It's all right this time, Matron, isn't it?'

'Well, it is if you say so, I suppose, Miss Topham. But don't you try it on again, Gwen Dobson, or it won't be.'

The girl went slowly towards the door, but before going through it she turned and smiled wistfully at Miss Emily.

'Why, she's a sweet child, Matron,' said Miss Emily, much moved. 'Surely you don't find a child like that a handful? I'm sure I could manage her. Kindness is what she needs. You see how she responded.'

'You don't know her, Miss Topham,' said Matron wearily. She was tired of walking round the building she had walked round so many hundreds, nay, thousands of times already. She wanted to get into her room, shut the door and put her feet up. In this heat they swelled cruelly. She glanced down at them. Like bolsters they were and looked as if they might burst the straps of her ward shoes at any moment. She wished Miss Topham would go.

At last Miss Topham did. She got into the car she had left at the gates and drove herself home through the hot streets. She had to incline the mushroom hat quite often as she went along. She was well known. She felt people respected and looked up to her and was grateful. She was altogether happy as she drove in at the gate of The Willows and put her car away.

The house was deliciously cool. In the drawing room Susan was playing Chopin's Nocturne in E Flat. Emily would not go in lest Susan should stop. She stood in the hall to listen for a moment, taking off her gloves. Through one open door she could see the chintzes and flowers of the drawing room, through another the table laid for dinner in the dining room. From beyond the green-baize door at the back of the hall there came a faint but appetising smell of cooking. As Emily went up to her own room she thought, gratefully again, what a happy life she lived with Susan and Cook and how lucky she was. As always when she felt this, an urge came over her to pass some of it to other people.

By and by the gong went. Emily came downstairs, Susan left the piano. They dined together and afterwards walked round the garden, admiring the roses. Then they sat in the drawing room, Susan sewing, Emily with the paper on her knee, discussing the details of their day. Susan heard about poor little Gwen Dobson, Emily heard about Cook. The evening went, if anything, even more pleasantly than usual.

It was about quarter-past ten when the telephone rang.

'Who can that be at this time of night?' exclaimed Susan.

Emily went to see.

'Is that you, Miss Topham?' enquired an agitated voice.

'Matron!' Miss Emily was startled. Her first thought was fire. Fire at the Home. 'What's wrong?' she asked sharply.

'It's this, Miss Topham,' said Matron in a low hurried voice, as if she were afraid of being overheard. 'I'm very sorry to trouble you, but I don't know what to do. I daren't ring up the Director, because it looks so bad, doesn't it, to be bested by a child? But I can't get Gwen Dobson out of the bathroom.'

It took Miss Emily several seconds to wrench her mind from fire and bring it to Gwen Dobson.

'You can't get Gwen Dobson out of the bathroom?' she repeated in amazement.

'No, Miss Topham. She's locked herself in. She's been there since eight o'clock. She's got the one bathroom nobody can get at from outside. The caretaker's tried. He's had ladders up, but none of them's long enough. He's fallen off now and torn his trousers, so he won't try anything else. I'm at my wits' end, Miss Topham. It's been a long hot day and everybody wants to get to bed. They're all getting cross and expecting me to do something, and there's that bad girl singing at the top of her voice and banging on the bath with what sounds like the lid of the slop pail. She's raising the neighbourhood, Miss Topham, and we'll have the police here soon. The Director won't like that. You know we're expected to manage.'

The word 'manage' was always a challenge to Miss Emily.

'I think I'd better come,' she said. 'Perhaps I shall be able to make her listen to reason.' She felt secretly as if she were the voice of Reason itself. 'I'll come straight away,' she said.

'Oh, thank you, Miss Topham,' said Matron fervently.

'Susan, dear,' called Emily, putting down the telephone. 'I'm going to the Home. Would you bring me my hat while I'm getting the car out? That poor child,' she said as Susan appeared in the hall, 'Gwen Dobson, you know, has locked herself in a bathroom and they can't get her out. I think I shall be able to. What she needs is kindness. I saw it at once this afternoon. Just my hat, dear. I don't think I need gloves.'

As soon as she stopped the engine of her car before the Home the din from the bathroom within fell on the quiet night. Miss Emily hurried in. Guided by the noise, she hurried upwards. By the time she was met by Matron in a white-tiled passage, neither could hear what the other said. At the end of the passage, women surged round a closed door like angry bees. One was beating on the wood with both fists, shouting: 'My word, when I get at you, my lady . . .' when Miss Emily laid a hand on the strong bare arm. The woman, her hair in curlers for the night, turned. 'That won't do,' said Miss Emily, unheard, shaking her head. 'No, no. That's not the way.' Waving both hands gently back and forth, she shooed the women from the door. To their resentment she shooed them right down the passage and away. 'I'd rather handle this affair alone,' she explained, blinking in the harsh glare of the electric light. 'Besides, this child must not be allowed to think she has created such a stir. Just leave it to me. I'll manage.'

The women reluctantly dispersed, only to trickle back again, out of sight but not out of hearing, as soon as Miss Emily went back to the bathroom.

Miss Emily, kneeling on the wet floor – it began to look as if Gwen Dobson had also turned the taps on – put her mouth to the keyhole and waited. At the first pause in the banging and the singing, she said clearly: 'Gwen dear.'

The effect was all that she could desire. Silence fell.

'Gwen, this is Miss Topham. I'm alone outside the door. The others have all gone away. Won't you open the door, dear, and let me in?'

The banging was resumed with such violence that Miss Emily clapped her hands to her ears. But she waited, and when the pause came again, said: 'Gwen dear, come out and no one shall hurt you. You saw me this afternoon, you remember, and you know you can trust me. No one shall touch you. You shall just go to bed as if nothing had happened.'

But that, evidently, wouldn't do. The banging started again. Miss Emily fell back on her heels. She waited.

'Gwen dear, what is it you want? Why are you doing this? Tell me what you want, dear.'

The silence prolonged itself this time, and Miss Emily held her breath.

At last, speaking so close through the keyhole that Miss Emily started, a voice said: 'I want to go home.'

'But, dear,' said Miss Emily, delighted to have reached a point where Reason could speak at last, 'you haven't a home to go to.'

The banging started again. Louder than ever. Miss Emily felt desperation rising within her. What if she couldn't get this child out of the bathroom after all?

In the next pause, the voice spoke of its own accord.

'I could go to the Wattses. They'd have me.'

'Who are the Wattses?' asked Miss Emily.

'They keep the pub,' said Gwen.

'Oh, Gwen dear,' said Miss Emily regretfully, 'that won't do.'

The banging began again. Miss Emily clasped the door-handle and leaned her forehead against it as if in prayer. The din was deafening. Far down the passage faces began to reappear. She turned and they scattered. But they reminded her that the situation must be coped with and quickly. She had said she would cope with it and cope with it she must. She rattled the door-handle. The noise ceased. Gwen paused to hear what she had to suggest this time.

'Gwen, you have no home to go to and you can't go to a public house but – now wait a minute –' implored Miss Emily on a rising note, 'if you will come out of this bathroom, you shall come straight home with me. Yes, I'll take you home now in my car and you shall have supper and go to bed in a very pretty room with roses looking in at the window. No one shall touch you. I promise you, Gwen,' said Miss Emily with solemnity. 'I give you my word.'

She waited with bated breath. If the girl rejected this offer, what on earth should she do? There would be nothing for it but to send for the Director and the police, and what a confession of failure that would be. And how unpleasant for poor Matron and for herself. And what would happen to the poor child? She might be sent to an Approved School. Miss Emily waited for what seemed a very long time.

On the other side of the door a key grated in the lock, two bolts were slowly moved back, the handle turned, the door opened and Gwen Dobson stood on the threshold, glowering under the mop of fair hair she had removed from the regulation plaits. 'You promised,' she said warningly, ready with the door.

'I did, dear,' said Miss Emily, fervent with relief. 'And I meant what I said. Take my hand.'

'Stand back, please,' she called out to the advancing horde of women. 'I'm taking this child home with me for tonight. The whole incident can be discussed tomorrow. Let us pass, please. Matron, this is all right to you, isn't it? I'll come round first thing in the morning. Now go to bed, all of you. Good night, everybody, *good* night.'

She passed rapidly through the women, Gwen pressing closely behind her like a little truck behind an engine. Gwen's eyes darted warily from side to side, to anticipate any blow that might be dealt at her. But the women dared only mutter their threats.

Before she disappeared round the corner, Gwen, clinging closely to Miss Emily's silken waist, turned and put out her tongue.

A gasp, almost a hiss, of anger and frustration, went up from the women.

'You wait, you monkey you,' said one. 'Wait till tomorrow.'

CHAPTER TWO

But tomorrow, as far as Gwen's return to the Home was concerned, never came. She did not go back. At first, the situation was fluid. Nothing was settled. The sisters had not thought anything out. Emily had brought the girl to the house, and Susan was full of sympathy, and that was as far as things went at first. Gradually, however, the Miss Tophams were pushed into a position they afterwards thought it impossible to abandon.

To begin with, the Director of Education considered that Miss Emily had exceeded her authority in taking a child from the Orphanage without permission. The committee thought so too. Miss Emily was both hurt and piqued. She resigned her chairmanship. Matron eventually followed her into retirement. The new chairman soon came to the conclusion that Matron was past her job and said so. So the Home knew Miss Topham, Matron and Gwen no more, and all because Gwen had locked herself into the bathroom.

Gentle people are sometimes very obstinate, and the more opposition the Miss Tophams met with on the subject of keeping Gwen, the more obstinate they became. Several friends and neighbours called, inspected Gwen with curiosity, said that of course it was just like Miss Emily to act with such impulsive kindness, but they hoped the sisters wouldn't feel bound to keep the child for ever. After every such visit, the sisters redoubled their attentions to Gwen to make up to her for the adverse comments she hadn't heard.

But the most continual and violent opposition the sisters met with came from Cook.

'See where you've landed yourselves now,' said Cook. 'If you don't look out you're going to be saddled with her for good. And she's a sly piece. Anyone with half an eye can see it. You're not the sort to deal with a girl like that. You're too soft, both of you. If that girl was the daughter of any of your friends, you'd see through her fast enough. But she's poor and comes from a bad home, so you're sure she must be nice,' said Cook caustically.

'That will do, Cook,' said Susan. 'You may be sure that my sister and I will do what we consider best.'

'Yes, but best who for? Not for yourselves, I'm warning you,' said Cook.

'Now, Cook, we are quite capable of looking after ourselves,' said Emily, coming into the kitchen.

'That's what you think,' said Cook, with a snort that caused Susan to exchange glances with Emily.

With every day that passed, Gwen was more firmly entrenched at The Willows. Then James arrived and clinched the matter.

How James got wind of the situation the sisters did not really know, but they suspected Cook. Anyway, one afternoon when they came in from town whither they had taken Gwen to try on a new coat, there was James with Doreen in the drawing room, with Cook making a flushed, triumphant exit.

Miss Emily, who could always deal with a situation within her own social orbit, dealt with this one.

'Ah, James,' she said as coolly as if they had met yesterday. 'It must be five years since we saw you. How are you? Is this Doreen? We shouldn't have known her, but that is not surprising.'

James had considered his approach. He drew his daughter forward. She was a little older than Gwen and looked sulky, as if she hadn't wanted to come, which she hadn't.

'Kiss your aunts, my pet,' said her father. 'She's grown, hasn't she, Emily? Don't you think she's rather like you, Susan?'

'I see no resemblance,' said Susan. 'She's like her mother, and I'm sure her mother would not be flattered to be thought like me.'

'Doreen,' said Emily. 'This is Gwen, who has come to be *our* little girl now, you know.'

So it was done. Cook, coming in with tea, stood stock-still in the doorway. James's hand, holding a cigarette, was arrested.

'The tea, please, Cook,' said Miss Emily. 'Where are you staying, James?'

Not here, her tone implied. She knew what he had come for. He had come to protest against their keeping Gwen, to prevent their spending money on her. He had come to protect his daughter's claim to his sisters' estate. He was always mercenary, reflected Miss Emily. But he had brought Doreen too late, and it was no concern of his what they did with their money, as she pointed out to him later when she had sent the children into the garden.

James made no headway with his sisters. They refused to alter their decision to keep Gwen, they refused even to discuss it. James was obliged to withdraw, which he did that evening, in a rage, leaving Cook, who had expected much from this visit, also in a rage.

And now that it was irrevocably settled that Gwen was to stay, the sisters had a serious consultation and prepared to admit changes in their lives. They were both secretly astonished to find how far-reaching these must be.

The first thing they decided was that Gwen could not at present be sent to school; that is, to a private school. They themselves had been to private schools and for them those were the only schools to go to. They must do for Gwen what had been done for them. But if Gwen were not to suffer at school, her speech and behaviour must be brought up to standard. Since Susan was occupied in the house and Cook was being very awkward, and since it was after all Emily who had brought Gwen to the house, Emily felt she must undertake to teach Gwen herself. Except for music, which should be Susan's subject. So it was arranged that Susan should teach Gwen to play the piano in the drawing room and that Emily should give up her public work, turn a bedroom into a schoolroom and establish herself there with Gwen for a fixed number of hours a day.

The preparations were interesting. Miss Emily thoroughly enjoyed her consultations with a headmistress of her acquaintance on the best course to follow in educating Gwen. She drew up an elaborate plan, to which she gave hours of study, but somehow when it came to the actual teaching, when she found herself shut up in the schoolroom with Gwen, things did not turn out as she had expected.

Gwen's attention was slippery; in fact, it seemed unfixable. Miss Emily hoped, by changing the subject of the lesson often enough, that she would find and hold the pupil's interest somewhere, but there seemed no subject whatever in which Gwen was interested. The tales of Joan of Arc, of Richard the Lion Heart, of Warwick the King-maker that had so thrilled her sister and herself, left Gwen cold; she didn't even mind that the little Princes were murdered in the Tower. The only English sovereign she could remember seemed to be Bloody Mary, and that, Miss Emily feared, only because the epithet was familiar. She didn't want to write nicely; she didn't want to write at all. She didn't want to read, except 'comics'. Miss Emily barred these from the house, but somehow Gwen got hold of them, and Cook kept triumphantly bringing them out, as evidence of Gwen's slyness, from under her pillow or mattress or from down the sides of the armchairs.

It was not that Gwen was dull; far from it. To further her own ends she was as sharp as a needle. She had a surprising memory for films she had seen, songs she had heard, and a lively imagination used mostly on making up tales about what had happened at the Children's Home or at her own home in Burns Street. She found that by relating these during lesson-times she could keep Miss Emily from teaching her. Miss Emily had a theory that all these dark memories must be got out of Gwen's system by allowing her to talk about them. So while Gwen talked, Miss Emily, the Lady of Shallott suspended, listened with grave patience. Gwen embroidered and elaborated, seeing how long she could keep it up and how far she could go. She could generally go as far as she liked because the old girl, it appeared, would believe anything. Gwen despised her for it. When Miss Emily at last began on the lesson, Gwen began on her nails, which she bit, not absently, but with fierce interest. Miss Emily could not get on with the lesson for saying: 'Don't do that, dear.' 'Gwen dear, what did I say?'

It was not long before Miss Emily was forced to admit to herself that she was not a good teacher. The discovery shocked and surprised her, because she had always felt sure she would be. 'I wish I could have been a teacher,' she used to say to teachers when she went round the schools in her public capacity. 'I envy you, you know.' And now she found she couldn't teach. It was another illusion gone, and Miss Emily did not feel quite the same without it.

What Emily was experiencing in the schoolroom, Susan was also experiencing below in the drawing room. Music meant so much to Susan that she felt it her bounden duty, she explained to Emily, to teach the child in their care to lay hold of such happiness for herself. But Gwen seemed as impervious to music as she was to history or literature. She sat with a wooden expression, her eyes mostly wandering round the room as if her hands had nothing to do with her, while Miss Susan, enthusiastic, explanatory, arranged the fingers on the keys, pressing one here, one there. It seemed as if Gwen would never learn her notes, but Miss Susan persevered. With something amounting to torture to herself she persevered. Not only did she give Gwen a lesson three times a week but she sat with her twice a day while she practised, flinching from her stumblings and discords. 'Persevere, dear,' she kept saying. 'You will be so amply rewarded.' Miss Susan had forgotten, she told Emily, that the beginnings of music were so painful; painful for the teacher as well as the pupil, if not more so. Teachers of music ought to be paid twice or three times as much as they were, she said; and they ought to be honoured as martyrs too. She finally resorted to bribery, and things went better after that. Gwen consented to learn, but not to enjoy. For the last ten minutes of the lesson, Miss Susan 'rewarded' her pupil by playing to her herself; to train her ear and to show what happiness lay in store for her. But while Susan played, Gwen lolled in a chair, her eyes on the garden, her face a blank, paying no attention whatever. It was very discouraging, thought Miss Susan, her hands falling from the keys.

In the schoolroom, Emily gave in to Gwen, in the drawing room, Susan bribed her; but they did not disclose their weaknesses to each other. They were ashamed, but felt helpless.

What both chiefly felt in dealing with Gwen was what they had never felt before; uncertainty. They were uncertain how to proceed with the girl. They were baffled by being faced with a nature, a life, an experience so different from their own. They became more diffident, hesitant. Their friends noticed it: 'That girl is too much for those sisters,' they said to one another.

'We're too old for her,' said the Miss Tophams. 'She must have companions of her own age.' They asked little girls in to play with her, but after running wild in Burns Street, mild play with the little girls was nothing in Gwen's line; and nothing, it seemed, in the little girls' line either. For they didn't come twice, and they did not ask Gwen to their houses.

To add to their difficulties, the sisters found it impossible to reconcile Cook to the change in the household. Like cat and dog, Gwen and Cook were natural enemies. Every time Cook crossed Gwen in the house, every time she came into the room with the pudding or the tea she sent a look at her as if to say: 'My word, I'd chase you out of here if I'd my way,' and Gwen slid her eyes about with a half-smile as if to reply: 'Yes, but, you see, you daren't.'

Gwen told tales about Cook, and Cook told tales about Gwen, and the puzzled sisters went from one to the other, not knowing what to believe. They appealed to Cook's better nature, but in vain. Cook said that as far as that brat was concerned she hadn't got one. 'I've only got me sense,' she said. 'And that tells me she wants a good hiding, and my goodness, if she doesn't look out, she'll get it.'

That was going too far, the sisters felt. It was presumption. They felt bound to speak to Cook about keeping her place. To mention place is always fatal, and matters came to a head. Cook gave notice.

'Yes, I'll go,' she said. 'She's ruined this house for me. I've served you faithfully for ten years and I'd have stood by you to the end, if you'd have seen sense, but you won't. So I'll go. It's like leaving a couple of canaries to the cat, but you've chosen. You've asked for what's coming to you,' said Cook darkly.

The sisters accepted Cook's notice with outward dignity and inward misgiving. Would she really go? After all these years would she really leave them? She did. The day came when the out-porter carried away her yellow tin trunk and Cook, after making certain that she had left everything scrupulously clean, appeared in her red straw hat to say goodbye. They all wept then, three middle-aged women crying in the dining room, with Gwen, lolling in a chair, chewing sweets, watching them.

Always making a fuss about something, was her comment to herself. She was glad the old bitch was going. She would be able to do as she liked now. There was nobody to stop her.

'I'll keep in touch with you,' sobbed Cook as they took her to the door. 'I shan't cut myself off. If ever that girl goes, I'll come back. That is, if you want me.'

'You need never have gone, Cook,' said Miss Susan, wiping her eyes.

'Oh, yes, I need,' said Cook. 'It wouldn't have worked. Well, I'll say good afternoon. Good afternoon,' said Cook, convulsed, and went.

The sisters were amazed at the chaos that followed. They hadn't been able to believe that Cook would really go and had made no attempt to replace her. Now, left with the work of the house, the cooking, the washing, they found themselves shockingly inadequate. Susan, who had always prided herself on her cooking, couldn't manage the kitchen range. Not only were the flues frightfully confusing, but she couldn't regulate the heat. Things that should have cooked slowly cooked fast, and vice versa. They sometimes had to wait hours for a meal to come to table; in fact, a fowl intended for lunch had to be eaten at supper. Late dinner was given up two days after Cook's departure.

Emily, always considered almost masculinely practical, couldn't even put the vacuum together. Neither could Susan. They had to get a man up from the shop. Washing day was a nightmare. They rashly attempted the sheets, since Cook had always done them. But after drenching themselves to the skin in their attempts to transfer them from boiler to wringer, and after having been encoiled in their python-like folds for what seemed half a day, they murmured that next week it would be better to send them to the laundry.

They avoided each other's eyes; they were ashamed. If they could have laughed at themselves, it would have helped, but good and sweet-natured though they were, perhaps the Miss Tophams had a restricted sense of humour. Miss Susan had puckish flashes, but they weren't connected with wet sheets. Besides, they were too tired in these days to find anything funny.

Tired though they were, however, they never let themselves off. They toiled earnestly at whatever came their way. They persevered to the end. They saw things through. This was one of their outstanding qualities. Or it may have been a defect? Perhaps it is a bad thing not to know when to give up? Perhaps this is the key to the story of Gwen and the Miss Tophams.

When, after a time, they got maids, they either couldn't keep them or they didn't want to. Spoiled by Cook, they expected more than they were likely to get in these times. They were shocked at the change that had come over the girls since the day, ten years before, when they last engaged a maid. For some girls, the sisters were too exacting; with others, it was Gwen who complicated matters. Either they were a bad example to Gwen, or Gwen was a bad example to them. The sisters, anxious to be just, could not be sure which.

So that, more often than not, the Miss Tophams were without a maid, and the house and they themselves suffered in consequence. Never now did Miss Emily come in from interesting work in the outside world and stand in the hall to admire the flowers and listen to Susan playing Chopin in the drawing room.

They tried to get Gwen to help in the house. Housework, they pointed out, provided the most useful lessons. But Gwen would never do it if she could avoid it; if she couldn't, she did it as badly as possible. If they put her in a room with a duster, she flicked over the tops of things, left the lower reaches undisturbed and spent the time, until called, lolling in a chair, sucking sweets. She had an inexhaustible cache of sweets, because the old softies never counted the money in their purses, or the change they left about. It was easy to extract a penny here and a penny there without arousing suspicion. In fact, you could sometimes 'win' so much as sixpence, if you did it in two threepenny bits.

Gwen had ample opportunity of buying her sweets, because, although she avoided housework like the plague, she was always willing to run errands. She took Rover, the old Airedale, with her. The sisters were touched by her apparent affection for the old dog. But though she always took him with her, he often came home without her. Much later, Gwen would arrive, hot and breathless with looking for him, she said, giving a detailed account of all the streets she had searched through. 'I know you don't like me to keep him on a lead too long, Aunt Emily. But when I let him off, I always seem to lose him, don't I?' she would say, opening her eyes in a way that would have been too wide for most people's confidence, but which seemed innocent to the sisters; as she meant it to.

She did not lose Rover often enough to rouse their suspicion. Other times when she was away too long, she came in with a lot of bright lies about the shops being full of people and the shopkeepers not giving her her rightful turn because she was only a little girl. 'I told them it was for you, too,' she would say, with the flattering implication that that really ought to have been enough for anybody.

The truth was that her mother was back and she kept making flying visits to Burns Street to treat her former friends to chips or ices according to the season, to look at the life she had no wish to return to but which still interested her more than any other, to show off, to give cheek and flash away before anyone could avenge it. Visits to Burns Street added excitement to her life with the Miss Tophams, and she was glad her mother had come back.

But it was a shock to her when, one wet afternoon, her mother paid a return visit to The Willows.

'Who's this?' asked Miss Emily, looking up from her chair in the window to see a bedraggled female figure coming in at the gate.

'Not a maid for interview, I hope,' said Susan, who saw at a glance that she didn't want a maid like this.

An exclamation from Gwen made both sisters look at her. She had gone quite pale. 'Who is it?' they asked. 'D'you know her?'

'It's my Mum,' said Gwen.

'Good gracious,' said Miss Emily, going to the door.

Before Gwen could escape, her mother was in the room.

'Well, Gwen,' said Mrs Dobson, displaying a few broken teeth in a smile.

Gwen didn't say anything. She sidled against the sofa. The sisters thought it a strange meeting between mother and child separated for so long. They didn't know they had seen each other but yesterday.

'Sit down, Mrs Dobson,' said Miss Emily coldly, but putting a chair near the fire.

Mrs Dobson had a fuzz of fair hair, a thin face and a furtive air. She reminded Susan of a ferret James once had. She didn't look directly at anything, but darted glances under her light lashes at the floor and the furniture. She wore a red mackintosh torn at the pockets. She could not, Miss Emily calculated, be much more than thirty.

'What is it you want, Mrs Dobson?' asked Miss Emily, sitting very erect.

'Well, Miss, I came to say, after thinking it over, that it's about time our Gwen came home,' said Mrs Dobson, her eyes on the coal-box.

The silence that followed was shattered by a howl from the sofa. Gwen rushed at Susan and burst into tears.

'Don't let her take me. I won't go! I want to stay with you. Let me stay. Let me stay!'

The sisters were much moved. Gwen must be attached to them after all. Often enough they had feared she wasn't. Often they felt their pains were for nothing, she seemed so unresponsive and cold-hearted. But if she could cry like this at the threat of leaving them, and cling so passionately to Susan, she must love them after all. Susan soothed her in her arms, and Emily went over to stroke her hair.

'Sh, dear, hush now. Go upstairs with Aunt Susan and leave me to manage things,' said Emily comfortingly. 'It will be all right, you'll see. Go along, dear, and don't upset yourself. Aunt Emily will look after you.'

Susan took the sobbing girl away.

'Poor kid, she seems fond of you, I will admit,' said Mrs Dobson. 'And no wonder, because I'm sure you're ever so kind to her. I said to myself as soon as I saw you, I said, she's kind, is this lady and your sister too. I say myself, it would be a shame to take our Gwen from such a good home. You keep her beautiful, too, I must say. But she's my child, Miss, there's no getting away from that. It was me that brought her into the world and a cruel time I had. My health's never been the same since. You can ask anybody.'

Miss Emily waited coldly, implying that she would not avail herself of this permission.

'My point's this,' said Mrs Dobson, warming to it. 'If Gwen was at home with me now, she'd be earning. She'd be a help to me, would Gwen, because she's as sharp as all the rest put together. I've had a good job promised her. Usherette at the Palace picture house.'

'Tch,' said Miss Emily, in strong disapproval.

'Oh, it'd just suit Gwen. She always wanted a job like that. But what I want to know, if you'll excuse me, Miss, is why I should let you have my child and be out of pocket by it?'

'Do you wish us, then, to *buy* your daughter from you?' asked Miss Emily stiffly.

'Well, I shouldn't put it like that, Miss,' said Mrs Dobson, uninsulted. 'But what I say is, our Gwen should come to her rightful mother and bring home good wages. Or if you want to keep her for her own good, you ought to compensate me.'

Miss Emily had been out of touch for a long time with the Children's Home. She did not know that Mrs Dobson had been refused the custody of her other children. The authorities had been forced to adopt them to keep them out of their mother's hands. Mrs Dobson, who had questioned Gwen very thoroughly, was banking on Miss Emily's ignorance. She was successful. She went away with five pounds, and it was the first of many such sums.

Mrs Dobson brought another dark element into the Miss Tophams' lives. It was not that the money mattered so much. They had more than enough money for their own needs. But their home was somehow breached now that Mrs Dobson could arrive when she liked, as she often did, usually on a wet day. She chose the worst possible day to arrive on, partly because she was sure of finding them at home, partly because she could look more wretched. Mrs Dobson, or indeed any poor person inadequately protected against the weather, could make the Miss Tophams feel guilty, as if they had no right to their comfortable surroundings; though their father had worked hard enough all his life to provide them. The Miss Tophams were disturbed to see Mrs Dobson come and relieved to see her go. They gave, and got rid of her for the time being. But it was as if, through their house now, ran a trickle from some dark source, which they couldn't turn off, but must submit to.

The Miss Tophams had none of the brisk acceptance of the born social worker; it would have been better if they had. They were at the mercy of people like Mrs Dobson and Gwen. They were hampered in any resistance they might have put up by delicacy of feeling and fear of hurting those who had not had what they called 'the same chance'.

CHAPTER THREE

It was with a sense of achievement that the Miss Tophams saw Gwen off for her first day at Laurel Bank School for Girls. In spite of their inadequacies they had brought their task as far as this, and now they could pass Gwen on to hands more capable than theirs. At last she would develop on the right lines; at last she would begin to benefit from what they had tried to do for her.

Standing together at the dining room window, Emily and Susan watched her go. She was dressed like a schoolgirl, but somehow she didn't look like one. There was something about the swing of the short skirt over her plump thighs that brought a strange, unbidden thought to Susan's mind. 'Too old for the chorus,' she thought irrelevantly, and was surprised at herself. How could a child of fourteen and a half be too old for anything?

'I didn't know we'd had that tunic made so short, Emily,' she said. 'I must let it down tonight.'

'I hope she won't find it too strange at Laurel Bank,' said Emily. 'It's late for her to start there, isn't it?'

Gwen disappeared from view, and the sisters turned from

the window. They spoke of her often during the morning. 'I keep wondering how she's getting on,' said one or the other.

Although they had had every evidence to the contrary during the year that had elapsed since Gwen's arrival at The Willows, they pictured her as a sensitive, shrinking child this morning. Because the situation would have been difficult for them in Gwen's circumstances, they thought it must be difficult for Gwen. The Miss Tophams were continually reconstructing people in their own image. No matter how often other people proved themselves to be entirely different from the Miss Tophams, the Miss Tophams, though shaken, sometimes considerably, at the moment of proving, obstinately started building them up again before long, sure that they must really be what they themselves were. Everybody was surely what they vaguely termed 'all right underneath'? 'Gwen is all right underneath,' they kept telling each other throughout the difficult months that had passed. And now that she had gone to a school like Laurel Bank for the first time and might feel uncomfortable and at a loss, their hearts went out to her and they were sure, once more, that she was everything that could be wished for.

But Gwen was precisely what she had been hitherto. Tough, and pretty well equal to anything. She could adapt herself when she wished to. She didn't want to go to the school and would take care not to attend it oftener than she had to, but she knew, without having it pointed out, as she frequently had by her mother, which side her bread was buttered. She might as well, she had decided, fall in with the old girls' ideas until she made up her mind what she wanted to do herself.

So, pulling her hair well out from under her hat in front as soon as she was out of sight of the dining room window, chewing sweets, eyeing the boys going in the opposite direction, Gwen went to school.

When she came home at the end of the afternoon – she stayed at school for the midday meal – the sisters had a special tea ready for her in the dining room. They had not had tea as usual at four o'clock, but had waited to have it with Gwen, and now they all sat down together to a table spread with the things she liked best. A poached egg, because they were sure she must be hungry, jam and cream, scones, biscuits and an iced cake made by Susan, who, after dire experience, had now mastered the kitchen range. From their places at the ends of the table, the sisters kept leaning forward to push the laden plates a little nearer Gwen, anticipating her every want. They liked something to play at, thought Gwen, well, let 'em play. Suits me, she thought, eating.

After tea, they said she mustn't help with the washing up. Not that she offered to, but they were sure she must be tired, and she also had homework to do. Miss Emily helped her with it. She was anxious that Gwen should not develop an inferiority complex by not being able to keep up with the others. She wrote to the headmistress to say she was sure it would be understood if she gave Gwen a little help with her lessons from time to time.

Now that Gwen was away all day, the sisters thought they might be able to get and keep a maid. They did, and things were better. Things seemed much better, and the sisters sailed ahead in blissful ignorance. Their experiment in adoption was going to turn out well, they were sure. When Cook, who had got herself a place nearby, called to see them, they told her that she had been wrong after all; Gwen was developing very well. The next time Cook called she saw Gwen for herself and was almost persuaded that the Miss Tophams might be right, the girl's behaviour had improved so much. But Gwen was not really different; only cleverer.

She had always been an adept at concealment, and now her scope was enlarged. She deceived at school now as well as at home. She acquired a mocking sparkle in the eye, due to getting the better of the people she lived with. She kept a nice balance; she never overdid things. At school, she explained her absences by saying Aunt Emily wanted to take her to the dentist, or Aunt Susan had such a bad headache she did some errands for her, and so on. At home, she said Miss Parker had told her to stay at home because she had been sick in school. She was so ingenious and various in invention that neither party suspected her. She was considerably helped by the fact that the headmistress, Miss Parker, although she liked the Miss Tophams and took their protégée to please them, did not like Gwen and was subconsciously relieved when she was absent. The sisters, for their part, were convinced by Gwen that she liked school so much she would never miss it unless she positively had to.

For weekend or evening absences from The Willows, Gwen invented a school friend at the other end of the town, a girl who couldn't come to tea because her mother was an invalid, but who often invited Gwen. She also invented tennis and other matches.

When she played truant, she went to Burns Street to see her mother or she went to the cinema. She always had money for the cinema, because what she didn't have given to her, she took.

After some months at Laurel Bank School, Gwen discovered the amenities of the Public Library. None of the girls seemed to have found out before this that the King's School boys went there to look things up in the Reference Room or wander round the shelves of the Lending Library choosing books. What could be more fun, asked Gwen, than wandering round the shelves too, or looking things up?

The boys, once they saw what the game was, joined in with zest. Enticement and pursuit went on round the shelves with much suppressed giggling and guffawing. Notes were tossed over the desks in the Reference Room, meetings arranged and very little work done. At first, Gwen annexed most of the older boys, and other girls watched with awe and envy as she sauntered down the street with five or six boys in tow. The Library was in a fair way to becoming nothing but a rendezvous for adolescents, serious students were being driven away, the authorities were considering stern measures, when the nuisance suddenly abated. Either their mothers got wind of what was happening, or the girls of their own accord withdrew. They gave Gwen a wide berth, looking almost childishly frightened if she approached them. The boys began to cut her, more and more boys cut her. The Library, from having been the rage, began to be a place nobody wanted to be seen in. Until, after some weeks, it resumed its normal place in their lives.

Gwen was not perturbed. She had found them all too young, the boys too young. She was older in experience than they were. She knew more. She forsook the Library, but began to go to the afternoon sessions at the Palais de Danse, or the first house at the Empire. She knew she was safe. No one who saw her was likely to be an acquaintance of the Miss Tophams, who had never set foot in either of these places in their lives.

Gwen's attitude towards the Miss Tophams was more and more the attitude of some men towards women. She looked upon them as creatures to be taken advantage of, deceived, humoured, played up to. Their principles were laughable, but she used them for her own ends. She had no scruples in taking all she could from them. 'Well, they've got it,' was the keynote of her conversations with her mother. And they liked lavishing things on her, and it didn't hurt anybody, so why not let 'em? The Miss Tophams were vaguely uneasy, but did not know why.

There were hundreds of children who, in the same circumstances, would have responded to their care, would have loved them and been grateful; but by mischance they had hit upon Gwen. They had not, however, come to any clear realisation of this yet.

Gwen struck up a friendship with a programme-seller at the Empire, a vicious little girl known because of her platinum blonde hair as 'Blondie'. Blondie let Gwen in at the back of the variety theatre and introduced her to men performing there. The men came by the week and were always on the look-out for girls to pass the time with. Blondie and Gwen had a fine time going out with different men every week. With the aid of make-up and a dress Blondie kept for her at the Empire, Gwen transformed her appearance so effectively it is to be doubted that if the Miss Tophams had met her they would have known her. She made herself look years older and always passed, with the men, for eighteen.

One day when Gwen came in from an afternoon out with Blondie and two negro singers who were in the bill at the Empire, she found that James had arrived with Doreen on one of his visits of reminder. He kept putting Doreen before his sisters, periodically presenting the claims of flesh and blood. But since Doreen was unwilling to be thus presented, she was usually sulky and did not show up well. She gave Gwen every chance to shine by comparison, and Gwen always took it.

Hastily washing her face – she had removed most of her make-up while changing her dress at the Empire – Gwen subdued her frizzy hair with a ribbon and appeared in the drawing room. Greeting the visitors, she hastened to establish herself at Miss Susan's side to hand round tea. She was the picture of one used to helping, of one taking her rightful place as the daughter of the house. It looked to the visitors as if she must come in from school every day like this, and James wondered if it was really any use bothering any further.

When Gwen approached Doreen with the sandwiches, Doreen, hitherto silent, said suddenly: 'What's that filthy scent you've got on?'

For a second, Gwen stood poised with the plate, her eyes sliding sideways.

'Oh, this?' she said, pulling out her handkerchief and prof-
fering it to Doreen's nose, which was withdrawn in hauteur.
'Don't you like it? A girl at school gave me a drop from a
bottle she'd taken from her mother's drawer. Fancy, wasn't
she awful?' she said, pressing her teeth on her lower lip in
disapproval.

'The scent's awful,' said Doreen tersely.

'I'll run and get another hanky if you don't like it,' said
Gwen, and with a bright, loving look at Miss Emily ran off.

She came back and sat on the sofa beside Doreen. She set
herself to entertain the unwilling guest. She prattled about
Laurel Bank, giving such a convincing impersonation of an
enthusiastic schoolgirl that the sisters almost bridled with
pride. They kept exchanging glances of satisfaction.

They were grateful to her. They were grateful for any
evidence that their adoption of her had not been altogether a
failure. Whatever they knew about it themselves they didn't
want James to know, and they were very grateful to Gwen for
putting up a good show, at any rate when he was there.

Their feelings were complicated. They were not only glad
that James should be taken in, they were very willing to be
taken in themselves. They *wanted* to think that Gwen was a
nice grateful girl, and on the slightest excuse they did think
so. Relief and warmth invaded their hearts again and they
were glad to have done, and be doing, what they did for her.
They smiled, and the world seemed a brighter place when
they were able to think that Gwen was a good girl after all.

But before long they were doubting again. Their hopes
that school and education would do for Gwen what they had

not been able to do began to ebb once more. There never seemed to be anything definite that they could pin their doubts to, but there was something going on that they could not define or understand. Over their books or their sewing, when they had time to sit down to them, they looked at Gwen as she chewed sweets and read her cheap papers. She grew bolder as she grew older, and brought the papers in openly now without any attempt to hide them. No mild hen hatching, say, a gosling or a turkey, could have been more amazed at what resulted from the egg than were the Miss Tophams at the development of the child they had taken from the Home. How had that small undernourished creature become this increasingly flamboyant young woman with over-developed figure, overshaped legs and strong frizz of hair?

As they sat in the room with her, the sisters were uneasy, as if they were in the presence of something powerful and alien. As if she were waxing, waxing all the time, and they were waning. They had never waxed like this. Growth in them had been tranquil and imperceptible, but Gwen was pushing up like some coarse, quick-blooming plant.

Things had changed at The Willows. The house had lost its air of peace; its atmosphere was changed by a whiff of Gwen's scent, a coloured scarf thrown down, the sight of her thighs under her short skirts, her breasts under her tight jumpers. The clothes seemed decorous enough when they came from the shops, but as soon as Gwen put them on they took on some mysterious change.

When the headmistress of Laurel Bank School at last steeled herself sufficiently to call on the sisters to ask them to take Gwen away, they received her as if they had been expecting some such visit for a long time. Miss Parker, who liked and was sorry for the Miss Tophams, said apologetically that she thought she had done all she could now for Gwen and that no useful purpose could be served by her staying at the school any longer. Miss Parker knew she had not done anything for Gwen. She had put up with her for the sake of the Miss Tophams, but Gwen was one of those overgrown superannuated pupils who constitute a danger to their schoolfellows and a nuisance to their teachers. The sisters did not ask Miss Parker for any explanation. They accepted, they said, her decision.

Gwen, who saw Miss Parker arrive, waited upstairs with apprehension. She thought her activities at the Empire must have been discovered. She stood on the landing, biting her nails, trying to hear what they were saying below. Her mind darted about trying to find a way out. When she came down at last and was told gravely by the sisters that Miss Parker had asked them to remove her from the school, she laughed aloud. What was there about being asked to leave a school that anyone need mind about? 'Suits me,' she said. 'It was never anything in my line.'

'We shall have to think of something for you to do after the holidays,' said Miss Emily.

'Do?' said Gwen sharply.

'You will want something to do, won't you?' said Emily. 'Have a career of some sort? At your age, I was full of ambitions.'

'They didn't come to much then, did they?' said Gwen. She looked at them angrily, her face red. She was outraged at being expected to do anything. Ladies didn't work. What was the use of them bringing her up to be a lady and then pitching her out to work? Her mother would be mad, and no wonder. She stood before the sisters, her eyes flashing rapidly from the floor to their faces and back again in a way she had when angry or disturbed. '*I* don't want to do anything,' she said.

'There's plenty of time to think it over before September,' said Emily calmingly. 'We thought you might like to take a secretarial course? Go to Sutton's College perhaps?'

'Oh, well,' said Gwen mollified, seeing herself in an office with a lot of men. 'I might do that.'

In September, she allowed them to fit her out with new clothes, an attaché case, a new fountain pen and the necessary books, and to despatch her, with more waving from the dining room window, with more hope, to Sutton's College. When she came home at the end of the day, they were full of interest and enquiries, but she wouldn't tell them much. Her policy was to keep them from nosing into her affairs at all.

'But do you think you'll *like* the work, dear?' persisted Miss Emily, anxious for a crumb of reassurance of some sort.

'Oh, I dare say,' said Gwen. 'It'll do, anyway.'

It would do to be going on with. It kept the old girls quiet and secured a continuance of comfort for herself while she pursued her own ends, went out with men from the Empire, giggled with Blondie, tapped idly on a typewriter, never exerted herself and lounged about the house when she was in it.

Then suddenly, she fell violently in love with the drummer in Percy Perryn's band. His name was Bern Johnson. He was pale, dark and handsome; his long lashes, waved hair and flapping bell-bottomed trousers all combined to infatuate Gwen beyond bearing. He seemed at first to prefer Blondie, and Gwen suffered agonies of love, hate and jealousy. She could neither sleep nor eat, and, unable to loll any more, ranged restlessly about the house, biting her nails. The sisters, much concerned, asked what was the matter.

'Oh, it's the exams at the College,' said Gwen, almost brutal at having to bother to find excuses.

They begged her not to take them so seriously and brought her hot milk to bed. But when they sat on her eiderdown, diffidently hoping to invite confidences, she humped over to the wall and mumbled that she wanted to go to sleep.

She managed at last to get Bern from Blondie and roused his interest by telling him that she lived in a big house and was a rich girl really. Her aunts would have a fit if they knew she had ever set foot in the Empire, she said.

'Go on,' said Bern. 'I don't believe you.'

'It's true,' she said. 'You walk home with me and I'll show you. I'll go in first and then you can walk past the house and I'll wave to you from my bedroom window. Only don't wave back. They might see you.'

'Waving from a window doesn't prove anything,' said Bern. 'I bet you're the maid.'

'The maid!' she gasped. 'Me the maid? D'j'ever see a maid wearing shoes and stockings like these?' she said furiously, displaying her legs. 'Or a wrist-watch like that?' Tears of mortification sprang to her eyes. 'Me the maid! I've a good mind to go home by myself.'

She scrambled up from the grass, and he got up with her, amused. He took her home and walked past the house a few moments after she had gone in at the gate. She was in luck. Miss Susan was in the garden, and Gwen was able to prove she was not the maid by hanging in an inexplicable access of affection to Miss Susan's arm. She cast a triumphant glance at Bern as he passed, and a few moments later ran out after him to arrange, round the corner, a meeting for the morrow.

On the Sunday afternoon, after seeing Bern off at the station, Gwen's eyes were red from crying. The Miss Tophams, touched, anxious to comfort, tried to find out why.

'Oh, I've failed in the exams,' she said, flinging away from them.

It was true. But even the trustful sisters could not believe that this accounted for the prolonged gloom that now fell upon Gwen. Sutton's College was closed for the holidays, and the Miss Tophams had to bear the unmitigated brunt of Gwen's almost savage melancholy. She did not go out as she used to, but mooned about the house, sighing heavily, biting her nails, looking at the sisters from under a neglected mop of hair as if she hated them and couldn't think why they should exist. She wouldn't get up in the mornings. Behind her locked door, she lay on her stomach, her face twisted sideways to gaze at the large close-up portrait of Bern that stood on the bed-table. 'Enough to drive anybody mad,' she said, through clenched teeth.

The photograph, showing in detail each stiffened eyelash, almost showing the tragacanth on each stiffened wave of his hair, stood under the girlish lampshade the sisters had given Gwen for Christmas, a coloured parchment whereon a lamb with a blue ribbon round its neck gambolled over daisies in the grass. The shade was symbolic of what the sisters thought Gwen, at seventeen, ought to be; the photograph of what she actually was. During the day, when her door was open, the photograph of Bern was locked away in a drawer.

Gwen's gloom was trying, but her periods of activity at the piano were more trying still. At times, she would get up from the chair she had been lying in, push back her mop of hair and bang out Bern's tunes by the hour.

Susan rued the day she had taught Gwen to play. All the patient hours, the weeks, the months, the years, she had spent in teaching Gwen had come only to this. It was the same with everything they had taught her, thought Miss Susan. Every source of beauty they had opened to her ran dry in the sand of Gwen's nature. She turned all she knew to vulgar ends, mused Miss Susan bitterly.

The drawing room was littered with songs about melancholy babies, dreams that wouldn't come true, waiting for you, being blue and one about how somebody called Johnny could love. The sisters sat trying to be broad-minded while Gwen sang, rolling her shoulders, throwing her eyes up to the ceiling. At last, when the song came to an end, Miss Susan could forbear no longer.

'And now could we have a little Chopin for a change?' she enquired.

'Oh, play it yourself,' said Gwen, and, goaded by love and frustration, she got up and left them.

They didn't look at each other. 'May I have the scissors, dear?' said Emily.

The sense of failure was heavy upon them. They ought to have been able to manage better than this. Some crisis of adolescence was going on and they didn't know what it was. Nor if they had known would they have been able to deal with it. They had come to realise that. Gwen was beyond them. To manage her, to help her, they would have had to be different themselves; and they weren't, and they couldn't be, now.

But perhaps no one could have done much with Gwen, thought Miss Susan mutinously. Something about silk purses and sows' ears rose to her mind, but she daren't mention it. Emily would think it was dreadful of her. Emily never admitted that there were any sows' ears. It was all silk purses, according to Emily. Or had been, once.

CHAPTER FOUR

At the end of the hot July afternoon the Miss Tophams, two tall, gentle-looking women in discreetly flowered silks, mushroom straw hats and long pale gloves, walked slowly along the tree-shaded road towards The Willows. They had been to a garden party in aid of the NSPCC, and were tired. They were without maids again, and it had been a rush to get off after doing the work of the house, cooking lunch and clearing away. It was so hot, too, that they had been more inclined to rest in their own garden than to walk some distance to someone else's, where they would probably have to stand all the afternoon because, at these affairs, there were never enough deckchairs to go round. After all, as Susan pointed out, struggling a little against Emily's sense of duty, since they had paid for their tickets and contributed to the cause, they had really no need to go. They had almost decided not to, but Gwen was persistent in persuasion that they should.

'I should go,' she urged. 'Be a change for you. Does you good to get out of the house sometimes. You go. I'll have supper ready for you when you come in.'

She even offered to wash up, which was unprecedented.

Usually she did not care what they did, but today she had seen them out of the house with such determination that their suspicions were aroused. Turning at the door, Miss Emily said nervously: 'You know, dear, you can always have your friends to the house. But we would rather you didn't have strangers – strange men, that is – when we are out.'

'Oh, don't bother yourself,' said Gwen airily, tea towel in hand. 'I don't want any men in.'

From the corner, she watched them go down the drive. When about to turn the corner, they looked back and saw that she was watching them from the gate. She flapped the tea towel at them, not, thought Miss Susan, in farewell, but as if they were two flies she wanted to get rid of.

And now they were coming home. The garden party had been very pleasant, but they had to stand all the time and they were tired. Coming home was not what it used to be. They didn't say anything, but in these days they shrank from coming back to Gwen.

They walked up the short drive, and Miss Emily turned the handle of the front door. It was locked. She turned to Susan in surprise. 'She said she'd be in,' she said.

'It's lucky I have a key,' said Susan. 'I don't usually carry one in this bag.'

They went into the house. Gwen had said she would have supper ready, but there was no sign of it. She hadn't even finished the washing up. Sighing, not because there was work to do, but because Gwen was always failing them, the Miss Tophams went slowly upstairs to take off their hats and put on their aprons. But passing Gwen's open door, Miss Emily, who was first, saw that the floor beyond it was strewn with papers and sundry oddments. With Susan behind her, she went into the room.

Chaos reigned; cupboard doors hung open showing empty shelves, drawers had been pulled out and the contents emptied – toffee wrappers, lengths of greasy ribbon, old powder puffs, hair curlers, nail files, empty bottles, showers of torn envelopes – all sorts of rubbish, and nothing but rubbish, littered the floor, the bed, the dressing table. The sisters stared in amazement.

'She's run away,' said Susan at last.

'She has,' said Emily, and stepping through the dregs of Gwen's life at The Willows she took a sheet of paper from the dressing-table.

With Susan looking over her shoulder, she read Gwen's backward scrawl:

'I have gone away to get married. Don't try to find me and don't put the police on to me. It would spoil Bern's job and he'd never forgive me or you either. Besides, even if you did find me, I wouldn't come back and you couldn't make me. You never legally adopted me, so you've no rights over me, so don't try any funny business. I shall be married before you could find out where I am. Now don't try to find me, or I'll never forgive you. I'll never forgive you if you come between me and Bern.'

The sisters looked at each other in silence. Then Susan turned and contemplated the rubbish on the floor. A smile dawned slowly on her face.

'Gone,' she said. 'She's actually gone.' She looked as if she couldn't believe it, as if it must be far too good to be true.

'Emily!' she cried, turning back to her sister. 'She's gone.'

'What a letter!' said Emily.

Not a word of regret or gratitude after five years. Miss Emily was not so immediately concerned with the fact that Gwen had gone, but that she could write such a letter.

But Susan was already scooping up the rubbish on the floor. 'I'm going to burn this,' she said briskly.

Emily bent down and picked up an envelope hastily torn across. 'What a lot of these envelopes there are,' she said. 'They must have been letters from the man – Bern, does she call him?'

She examined the postmarks. They were from many different provincial towns. 'He must be a commercial traveller,' said Susan. 'Well, he's welcome to her.'

'Susan, Susan,' chided Miss Emily. 'That's not quite the way to look at it.'

'I know,' admitted Susan, shovelling litter into the waste-paper basket. 'But I don't care.'

She moved briskly about, clearing up after Gwen. She took the sheets from the bed, threw up the windows, brought the vacuum cleaner. Already it seemed to her that the house felt cool, different, itself. She went through the rooms, looking at them all, as if she hadn't seen them for a long time. The house, a friend, had been restored to her,

Emily wandered after her, temporarily disorientated. She had a guilty feeling that she ought to go off and look for Gwen, and a guiltier one that she didn't want to. But to marry at seventeen and a half ! And what sort of a man? What sort of a life had she gone to?

'Nothing to do with us,' said Susan firmly. 'If she's married, she's married, and going after her wouldn't undo it.'

'She's taken the money from the bureau drawer,' she called out later. 'There was about seven pounds there.'

'Well, I suppose she had to have some money,' excused Miss Emily.

'Huh,' said Susan. 'I think you'll find she's emptied her bank account.' Susan was right; she had.

The sisters at last remembered that they hadn't had supper, and set about boiling eggs. Anything would do tonight, they agreed. Halfway through the meal Susan got up and went into the drawing room. The strains of the Nocturne in E Flat poured from the piano. When Emily came in, napkin in hand, to remind her of her egg, Susan got up and kissed her sister. 'Isn't it nice to be alone together again?' she said, and returned to the kitchen.

Emily wondered how she should explain Gwen's absence, when discovered, to the neighbours, to the people in the road. But she had no need to worry. The neighbours knew almost as soon as the Miss Tophams; in fact, some of them knew, or guessed, before. They saw Gwen going away with her luggage in a taxi and hoped it was for good. The neighbours appeared to be delighted when this proved to be so. It seemed, from their nods and smiles, as if they with difficulty refrained from congratulating the Miss Tophams on their loss.

A few days later Emily met Susan coming out of the house with a letter for the pillar box at the corner. 'I've just been writing to Cook,' she said, waving it aloft.

And as soon as she had served her notice, which she gladly did, because good mistresses are as rare as good maids and she had never found any like the Miss Tophams, Cook came back. She came back to her old room, which had been freshly painted and papered, to the view from the windows she was so fond of, to a tin of her favourite humbugs on the dressing table with a card propped against it to say: 'Welcome Home'.

She came downstairs with red eyes and a watery smile.

'I'm glad I've got back in time for the bottling,' she quavered to the sisters. 'I've missed the straws and the rasps, I know, but there's the currants yet, and the plums and blackberries and apples. I'll not do so badly. Now, I'll have your tea ready in no time. You go and sit down. You can rest now.'

Everything at The Willows was now as it had been before Gwen's advent, only better. Better, because of the contrast and because the occupants appreciated one another even more than of old. Separation, uncomfortable experience of others, had brought it home to them that they were eminently suited to one another.

The months went by, tranquil, happy, with never a word of Gwen to disturb them. A year went, one of the happiest years, they said to each other, that they had ever spent. They were so far restored to themselves that Susan was talking about 'her' strawberry jam again, and Emily was seriously thinking of putting up once more for the Council.

Then, one wet summer afternoon, they looked up from where they sat at the open windows and saw a shabby, shapeless figure, carrying a suitcase, coming in at the gate. Their sewing falling from their fingers, the sisters saw that it was Gwen.

II

'And when do you expect your baby?' asked Miss Emily, much as if she were interviewing one of the girls at the Moral Welfare Centre.

She and Susan were determined not to be moved by the pitiable change in Gwen. They would do their best for her, they would see that she had everything she needed, but she could not come back. As soon as she was rested, they would make arrangements for her to go to a Nursing Home, and when the baby was born, they would settle her somewhere. But not at The Willows. They were firm about that.

'Oh, ten days to a fortnight,' said Gwen, pushing back her hair.

Cook brought tea, looking daggers at Gwen, who did not look at her, but sat with her eyes on the newly lit fire, close-lipped, dirty, wet, and with a bad cold.

'And why didn't this man marry you?' asked Miss Emily stiffly.

'He's got a wife,' said Gwen. 'He doesn't live with her,' she added, after a moment.

'Did you know that when you went to him, or with him?' pursued Miss Emily.

'No,' said Gwen. 'No, I didn't know.'

It was the first thing he told her when she turned up at his rooms in Derby that night a year ago.

'But I've got a wife, I tell you. I'm married. Blast you, you'll get me the sack coming after me like this. What the hell do I want with you? I can get women wherever I go, can't I?'

But she managed him. She frightened him into helping to hide her by telling him what her rich people would do if they ever found him. He was weak and easily influenced, and she knew how to get her way. She lied and cajoled and stayed with him. But he had a wretched year, being terrified of his wife, who had a dress shop in London, terrified of the police, terrified of the bandleader, who would not countenance trouble with women.

An offer to go abroad with another band for the summer came as a godsend to Bern. He decamped, leaving Gwen without a word or a penny. To get the money for the fare to The Willows, she pawned her last remaining article of value, her wrist-watch.

When Susan went upstairs to get the room ready for the unwelcome prodigal, Cook followed her.

'Miss Susan,' she said. 'That girl's further on than what she says. If you take my advice, you'll get her into a Nursing Home straight off.'

'We will, Cook,' said Susan heavily. 'My sister will go round to Brooklands tomorrow.'

But tomorrow wasn't soon enough. Gwen had reached The Willows just in time. After a night such as the Miss Tophams had never experienced, Gwen's child – a boy – was born towards ten o'clock the following morning.

Neighbours, the people in the road, looked up at the house as they went past. They stopped to tell one another the news. The poor Miss Tophams! Fancy that girl coming back and having a baby like that, they said. What brazen impudence!

But to the occupants of The Willows it no longer seemed any such thing. If Gwen had wished to reinstate herself, she could not have found a better way to do it than to come back and involve the three childless women in the pain, confusion and anxiety of birth. The Miss Tophams and Cook were shaken to the depths of their being by the events of the night, and by morning their attitude towards Gwen had quite changed.

As far as Cook was concerned, Gwen had found the one possible way to her sympathy; she had been badly treated by a man. And so, long ago, had Cook. In the small hours of the strange night, she revealed this piece of information to the astonished sisters.

'But not like this?' faltered the horrified Susan. 'I mean – you didn't have a baby, did you, Cook?'

'Miss Susan, I'm surprised at you,' said Cook. 'Certainly not. But I had my ring and dress and veil and everything – when he came and said he'd rather not go through with it. So I left home, and I've never been back. But it's all for the best. He was a proper cissy; he's living with his mother still. But I'd never trust a man again. I never liked that girl, so it's no use pretending I did, and I don't really think I ever could like her, but I feel for her now, I must say.'

As for the sisters, it seemed to them that by such pain Gwen had atoned for everything. You couldn't suffer like that and remain the same, it seemed to them. 'And the baby will make a new woman of her, you'll see,' they told Cook.

When the baby was born at last, the Miss Tophams and Cook greeted him as if he were the long-hoped-for heir to their affections. They clean forgot that his father was a weakling, his mother a bad lot and himself a bastard. He was a baby, and none of them had ever had a baby at such close quarters before.

'I'd no idea newborn babies looked like this,' said Susan with awe and delight as she washed the child. 'Why, he's a person already. See the way he turns his head to look at us. We're the first things he has seen in his life, Emily.'

'If he sees,' said Emily, bending over the child on Susan's lap. 'Which I doubt.'

'I don't,' said Susan stoutly. 'He knows he's here. It's wonderful to produce life, Emily,' she said, looking up wistfully at her sister.

'It's wonderful to preserve it too,' said Emily, smiling down at Susan. 'That baby might have died, but for us.'

'He might indeed,' said Susan, restored. She wrapped the baby in the shawl she used to go to parties in when she was a child. 'You know, I've never handled a baby before, Emily, and yet I feel quite used to doing it. I don't feel at all clumsy or nervous.'

'You don't look it either,' said Emily. 'But all the same I must go and try again on the telephone for a nurse.'

III

So life at The Willows underwent another change. The household now revolved round the baby. The Miss Tophams were as glad as any devoted young mother to see what Cook called 'the back of the nurse', so that they could have the baby to themselves.

Gwen let them take charge. She let them play; again, it suited her. 'Having that kid fairly took it out of me,' she told her mother, who promptly reappeared upon the scene.

'I don't know about that,' said Mrs Dobson, eyeing her daughter lying back on the frilled pillows with a tea tray beside her. 'Wherever you fall you manage to land on your feet. Trust you.'

Gwen resented this, and a quarrel blew up like a sudden squall at sea.

'Don't let her up again,' said Gwen to Miss Emily. 'She upsets me.'

Miss Emily was only too glad not to, and in protection more of the baby than of Gwen, paid Mrs Dobson a considerable sum of money to keep away.

Gwen did not feed the baby herself. The Miss Tophams, taking it in turn, gave him his bottles. She didn't attempt to bath him. She said, making the sisters shudder, that she'd probably drop him or drown him. Besides, she said, she was too tired. She stayed in bed, or sat about, letting them bring her nourishing broths and Bengers, which the sisters did willingly, their reawakened benevolence overflowing from the baby to Gwen.

Exhaustion and depression had so subdued Gwen that she did indeed appear to be changed. But as the weeks went on, the sisters might have noticed that she was becoming, as people sometimes say, more like her old self; which in Gwen's case was not an improvement. The sisters, however, were too wrapped up in the baby to notice.

Gwen let them choose his name and take him to church to be christened. They called him Philip, after a brother who had died in infancy. They had always felt he would have been much nicer than James, had he lived. They bought a handsome perambulator and wheeled the baby out morning and afternoon, Cook sometimes taking her turn instead of going to the pictures.

The modern idea, they knew, was that the baby should spend the day in his pram in the garden, but Miss Emily said she was sure that the movement of the perambulator travelling over the pavements was a form of gentle exercise beneficial to his muscles, and Miss Susan heartily agreed, only too glad of an excuse to take him abroad and collect admiration from friends and neighbours. These came to hang over the pram at first from curiosity and love of scandal, but later, when they were used to the situation, they hung over from genuine interest in the baby and from a wish to please the Miss Tophams, who really were, everybody said, rather sweet.

James, who had not visited them during the year Gwen was away, now came again, without Doreen, to remonstrate with his sisters on harbouring that girl and her baby. But even Cook greeted him coldly, and when he used the word 'bastard', the Miss Tophams requested him to leave at once and said they would rather not see him again.

The months passed. Philip throve and cut two teeth. Physically Gwen throve too. She put on weight, acquired another bank balance and many new clothes. But she was restless and dissatisfied and was out a great deal. It did not occur to the Miss Tophams that Gwen could be anything but happy. She was a mother, and all mothers, according to their simple conception of such, were surely happy when their children were well? They were grateful to Gwen for letting them do so much for Philip, and when they very rarely noticed that time seemed to hang on her hands, they wondered guiltily if it was because they did too much for him, usurping a mother's place? But somehow when there was anything to be done, they did it as a matter of course, and did not notice that Gwen made no move to do it herself. Then they blamed themselves.

When Gwen said she would go and stay at Southend for a week or two at a boarding house she knew of, the sisters accepted it as quite natural. Gwen was Philip's mother now; she was a mature woman. She must go away for a change if she wanted to. They were only too glad she didn't want to take Philip, who was cutting more teeth. He gave them a wakeful night before Gwen was due to leave in the morning. They were rather tired and worried at breakfast, and it was not until she was gone that they realised they hadn't got her address.

'Never mind,' said Miss Emily. 'She'll be writing.'

But when the postcard came from Southend to say she had arrived, there was still no address on it.

'It's very careless of her,' said Miss Emily. 'How are we to let her know how Philip is?'

She could not imagine that anyone, least of all his mother, should not be concerned about Philip's new tooth.

When at length a letter came from Gwen, it was the very last kind of letter they expected. Gwen announced that she was not coming back.

'I've got a chance to go to America,' she wrote. Bern would have been horrified to hear that she meant to go with him. Through his agent, she had tracked him down again. 'So I'm going,' she wrote. 'You'll probably never hear of me again and I don't suppose you'll be sorry. I'm leaving Philip with you. You seem so fond of him it would be a shame to deprive you. Besides, what should I do with a baby in America? I don't want him. You do. So we're both suited. You can adopt him legally. I'll give him to you. You can use this letter as proof that I give up my rights in him.'

Miss Emily, gasping frequently, read aloud to Susan, who was holding Philip. She read in amazed sentences, stopping to read for herself what came next.

'Go on – Emily! Emily, don't stop like that – go on,' urged Susan.

'That's all,' said Emily, turning the single sheet over and seeing that there was positively no more to this amazing document.

'Give it to me,' said Susan, reaching over the breakfast table. 'Let me see it.' Her eyes ran rapidly over Gwen's scrawl. 'Well, I never heard anything like it,' she said, dropping the letter to the table and staring at her sister. 'She's gone again, and she gives us Philip. Look, Emily,' she said, holding up Philip, rolled like a little cocoon in his shawl. 'She'll give him up. His mother . . . this little, helpless, living creature. She'll hand him over. Well, Emily, all I can say is that she's an unnatural wretch, and I hope we never see her again. Never,' said Susan vehemently, and getting up from her chair with Philip in her arms she went into the kitchen. 'Cook,' she said. 'He's ours. His mother's gone, she's never coming back and she's given him to us. She never did a better day's work in her life because she's not fit to have him and she never shall. We'll see the lawyers this very morning.'

CHAPTER FIVE

For nineteen years the Miss Tophams were happy, and time passed almost imperceptibly at The Willows. The virginia creeper, once no bigger than the spread of a hand low down by the front porch, now covered all the house; a bower of green every spring, a glory every autumn and a great nuisance when the leaves fell. Nowadays, Miss Susan let the gardener sweep them up. They employed a gardener now, and Cook had a young maid to help her, because they were all getting older. Every year the tall Miss Tophams were a little more bowed, their hair a little whiter; every year Cook was a little stouter, and Philip taller and stronger.

Philip was a good-looking boy, with a clear pale skin, beautiful teeth and dark hair. If the Miss Tophams had ever seen the photograph that once stood under Gwen's bedside lamp, they would have been startled by the resemblance. But since they had never seen it, they were untroubled, and complacently considered that Philip was by far the handsomest boy in the district, as he had been the most beautiful baby.

He had left school and was doing the engineering course at the town's college of technology. The Miss Tophams and

Cook adored him, but they tried very hard not to spoil him. They tried to profit from what they had learned in their treatment of his mother. They continually checked one another.

'Susan dear, no more money this week,' Emily would say. 'He'll never keep within his allowance if he knows he can come to you every time he overspends.'

'Emily, you said he mustn't be out late again this week, but it was after midnight when he came in last night,' said Susan.

'Cook, you really should not keep getting up these dress waistcoats yourself. You must send them to the laundry.'

'They don't do them as well as me,' said Cook. 'And you know we all like to see him look nice.'

It was painful to the Miss Tophams not to give Philip everything he wanted, but for his own good they rationed themselves in giving. He had everything suitable to his age as he grew; he had the best bicycles, the best bats, the best tennis rackets. He had at present the best motorcycle, but he must not have a car of his own until his twenty-first birthday, the Miss Tophams decreed. No, positively not until then. If they gave him a car before, there would be nothing left to give him on that great day. Besides, if he waited for a car, he would value it when he got it.

Philip liked the best. He would not pick up any old car for a few pounds as he might have done. He wanted one he didn't mind being seen about in, he said. As it was, he could drive any car or do any repairs to any car he came across.

In addition to this talent for motor-engineering, Philip had another. He played the piano, in his own particular way, with something amounting to brilliance. Miss Susan had had no unwilling pupil this time. He gave her no trouble. But she was dismayed and rather rueful when later he was seized with a passion for jazz and swing. She was still more dismayed and rather more rueful when she herself, and Emily too, caught the infection from Philip. When he began to play, they were drawn irresistibly to the drawing room, and there they sat with their knitting, tapping their toes on the carpet, while Cook hummed in the kitchen. Philip played, with the most dazzling feats of technical execution, turning his handsome, laughing face towards them, egging them on, beating them up.

'His sense of rhythm is really remarkable,' thought Miss Susan, proudly. 'A very hot number,' she said aloud, smiling as she turned her needles.

He got up and kissed her for that. 'That's the style,' he said. 'I certainly keep you up to date, don't I?'

They smiled fondly. That was just what he did. He had drawn them into life, made them live. Their boy, their dear, dear boy, they thought, and longed for his twenty-first birthday so that they could give him the car.

Philip was very fond of his aunts and showed it. He had a gay, lovable nature. They thought he was perfect; and had no reason to think otherwise since he had not, so far, been put to the test in any way.

When he came in from tennis or football the Miss Tophams, elderly ladies now, sat beside him at the table, pushing first one plate towards him, then another; just as they had done for his mother, but with how much more love now on their side and affectionate acceptance on his.

It was as they sat thus at the table one warm summer evening that they heard the crunch of the gravel on the drive, and inclined stiffly backwards to look out of the window. Philip looked too.

'Who on earth is it?' he said laughing. 'Looks like a trio of organ-grinders.'

The Miss Tophams had no idea who they were. A bulky woman, a man in yellow shoes with something shady in the tilt of his hat, a young man, a boy of eighteen or so, bare-headed, with a bold reckless swagger.

Cook was out and the little maid had gone to the post. When Miss Emily got up from the table and crossed to the open window, the woman waved. She came towards the window, waving. 'Coo-oo,' she called.

Miss Emily stood where she was, staring. 'She can't know us,' she said. 'Who is she?'

The woman had reached the window and now thrust her head and shoulders through it.

'Well?' she said. 'Don't you know me? I'm Gwen,' she said.

Susan got up so abruptly from the table that she took the cloth with her. Plates and glasses slid in an avalanche to the side, but no one noticed them. Susan stood staring. A feeling of danger, of apprehension had rushed over her, making her heart beat heavily, drying her mouth. Gwen. Philip's mother. Her thoughts flew up like disturbed bees. But Gwen couldn't touch Philip, she reassured herself. He was theirs. Everything was in order. Gwen could do no harm.

'You seem surprised to see me,' said Gwen jauntily to the transfixed sisters. She leaned further into the room and looked past them. 'Is that my boy at the table? My Philip – why . . .' she faltered, 'he's the very spit and image . . .'

Miss Emily took a rapid step forward.

'What's up?' asked Gwen. 'D'you mean to say he doesn't know I'm his mother?'

'He knows,' said Miss Emily with dignity.

'That's all right then,' said Gwen. 'Perhaps you were bothered about Ken and Ronnie here? Well, there's no need. They know all about it too. No secrets in this family. But I forgot, you haven't met my husband and son yet, have you? I'll bring them in and introduce them. Is the door open, Aunt Emily? I remember you used to keep it on the catch, didn't you?'

Steps receded on the gravel. In the room, no one moved. Their eyes turned to the door, which in a moment opened to admit the intruders.

'Well, well, well,' said Gwen, advancing into the room. 'Funny to be back after all these years. And funniest of all is that big boy at the table.' She went over to him and put a hand on his shoulder. 'Well, ducks, what d'you think of your mother? Not much, judging from your face,' she said with a hoarse laugh.

Philip stood up, partly from courtesy and partly, the Miss Tophams thought, to remove himself from her hand. He looked as if he didn't know how to deal with the situation at all.

'Let these boys go out into the garden,' said Miss Emily, sending them away from the scene as, years ago, she had sent Gwen and Doreen.

'Righty-ho,' said Gwen. 'Go on, Ronnie, with your brother.'

At that word, Philip whipped round startled and looked at the other. Ronnie, his hands in his trouser pockets, his feet apart, met his eyes with amused equanimity. Then he jerked his head towards the garden door.

'Come on, old son,' he said with rough sympathy. 'You'll soon get used to the idea.'

Philip's face cleared a little as he followed his newly sprung relation from the room.

'Sit down, Gwen,' said Miss Emily when the boys were gone. 'Sit here, Mr——er?'

'Gordon's the name,' said Gwen promptly.

A good Scots name, thought Miss Emily, but glancing at the man, she wondered. Was it his own?

'I'm married this time all right, Aunt Emily,' said Gwen, exhibiting a thick gold ring embedded in the flesh of her third finger. 'So don't be thinking otherwise. Been married nineteen years, haven't we, Ken? Ron's eighteen next month, isn't he?'

'That's right,' said Ken, and coughed behind his hand as if to apologise for speaking. The two old ladies, the settled, sober, cultured atmosphere of the room seemed to upset him. From the yellowish whites of his eyes showing in his dark face, he looked as if he might bolt at any minute. His hands were thin, dirty, restless, the sort of hands, thought Miss Susan, who had once been to the races, that would be good at the three-card trick.

'And why have you come here?' asked Miss Emily.

'Well, I like that,' said Gwen with another of her hoarse

laughs. 'I came to see how you were all getting on. It's natural, isn't it, that I should want to see my own son?'

'You've managed pretty well without seeing him for nineteen years,' said Miss Emily. 'And legally he isn't yours, you know. You can't take him away from us.'

'I've no intention of trying,' said Gwen. 'So you can set your mind at rest.'

That wasn't her game at all.

What her game was soon appeared. They had had a bad time. Ken had lost his job – unspecified. They decided to leave the London district in which they had been living, and though Ron had a good job as motor-salesman, secondhand cars, Great Portland Street, he threw it up to come away with his parents.

'They thought the world of Ron, didn't they, Ken? But he's always ready for something new. He'll pick up something here in no time. Trentham's not a bad place to make a living in,' said Gwen. 'There's always plenty going on, and it's not as if I was a stranger. After all, I was born here. It's only natural I should want to come back, isn't it?'

The Miss Tophams did not assent. Their minds were busy all the time, sifting what Gwen said to see where any threat to Philip might lie. Apart from anything else, and no matter how sweet-natured he was – and they knew he was that, he could not help but be shocked by the sudden appearance of such raffish relations. Years ago, the Miss Tophams had told him about his mother, but they had not imagined that he might some day be confronted by such a step-father and half-brother.

Suddenly, Gwen's tale was broken in upon by the urgent spitting of a motorcycle. Miss Emily rose and went quickly to the window. The revelations of the evening must have been too much for poor Philip. He must be rushing away somewhere to escape from his brother.

But it was Ronald who was rushing out of the gate on the motorcycle while Philip, his hands in his pockets, stood smiling on the drive. At Miss Emily's exclamation the others came to stand at the window behind her.

'Is that Phil's bike?' asked Gwen. 'Ron'll be trying it out.'

She was right. In a few moments Ronald came flying back. He dismounted, and the young men stood laughing together, bending lovingly over the machine.

'Seem to have made friends,' said Gwen with satisfaction. 'Trust Ron to get round anybody. He's always like that, isn't he, Ken?'

'That's right,' said Ken.

Afterwards, Miss Susan reflected that, throughout the evening, those were the only two words he said, though he said them several times.

By and by the boys came back into the house. Philip had evidently got over the immediate shock of finding that he had a mother and a brother.

'I've asked Ron in on Sunday,' he said. 'It's all right, isn't it?'

'We'll all come,' said Gwen. 'We don't think much to our rooms, do we, Ken?'

When at last they took their leave, the Miss Tophams went to their chairs and sat down. The evening had been too much for them. Their foreheads were damp, their hands trembled a little as they wiped their glasses. There was Cook to be told yet, and they must help Philip to readjust himself to this sudden acquisition of near relatives. But Philip seemed in no need of help. He walked up and down the room, restless, but not troubled. His chief reaction seemed to be that it was hard lines on Ronald as well as on him to have such a mother.

'Gosh, she's awful, isn't she? Yet I suppose she was quite good-looking once in her way. I wish she wouldn't wear that appalling hat. Do you suppose Ron, as she calls him, is the son of that man, as she says, or the son of my own father, Aunt Emily?'

'I have no idea, Philip,' said Miss Emily gravely. She didn't quite understand how he could touch on these matters. But she could see he was taken with the idea of having a real brother. He had no wish to repudiate Ronald, whatever he felt about Gwen. It was really very sweet of him to be so devoid of snobbery. They must look at it like that, she thought. This was the fruit of their training. She ought to be proud, not uneasy, she told herself. His next remark showed their influence again.

'I wish Ron could have grown up here with me,' he said. 'It's tough luck on him that I should have had so much and he should have had nothing, isn't it?'

'He's a decent chap, too,' he added after another turn round the room. 'What he doesn't know about cars isn't worth knowing.'

II

'Always turning up, like a bad penny,' said Cook. 'Eh, I don't know,' she sighed. 'We can't seem to get rid of her. It was a bad day for us all when Miss Emily took her from that Home.'

'But, Cook, without her we shouldn't have had Philip,' said Susan. 'We mustn't forget that when we are totalling things up.'

'No,' agreed Cook. 'That's true. Well, all we can hope is that she'll go away again. She's gone before. Let's hope she'll go again – and soon, too.'

But this time Gwen seemed to have no intention of going. She said it was time they settled. If only they had the money, she said, looking expectantly towards the Miss Tophams, they would buy a little business of some sort; something they could put Ronald into, since jobs were not turning up, even for him, as they had expected. A little business in Swanley, she said, would be just the thing.

At that, for the first time, the Miss Tophams felt some relief. Swanley was a new housing estate; it was not only respectable, it was a long way off, right across the city. The further the better, felt the Miss Tophams, and for the first time displayed a faint, but promising interest in Gwen's plans.

Gwen saw at once that she had hit the right trail at last. She enlarged on the advantages of Swanley, but said it had one drawback; it was so far away that they wouldn't be able to visit The Willows very often. But it was a good neighbourhood, and she was anxious that Ron should live in a nice part. Since she'd seen Philip again, she said she realised what poor Ron had missed. If only they had the money to buy a little business, say a greengrocer's or a stationer's, she said, they'd be set up for life. They'd never need to bother anybody again. Her eyes bright on Miss Emily, she waited.

'Have you looked about to see if there is a business for sale in Swanley?' asked Miss Emily.

'Oh, no,' said Gwen. 'Not much good looking out if you've no hope of buying, is it? I mean, I don't go looking in shop windows when I've no money in my pocket!' she said with one of her hoarse laughs.

'You'd better look for something then,' said Miss Emily. 'And we'll see what we can do.'

'Well, that's ever so good of you, Auntie,' said Gwen. 'I'm sure we'd be ever so grateful, wouldn't we, Ken?'

'That's right,' said Ken.

It was not long before Gwen reappeared at The Willows with news of a business in Swanley for sale; a stationer's shop with a circulating library attached.

'I knew you'd be interested in that, Auntie,' said Gwen brightly. 'Books, you know. The man's just died. Bit of luck, isn't it? Spurr's the name. And the widow wants to sell. But we shall have to be quick, because there's several after it, and no wonder, it seems a little gold mine. Ken made enquiries and dotted it all down, didn't you, Ken?'

'That's right,' said Ken, bringing a wallet full of newspaper cuttings from his inside waistcoat pocket. With long, soiled fingers he selected a scrap of paper with figures scribbled over it.

The stationer's widow, it seemed, would sell for two thousand pounds.

'Two thousand pounds,' repeated Miss Emily. She had not expected a small stationer's shop to cost so much. But she knew nothing about these things.

'I must think it over,' she said.

'Certainly,' said Gwen. 'But you'll let us know fairly soon, won't you? As I say, there's others after it.'

'I think I'd better see the place,' said Miss Emily reluctantly. She didn't want to occupy herself with the affair, feeling inadequate to cope with it, but she must. She could not trust to Gwen's account and she would not consult the family lawyer. She knew the lawyer kept James informed of his sisters' affairs, so she never went near him unless obliged to. He certainly must not get wind of this project or James would reappear at The Willows. He had not been for years. Doreen might have competed with Gwen, but he knew she had no chance against Philip, so James gave up coming and contented himself by writing at Christmas or when some financial indiscretion of his sisters aroused him to protest.

She sighed at the thought of going into this affair of the stationer's shop, but could not part with such a sum without making sure that it was being given for a sound project. Given it would have to be. She knew they would never get any of it back; not from Gwen. She would not ask for or accept interest. There was nothing for it, if they decided to provide the money, but to give it outright. But she owed it to Susan and Philip to see that the money was properly spent.

Then, with a feeling of relief, she decided to let Philip handle the matter. He was old enough now to be the man of the family, and Gwen would never cheat her own son. Yes, Philip should manage everything. Except that she and Susan would just go and give the place what Philip called 'the once-over'. She smiled as she thought of that expression. Dear Philip, he was going to be such a comfort to them, such a help and stay in their old age. More and more they would be able to rely on him. It seemed almost too much, they were being altogether too much rewarded, that in addition to the happiness he had brought them as a child, he should be going to be such a comfort to them as a man. In adopting him they had meant to do the best for him, but they had, unconsciously, done the best for themselves too, thought Miss Emily, feeling almost guilty about it.

The sisters, taking four different buses to do it, went across the city to Swanley and back. The inconvenience and length of the journey did not annoy them in the least. It made them sure the indolent Gwen would not often make it. Spurr's shop, with a flat above, seemed a nice respectable place and looked flourishing. Having seen this, the Miss Tophams sat back and left the rest to Philip. All they did, though it was not the least important part, was to make out to Gwen a cheque which amounted in the end to a sum nearer three thousand than two. They felt relieved when they had done it; as if they had once more got rid of her. At least, she would have something to occupy her now and would not keep arriving at The Willows, rousing in the Miss Tophams and Cook the old feelings of uneasiness and apprehension.

The cheque seemed to work at once, too, because Gwen and her family seemed to drop completely out of the Miss Tophams' lives. No news whatever came from them. Winter had set in, and Philip always went to a good many dances and parties in the winter, so that the Miss Tophams saw little of him. When they did see him, he didn't speak of the Gordons, and the Miss Tophams were only too glad to let sleeping dogs lie.

For a time. At first they congratulated themselves on Gwen's silence, but after several weeks had gone by, they grew uneasy.

'It's rather strange,' said Susan. 'That boy seemed so attached to Philip. Of course, it's all for the best, but it *is* rather strange, isn't it?'

It seemed increasingly strange, and at last the Miss Tophams decided to take a surreptitious journey to Swanley and have a look at the shop from across the road to see if Gwen had settled in properly. 'And if we feel like it when we get there,' said Miss Emily, 'we'll just go in and ask how she's getting on. After all, it's perfectly natural.'

They crossed the city to Swanley. There was such a sameness about the roads and houses of the estate that they found themselves considerably confused, but at last, from across the road, Miss Emily pointed her stick at the opposite corner.

'There's the shop,' she said.

They stood, surveying it. 'They haven't changed the name over the window,' said Miss Susan. 'It's still "Spurr – Stationer."'

'Perhaps they aren't going to,' said Miss Emily. 'Perhaps they think it best to keep the old name.'

'They dress the window very well, don't they?' said Susan. 'Quite as if they were used to it.'

Miss Emily agreed. But at that moment a woman appeared at the door of the shop and stood there for a moment, looking out.

'Why, that's the woman we saw when we went over the place,' said Emily. 'That's Mrs Spurr, the widow, Isn't it, Susan?'

'It is,' said Susan. 'Emily, what's the meaning of that?'

'I don't know,' said Miss Emily. 'Unless they've kept her on.'

'Of course, they might have done that,' said Susan.

'But I think we'd better go and see,' said Emily.

They crossed the road and went into the shop. But for the woman behind the counter, it was empty.

'Good afternoon,' said Miss Emily, bowing her head under the dangling magazines. 'You're still here, Mrs Spurr?'

The woman looked surprised. 'Yes, I'm still here,' she said with a laugh. 'Why not?'

'I thought you were going to leave,' said Miss Emily. 'I thought you were going to sell the business.'

'Oh, I changed my mind,' said the woman. 'I found I could manage, so I'm managing. But what's that to you, if you don't mind my asking?'

'Well,' said Miss Emily, faltering a little, 'some friends of mine thought of buying it, you know, and I came with them to look over the premises.'

'I thought I'd seen you before,' said the woman. 'Those people – yes. No, I never heard from them again,' she said.

A man came into the shop and she turned to serve him.

'Well, good afternoon,' said Miss Emily, relieved to be able to escape.

'Good afternoon,' called the woman indifferently.

'Susan,' said Emily, clutching her sister's arm as they recrossed the road, 'what can it mean?'

'She's cheated again,' said Susan sternly. 'That's what it is.'

'But it's more than that,' said Emily, her lips trembling. 'What has Philip known about it all?'

'Philip!' exclaimed Susan. 'Philip?' She halted on the pavement. 'Philip can't have known anything about it. What do you mean?'

'I think he must have known they didn't buy the shop,' said Emily.

The sisters looked into each other's eyes.

'Oh, no,' said Susan. 'He would have told us.'

'I think he must have known,' said Emily.

'Oh, Emily, don't say that. He couldn't have known. Come along, let's hurry home and talk to him. Don't suspect Philip like that. Why should you?'

'Because I think it is very strange he never spoke of them again. We had a reason for not speaking of them, but what reason had he – except that he didn't want to bring the subject up? Susan, I'm old. I see things too late. I feel very old this afternoon, Susan. I wish the bus would come so that we could sit down.'

'It's coming,' comforted Susan, holding her sister's arm. 'We'll soon be home, and I know we'll find that Philip knew nothing whatever about it.'

But Emily was right. Philip had known. He had known that his mother made no attempt to buy the stationer's shop, but had bought a share in a dance hall in Lower Marsh instead.

'But I didn't know until they'd done it,' he said, looking at the sisters across the table.

They looked at him in silence. Emily's hands trembled as she clasped them on the cloth. Susan had tears in her eyes.

'Why didn't you tell us? Didn't you think we had a right to know?' asked Miss Emily. Never had she thought she would have to speak in such a tone to him.

'Well, I knew it would only upset you,' he said. 'Besides, it was too late, what was the use?'

'But you couldn't expect it not to come out?' said Emily.

'I *wanted* it to come out,' cried Philip. 'I was hoping every day you'd get to know, but not from me. D'you think I've liked keeping it dark? I have not, let me tell you.'

Very slightly, Miss Emily's face cleared. Susan laid a hand in appeal on her sister's arm.

'Besides, you know, Aunt Emily,' reasoned Philip, leaning across the table earnestly. 'You'd given them the money. We really ought to let people earn their living in the way that suits them best. What would my mother and Ken do in a book-shop? And Ron? It was absurd, wasn't it? Ken knows all about dance halls. He's run one before, it seems. They'll make far more money and be far happier where they are, than in that shop.'

'In Lower Marsh?' said Emily. 'A district like that?'

'Oh, it's not so bad,' said Philip. 'In fact they've made it into a very nice hall.'

Miss Emily's face clouded again.

'So you've been there?' she said.

'Well, yes, I have.'

They looked at each other, Philip's dark eyes on his aunt.

'As a matter of fact,' he said, his face breaking into a smile in spite of himself, 'I've been playing in the band.'

'Playing in the band?' said Miss Emily aghast.

Philip got up and flung himself round the table to throw his arms round her.

'Oh, I couldn't resist it,' he said. 'Don't look like that, Aunt Emily, I can't stand it. Don't be cross, darling. Think of it – there was that gorgeous piano and a complete band. It was such a chance and they were so decent. They practised with me no end, and the regular pianist went off on his holiday and left it to me. I've had the time of my life. Don't spoil it, Aunt Emily. Don't! And I say, you and Aunt Susan must come and watch me playing. You must. Oh, don't be narrow-minded, darling. Don't be a spoilsport. What's wrong with a dance hall? There are thousands of them. Young people will dance, you know, you can't stop 'em, and they might as well dance in a respectable place while they're at it, and this is, I promise you. You must come and see. They're dying for you to see it.'

And, surprisingly, they went. He talked them round, though it took time. Miss Emily was badly shaken by the incident. She felt that Philip's behaviour had been secretive and somehow devious. Anyway, it wasn't what she would have *liked* him to do, she said to Susan. Cook, too, when they told her – they always told her everything – took it as seriously as Emily. She shook her head over it. She saw his mother's hand in it. It didn't sound like their boy, she said. From this day she added a petition to the prayers she said every night, kneeling by her high bed. 'Please God,' she prayed, 'don't let him be like his mother.'

But Susan tried to persuade them that it was really nothing. He hadn't known until too late, and then, boy-like, he had been so very tempted to play in the band. They mustn't blame him, he was so young. And Emily had given him too much responsibility. How could a boy control a sharp, experienced woman like Gwen? It was too much to expect altogether. They must forget about it, and they must go to the dance hall as he wanted them to. They must keep up with him, keep along with him, said Susan. It was much safer that way. If they didn't, they might lose him altogether, being old as they were, and dull company for him.

In the end, she got her way. They went to the dance hall. They donned their 'semi-evening' dresses of black moiré silk, the ones that Philip liked best. Each wore a black velvet ribbon round her throat to conceal, a little, the ravages of time. Susan actually put a star of dim diamonds in her hair. They took floating ninon scarves to throw round their shoulders if the place should be draughty – and filled with trepidation and excitement, they took a taxi to the hall.

'This is something very new for us, Susan,' said Miss Emily, as they walked over the soundless rubber carpet of the foyer.

'It is indeed, dear,' said Susan, her eyes going past her sister to the dance floor beyond.

It was clear for the moment. The dancers had drifted from the floor when the band stopped and were now crowded against the walls, or seated, the lucky ones, at the small tables scattered under the balcony. There seemed to be an immense number of young men and girls, all very noisy. The Miss Tophams stood at the entrance peering in, much to the amusement of the young people about them.

'See what's come!' said one. 'Mike and Joe – two partners looking for you! Go and ask them for the rumba.'

At the far end of the room, on a low dais, the Miss Tophams saw Philip at the piano, his back for the moment towards them. 'Let's go across to him,' said Miss Emily, and would have started had not Susan laid a hand on her arm. 'Perhaps he wouldn't like it,' she said.

Then they saw Gwen coming across the floor towards them. They waited for her, concealing their astonishment, she looked so unfamiliar. She wore a long tight black dress with a glittering design of sequins climbing up the front. The design was so bold and brilliant that from a distance you couldn't see the woman behind it. She looked like a tree walking, thought Miss Susan. Like a palm with the leaves heaved by an ample bosom. Her bleached hair was piled immensely high. Her mouth was shaped into a strong, orange-coloured cupid's bow and her lashes were balled with mascara.

But she looked completely at home, completely mistress of herself and the place.

'Nice of you to come, Aunties,' she said, reaching them. 'Come this way. I've kept a table for you.'

She led the way to a table under the balcony and pulled out the small gilt chairs for them. 'You be all right there?' she enquired. 'I'll send a waitress later. Order what you like. It's on the house tonight.'

The Miss Tophams had no idea what that meant, but they

thanked her. Miss Emily had intended to tell Gwen what she thought of her misuse of the money. Over and over again she had rehearsed what she would say, but she felt it was not the moment. She sat at the table, arranging her scarf, looking at Philip, who was chatting with the band, looking at Ken, who, his face sallow above his dress shirt, was gliding among the tables diffusing an air of stealth and wrongdoing, though in all probability, thought Miss Susan, he was only asking them if they would take tea or coffee.

Gwen stood beside the table. She hadn't time to sit down, she said, she must be off in a minute.

'D'you know who we've got in the bar?' she said, amused. 'We've got Blondie.'

She saw that it conveyed nothing to them.

'Oh, I forgot,' she said, laughing at herself. 'You never knew Blondie, did you? She was a friend of mine in the old days. She was at the Empire. Introduced me to Bern, as a matter of fact. My God, you should see her now! Enough to turn the milk sour. But I chose her on purpose. Because of the boys. She's no temptation, isn't Blondie. Not now. Phil and Ron'll be safe with her, you don't need to worry.'

In spite of this reassurance, the Miss Tophams looked troubled. They had not thought to reckon with a bar and a woman behind it, in addition to the dance hall, for Philip. It was another disturbing idea to assimilate. But before the process could do more than begin, the band struck up and the dancers crowded out on to the floor.

The Miss Tophams leaned forward. They had come to watch Philip play, and for them, now, the evening had begun.

But the dancers were a nuisance. They obscured the view. Miss Emily waved her hand as if she would brush them from the floor. Miss Susan craned over their heads. 'I can't see him properly,' she complained.

'Half a mo',' said Gwen indulgently. 'You will.'

Gwen was in an amiable mood. Everything was going her way. The place was crowded. Philip was a draw, the girls were mad about him, and Gwen enjoyed saying: 'That's my son at the piano.' It made a sensation, and everybody made up to her, hoping for an introduction. It was something of a triumph, too, to get the old girls in, and though they looked a scream, really, with their black velvet neck-bands and starchy ways among the boys and girls, they somehow gave a bit of tone to the place, and Gwen wasn't sorry to be overheard calling them 'Auntie'. And nothing had been said about the money. It was all passing off very well, and Gwen was pleased with herself.

The hall grew dim and a spotlight picked out Philip at the piano. There he was, dashing music from the keys like brilliant water-drops, playing with incredible speed and verve, laughing up into the light, having the time of his life and looking so handsome, young and altogether irresistible, the Miss Tophams thought, that tears came into their eyes and they watched him through a blur.

'It takes me back,' said Gwen, standing above them, her arms crossed over the sequins. 'Many's the time I've seen his father look just like that. You don't wonder I fell for him, do you?'

Miss Susan looked up. Gwen, in her good humour, was inclined to be communicative.

'He died, you know, did Bern,' she said. 'Yes, died in America about six weeks after we got there. Scarlet fever.'

'He was only twenty-five,' she said. She poked a finger here and there into her pompadour and scratched her scalp. 'What's that, Ken? You want me? Righty-ho. Well, you'll be all right, won't you?' she said to the Miss Tophams. 'I'll send a waitress along. Not a bad place, is it?'

She smiled a hostess smile, and without waiting for an answer walked away between the tables, trailing her hand proprietorially over the back of the gilt chairs as she went.

With a crash of chords, Philip's playing ceased, and, running the gauntlet of unbridled applause, he came sliding over the floor to his aunts. He threw himself into a chair and mopped his brow. 'Phew,' he said.

'That was splendid, dear,' they said. 'You surpassed yourself.'

'It was all right, was it?' he said. 'Oh, Phyllis, bring me a large lager. I could drink a well dry,' he said to the waitress. 'And tea for my aunts. China, if you've got it.'

A large semi-circle of girls was crowding slowly nearer, like calves approaching an object of curiosity or fascination in a field, thought Miss Susan.

'No autographs tonight,' cried Philip, waving a hand at them. 'Let me off. I'm otherwise engaged.'

Laughing, he picked up his chair and sat down again with his back to them.

'It's beyond a joke,' he said. 'Ah – my beer! And your tea. Well, what do you think of it all? Eh?'

The Miss Tophams looked at the girls, all eyes on Philip.

'It's most interesting, dear,' said Miss Emily, blinking anxiously. 'Most interesting.'

'Where's the boy?' asked Miss Susan. 'Where's Ronald?'

'Isn't he about?' asked Philip. He looked round, and smiles rippled over the admiring semi-circle. 'He slips out, the beggar. There's a car park behind the County Club. He knows the man at the gate, so he takes his girl and spends a comfortable evening in a Rolls-Royce now and again.'

He laughed and drained his glass. He was excited at his own performance and the girls at his back, or he would not have spoken so freely.

'Phyllis,' he called. 'Another lager. Don't be shocked, Aunt Emily. It wouldn't hurt a fly.'

Victorian parents, foster or otherwise, had an easier task. Black was black, white white in those days, right was right and wrong wrong; there were no half shades to confuse. The Victorian elders could lay down the law in these matters, and the young, mostly, took their word for it.

But nowadays it is different. The Miss Tophams were modern in that they were apologetic about what they thought to be right and diffident in condemning what they felt to be wrong, in case it wasn't.

The conversation that took place in Miss Emily's bedroom that night, over the glasses of hot water they always drank on retiring, might have amused a sophisticated listener.

'I don't suppose, Emily,' ventured Susan, sipping the hot water, 'that there's anything actually wrong in playing in a band?'

'There isn't,' said Emily, also sipping. 'All boys nowadays seem to want to play in a band, or have a band at home, just as they want to fly or drive fast cars. Speed, noise and danger, preferably combined, are what they want, and if they can't have them altogether, they'll take them singly.'

'Well then?' said Susan, who wished very much to let Philip do as he wanted, but feared for him if he did.

'Don't you think we ought to let him?' she said, since Emily did not speak.

'My dear, we can't stop him,' said Miss Emily rather grimly. 'What can two old women do against youth, high spirits, excitement and novelty? What chance have we?'

They pondered on this, Emily sitting on the bed, Susan in a chair.

'Lager's very light, dear,' said Susan, beginning again. 'I had it once in Switzerland, I remember, and I didn't feel the slightest ill effects.'

'Oh, we've no need to fear lager,' said Miss Emily, still without saying what it was they had need to fear.

'There are so many different kinds of lives and so many different kinds of people and natures, aren't there?' said Susan, trying to figure things out. 'I suppose even Gwen has her good points.'

'She probably has,' admitted Emily. 'For one thing, she's not timid, and we are, rather. She's not bound by comfort or ease, as we are. She broke away from them and went to much worse conditions. She went halfway across the world after a man. He didn't want her, but she went.'

The sisters sat in silence for a moment.

'But we can't trust her,' Emily broke out again. 'And we don't want Philip to be mixed up with her. Yet I hesitate, you know, to try to prevent Philip from seeing his own people. It doesn't seem to be quite the kind thing to do, does it? Besides, if we did try to prevent him I don't suppose we should succeed.'

'He seems to be quite taken up with that brother of his,' said Susan. 'I didn't like to hear he was sitting out with a girl in someone else's Rolls-Royce, did you?'

'No, but I liked even less that Philip should think it was funny,' said Miss Emily.

'And yet I don't suppose there's anything actually wrong in sitting out in someone else's car?' puzzled Miss Susan.

'I don't suppose there is,' admitted Miss Emily. 'I don't know why we think so badly of it.'

'Well, dear, I think we'd better go to bed,' she said. 'I don't suppose we shall get anywhere, with all our talking. We can only pray for our boy and do our best.'

'Good night, dear,' said Susan, kissing her sister's insubstantial cheek. 'I don't know what I should do without you. You know so much more than I do.'

'Don't say that,' said Miss Emily, shocked. 'I've just lived long enough to know I know nothing at all.'

CHAPTER SIX

Gwen's Ronald seemed to have the same faculty of upsetting the atmosphere of The Willows as his mother before him. When he arrived, which was often, confusion came with him. Philip hailed him with joy and took him up to his room, which the Miss Tophams had fondly furnished as a bed-sitting room so that he should have a place entirely to himself.

As soon as the boys got upstairs the house was filled with a blare of noise from Philip's wireless set, with the sound of the bath taps turned on full, with the amazing bumpings and thumpings that accompanied the bathing and changing that followed. Ronald used Philip's shirts, socks, shoes, suits as if they were his own; to Cook's extreme annoyance.

The Miss Tophams sat below in a state of agitation. They said it was the loud throb of the music that upset them, but it was probably because Philip had a cupboard full of sherry, gin and vermouth upstairs, bought with his earnings at the dance hall and at Fell and Brownings, the engineers, where he now worked. He was boyishly proud of his cocktail cabinet, arranging and rearranging it like a little girl playing with a doll's house. But the Miss Tophams looked upon its contents as dangerous stuff, especially in Ronald's company.

By and by the boys came bounding down to raid the pantry, eating largely of anything they could lay their hands on. Then with a hug for each aunt – bent on haste and pleasure though he was, he kept his charming, affectionate ways – Philip mounted his motorcycle and, with Ronald pillion behind him, rushed off, leaving the Miss Tophams in anxious ignorance as to where he had gone and when he would be back, and Cook full of dark conjecture.

'That Ronald's his mother's son,' she said. 'He'll get our boy into trouble before long.'

'But Philip shouldn't be so easily led,' said Miss Emily. 'Though I know boys will be boys,' she added, trying to be reasonable. 'This stage will pass. I'm sure Philip's all right underneath.'

They would go upstairs, then, the three of them; Emily and Susan to put Philip's room to rights while Cook mopped up the bathroom. But the next morning, if Ronald had come back with Philip as he often did, to sleep on the sofa, it was all to do again. 'I've never seen anyone make such a mess,' complained Cook. 'I don't know what our boy sees in him.'

If it had been any other friend of Philip's, the Miss Tophams would have taken a fond pride in the noise and upset. They always had until now. But Philip had deserted his former friends. Ronald had become his sole companion and the dance hall his chief interest. And the Miss Tophams distrusted Ronald almost as much as they distrusted his mother.

'It's as if he doubles Philip's own weaknesses,' said Susan suddenly, having worked it out. 'We've tried to bring Philip up with a better sense of values, and then at a crucial age his mother and brother come to reinforce the characteristics he probably has in common with them.'

'I think that's what it is,' said Miss Emily wearily.

They were worried. Philip was not taking well to the work he had once looked forward to. He came down late in the mornings looking tired and even, the Miss Tophams feared, dissipated after his night at the dance hall. When Miss Emily inferred that he might lose his job if he didn't attend to it better, he said it wouldn't matter.

'I can earn five times as much in a professional band, or on the halls,' he said, horrifying them.

They feared limelight was getting into his blood; he never wanted to be out of it. He wanted more and better limelight.

Then he worried them still further by losing his appetite, by looking even worse when he came down in the mornings, by being silent and forgetting to hug them before he went out. Many a time they might not have been there at all, they felt. They decided to go and see Gwen and insist that she should not employ him any more.

Gwen lived in the flat over the dance hall, and when the Miss Tophams, passing through the shrouded ballroom which smelled stale, rang the bell at the foot of a stair, Ken opened the door, cautiously as he did everything, and looked down at them. Sallow, collarless, unshaven, a cigarette stuck to his lip, he motioned to them to come up, called to his wife and glided away. He scented trouble, and his instinct was always to avoid it.

In the sitting room, Gwen lay before a hot fire on a short sofa with high ends. She looked like a woman in a bucket, with her head, her back hair dangling in tin curlers, protruding at one side, her feet, in old pink satin slippers, at the other.

'Hello,' she said, without getting up or putting aside the newspaper she was reading. 'What brings you? We're resting. But sit down. Chuck the bag off that chair, Aunt Emily.'

The room was like a deep box with windows set so high that, in a corner, there was a pole with a hook to open them. Miss Susan felt sure it was never used. The room smelled of new carpet, a harsh ochre; everything was new, varnished, and in the Miss Tophams' opinion, hideous. On a stand was an art vase of honesty, its delicious parchment interspersed with coloured tinsel balls to brighten it up. Gwen lolled on the sofa, her feet so high she showed her knickers. The Miss Tophams averted their eyes.

'Well, what have you come for, ducks?' said Gwen, scratching her arms. 'Not for love of me, I'm sure. Something wrong with the precious boy? You're not going to say he can't play tonight, I hope?'

'We don't want him to play here at all,' said Miss Emily. 'We understand that he can't leave you in the lurch at once, but at the end of the week we want you to tell him you don't need him any more.'

'And can you see me doing it?' asked Gwen. 'I would be a fool. He's a draw, is Philip, and he knows it. He's having the time of his life. You came here and saw him, you made no objection. What's got you now?'

'It's not good for him,' said Emily. 'It's affecting his health. He can't play night after night, in a bad atmosphere, after his day's work at Fell and Brownings.'

'Let him give up the day work then,' interrupted Gwen. 'He'll get twice as much here in time.'

'We would never agree to that,' said Miss Emily sternly. 'It's not the sort of life we want for him.'

'It won't matter much what you want,' said Gwen. 'Phil takes after his father. You'll not root his playing out of him. If he doesn't play here, he'll play somewhere else. I should have thought you'd have thanked me for keeping him under your eye, instead of carrying on like this. Phil'll go his own way. I always went mine, didn't I, in spite of you? Well, Phil's my son, though I dare say you'd like to forget it. You know, you two,' said Gwen, drawing in her feet, raising her knees and showing even more of her knickers, 'I dare say you've been very good and you meant well and all that, but your sort shouldn't really mix itself up with ours. Your life drives us bats, you know. A bit of reading and playing the piano, but nothing loud, oh no, and nothing with a tune to it. A bit of gardening and going to church – and what else? Nothing. How d'you expect anybody with guts to stand it? I couldn't, and I bet Phil doesn't, either.' She looked at them with her bright, mocking eyes.

'Philip was happy until you came,' said Miss Emily, her lips trembling. She was struck to the heart by Gwen's version of life at The Willows in case it was at the root of the trouble, in case it was what was driving Philip to his wild ways. Parsons'

sons, boys brought up by maiden aunts, always went wild in reaction.

But Susan drew herself up in the hideous plush armchair. She was extremely indignant that the raddled Rubens on the sofa should attack Emily in this way – Emily, so gentle, unselfish, good, tolerant – far too tolerant. That was where the trouble was. Emily, she herself, they had both been far too tolerant.

'Gwen, you're a viper,' she said. 'We nursed you in our bosom far too long. After the first half-dozen bites we should have thrown you out. I don't like gratitude and we never wanted any. Which is a good thing, because we should never have got any from you. But you haven't even any decent feeling. You've treated us abominably. You've cheated and lied since the day you came to the house. Your latest trick has been to get three thousand pounds out of us under false pretences, and you use it to undermine our influence with Philip and our hopes of a good life for him.'

'Phil's as keen on this dance hall as we are,' said Gwen, her curlers clashing.

'The fact remains that but for you he would never have thought of it,' said Susan. 'You came back to get what you could out of us, you introduced him to a life he would never have known but for you. You can make out a case for your sort of life against ours, if you like, but under your eyes at this moment is a proof which life is the better. Look at my sister's face and look at your own, twenty years younger and more though you are. My sister's life shows in her face and yours shows in yours, and a vulgar, self-indulgent, low thing it is . . .'

'Susan!' cried Miss Emily amazed.

'I don't care,' said Susan. 'It's time we spoke out. It's no use sparing her feelings. She hasn't got the feelings we're soft enough to credit her with. She's a bad influence. She's dogged our lives for twenty-five years, turning up again and again to see what more she could get out of us. I know you'd never have said this, Emily, so I've said it for you. And now come away. I'll speak to Philip myself.'

She got up from the plush chair, and Emily got up too.

'Well, thanks a lot,' said Gwen. 'Now I know where we stand. But I bet Phil won't listen to you. You'd better tackle that girl, that Sonia Smith they're both after,' she said, narrowing her eyes at them as if she were glad to give them something else to worry about. 'Phil'll go where that girl is, and she's always here. I don't suppose you knew about her, did you? There's a lot more danger in a girl like Sonia Smith than there is in any piano-playing. And there's danger in men themselves, it's *in* them,' said Gwen. 'So what are you going to do about that?'

The Miss Tophams had halted at the door. A girl. This was a new threat to Philip. They looked almost blankly at Gwen, unable to deal with it. Susan recovered first. 'Go along, Emily,' she said, gently impelling her sister through the door. 'It's no good looking to her. She can't tell us what to do.'

'Well, ta-ta,' said Gwen, resuming the paper.

They shut the door and went carefully down the stairs, much shaken.

II

Susan had what she thought of as a 'talk with Philip,' though the talking was all on her side. He listened, half-smiling in affection, but looking as if she didn't really know what she was talking about. And facing him, she almost felt she didn't. It was all very well to talk, to point out, but you couldn't do away with the blind drive of youthful passion. Parents might go about congratulating themselves that because they have explained the 'facts of life' in good time their children can't possibly come to any harm. But facts have little or no effect on feelings; you can't reason with passion.

Philip listened, assured her that there was nothing to worry about, patted her on the shoulder and went on as before. The only difference was that Ronald did not come to the house. There was no more noise upstairs; but that only made things seem ominously quiet. The Miss Tophams were soon inconsistent enough, as they acknowledged to each other, to wish that Ronald would come back and things be as they were.

Philip was increasingly tired, strained, silent, and the Miss Tophams, remembering their last experience of adolescent love, were haunted by the idea that like his mother he would run away. They got into the habit of not being able to go to sleep until they heard him come in at night.

Gradually they gave up the idea of going to bed at all until he came in. They wandered in and out of each other's rooms, and about midnight Emily made tea with her electric kettle. If he was very late, she made it again during the night. They wore silk caps with deep lace frills and dressing gowns of quilted silk, Susan's crimson, Emily's peacock blue. The gowns were old and the stuffing was coming out in places, and Cook had lately turned the cuffs and collars to make them do a little longer. The Miss Tophams were cutting down their personal expenses.

They had learnt with mild surprise that if you reduce your capital you reduce your income. Gwen's three thousand pounds had taken a large slice of their remaining capital, already considerably eaten into by the cost of Philip's upbringing and education. The sisters had always lived with comfort and elegance and had never thought of doing otherwise, but lately it had been brought home to them that they must make some economies. It would be dreadful if it came about that they had to leave their beloved Willows, they said to each other. Only one more raid must be made on their capital, they agreed, and that was for Philip's car on his birthday which was only two months away now. After that, positively nothing more must be taken out, for it was not only themselves they had to think about, but Philip and Cook too.

So they waited up for Philip in dressing gowns they would once never have dreamed of wearing. They made tea, they talked a little and sighed a good deal without knowing it. Each sometimes noticed that the other sighed and was compassionate, without noticing that she sighed herself.

'He gets later and later,' sighed Emily.

'I think he'd been drinking last night,' said Susan.

'I feel we've failed as foster parents,' said Emily.

'It's only what many a real parent has to put up with,' said Susan. 'Why should we escape?'

Cook sometimes came in, her hair screwed into knobs with lead curlers, to remonstrate with them, or have a cup of tea herself. She often told Philip what she thought of him keeping his aunts up night after night, distressing them, wearing them out. But he said they had no need to wait up for him; he hated them to wait up for him, he said, it was their own fault. He spoke savagely sometimes, shocking Cook into silence.

One night, a mild summer night with a fine rain falling, the Miss Tophams wandered about the landings as usual. From time to time Susan looked through the thick curtains by way of something to do. The moon showed through a slit in the clouds like an eye through a half-closed lid.

At midnight Emily made tea; at half-past one she made it again. As she was drinking hers, Susan paused to listen. She had heard a quick padding of footsteps on the gravel.

'He's coming,' she said to Emily, thankful that their long vigil was over. They heard his key in the lock, the front door was stealthily opened and closed.

'He's not been drinking tonight,' said Susan. 'He's trying to be quiet.'

'We can go to bed now,' she said, kissing her sister. 'Good night, dear.' She went to the door to steal to her own room. They didn't like Philip to know they waited up for him, it annoyed him. She stood with the door in her hand, wondering if it were safe to slip across the landing now, or if it would be better to wait until he had come up and shut himself into his room.

But as she stood, a strange sound made itself heard in the

silence of the night. The sisters turned their startled eyes to each other. It was the sound of very fast, very difficult breathing. It was the noise of sobbing, straining lungs, struggling for breath in the hall below.

Without a word the sisters were through the door and on to the landing. Emily switched on the light, Susan was already halfway down the stairs. Beyond the threshold of the dining room, the darkness behind him, stood Philip, his collar burst from his neck, his soaked clothes hanging on his body, his hair streaked over his brow. His staring eyes upon them, he struggled to breathe, his chest heaving.

'Philip!' they cried. Miss Emily made to turn on the dining room light, but he raised an arm as if it were a dead weight and shook his head.

'No light,' he gasped.

'Philip, what on earth is the matter? Where have you been? What is it?'

Miss Emily grasped him firmly by both shoulders. He staggered in her hands.

'The light, Susan,' she said.

'No, no,' he said hoarsely. 'No one must see . . .'

'No one can see through those curtains,' said Miss Emily sternly.

The light on, the Miss Tophams stared at him in horror. Blenched, distraught, shuddering, he stared at them with fixed eyes.

'I've killed them both,' he said, hanging between Emily's hands. 'They're both dead, and another man in the road . . . they're dead, all three . . .'

'Philip, pull yourself together . . . you're drunk . . .'

'No, I wish I was. . . . They're dead, I tell you. I didn't see the man in the road till the last minute. I ran up a bank to avoid him, the car overturned. Sonia and Ronald are dead, I felt their hearts . . . they've stopped. The man's dead too. And you see, I'm not touched. Oh, Aunt Emily,' he said with a dry sob. 'I was jealous of him, but I never wanted him to die – and I love her so much and I've killed her.' He bowed his head and sobbed, while Miss Emily held him off, staring at him.

'It can't be true,' faltered Susan, stooping to look closely into his face. 'You've no car . . . what car . . .?'

'Ronald took it from the car park at the back of the hall. I saw him coming with Sonia. I stood in the road and made him stop. I forced my way into the driving seat. We were all a bit tight, I think. He and Sonia climbed over into the back. I was mad because she did that. I drove all out on the Orton Road, and then I had the accident, and then I found they were dead. I left them lying there and I've run across the fields – it was near the White Posts.'

'More than four miles out . . .' said Emily. 'You've run four miles.'

'I've never seen a soul,' said Philip, as if he were pleading with her. 'No one saw me. No one knows I was there. Don't let anyone know, Aunt Emily. I'll be had up for manslaughter and for taking a car that doesn't belong to me. I'll get years in prison. Hide me, Aunt Emily. No, no,' he said, breaking away from her and throwing himself into a chair, leaning over the side distractedly, clasping his head, 'I don't need hiding. I must just stop here and go on as usual. I mustn't hide. No one knows I was in that car . . . no one must ever know that I killed them.'

At an exclamation from behind, the sisters turned. Cook came into the room, her face set.

'You're right,' she said harshly. 'Nobody must know. No need for anybody to know. What good can that do, now they're dead? You must go to bed. We must get the lights out and the house quiet. But you must stop shivering. Stop chattering your teeth. Put your hand under his chin, Miss Emily. I'll get him some hot milk. Hot milk for shock, they say. We must think up a tale – of how he came home at the usual time and went to bed. Go over him, Miss Emily, and see he has no stains on his clothes. We must think of everything. Get his shoes off, Miss Susan, and bring them to me. I'll burn them. They'd give him away. We must think of everything,' she said again, hurrying out to the kitchen.

Emily put one hand on his head and the other under his chin, her thoughts whirling. Susan knelt on the carpet and took off his thin burst shoes.

'Gwen knows, surely,' she said. 'She must know you went to the car . . .'

'She doesn't, she doesn't!' he said, rolling himself free from their hands in the chair. 'He went out with Sonia hours before. I saw him go. I know where they were going. I had to play. I had to go on playing. I'll never play the piano again – never, never. It was torture – those damned tunes . . .'

He clasped his head.

'I wish I'd died. I wish I'd been killed too. I'll go to prison. I'll be years in prison. It's manslaughter. I'll never forget I've killed them. I'll be shut up for years with nothing to think of but that I killed them.'

'Philip, Philip,' said Susan, trying to stroke his hands.

'She was eighteen,' said Philip. 'Her neck's broken. She must have hit the roof of the car.'

'Philip, stop. Don't go on like this. They'll never get you. No one will ever know,' said Emily. 'Try to stop shivering, darling. Susan, do you think he ought to have brandy?'

'No,' said Susan. 'He needs a sedative, not a stimulant. I'll go and get those tablets from my room.'

She went out. Philip lay back in the chair, his eyes closed, his face streaked with sweat and rain. Emily stood beside him, looking at him. The whole thing was a nightmare she could not credit. His face was a nightmare. That he should ever look like this, that he should ever suffer such remorse and fear . . .

Susan came back with the tablets. She stood with her sister, looking at him too. His face frightened her. There was some struggle going on in him that they dared not break in on. When Cook came in with the hot milk, Susan put out a hand to keep it aside.

Philip opened his eyes and looked at them as if they were not there. He sat up and leaned forward in the chair, his chin in his hands, his elbows on his knees. He had finished shivering; he sat still and silent, staring blindly before him, and the three women stood round him, silent too.

The clock in the hall ticked audibly; ponderous, slow. The women waited, not knowing what they waited for.

Suddenly Philip bent forward and seized the shoes Susan

had taken off. He began to put them on, his fingers sure and quick on the laces.

'Philip,' said Miss Emily. 'What are you doing?'

He did not answer until his shoes were on. When he spoke it was in a different voice, resolute, almost calm. He got to his feet and fastened his collar.

'I'm going to give myself up,' he said.

They stared at him, petrified.

'Philip,' cried Susan, darting to pinion him in her arms. 'You mustn't. No one saw you, no one need ever know, what good can it do – since they're dead? You're not going. You're mad.'

Gently, almost smiling, he tried to free himself. 'I was mad when I ran away,' he said. 'I've come to my senses now.'

'Not you, you're crazy,' rasped Cook. 'Clean crazy. You'll ruin yourself. You'll never live it down. You'll go to jail for two years or more. You at your age, just beginning your life. And what about your aunts? You'll kill them. Nice reward this, for all they've done for you. And what will it cost them trying to get you off ? They'll spend their last penny. You and your mother between you, you've taken pretty near all they had. The only thing you can do now for your aunts is to swear you've never been in that car, and stick to it. If we're prepared to lie, you've got to lie too.'

Philip shook his head. 'It's no good. I've got to go. If I don't I'll never have any peace again. Sonia and Ronald are dead, I'm sure of that. But that man in the road may not be. I don't know now. I can't remember what I did when I found the other two were dead. That man at the car park, I must let it be known that he wasn't there when Ronald took the car. He'd let Ronald sit in the car before, but he never thought he'd take it away. He'd lose his job and never get another . . . there are too many things involved, all sorts of things will come out. I must go. It's no good,' he said grimly. 'I must face it. If I'm going to keep a shred of self-respect, I must face it.'

'Philip,' wept Susan. 'For our sakes, don't go. We're old, Philip, we can't stand it. We'd never live to see you come out of prison.'

He put his arms round her.

'I'm so sorry . . . I'm so terribly sorry, Aunt Susan. I wish you'd never kept me when I was born. See what I've brought on you. But I've got to go. Aunt Emily,' he said, looking to her, his arms round Susan. 'You see that I've got to go, don't you?'

Emily stood with the tears running down her face.

'Yes, dear, I see. So go, my dear, dear boy, and God bless you.'

A look of relief came into his face.

'I'm going on my motorbike. I'm going to the police station in Carden Street, it's the nearest. I shall take them to the place,' he said, catching his breath. 'I'll get a message through to you as soon as I can. I don't know what they do. Perhaps they'll let me out on bail. I wish you'd go to bed now, all of you. Try to get some sleep. Try not to worry.'

He kissed the weeping Susan, he kissed Emily, who stood stiffly like a post, he kissed Cook, who sobbingly abused him: 'You silly, silly boy . . . you young fool, breaking our hearts. You've no right to go . . . no right . . .'

The door closed behind him. They stood rooted. They heard him start his motorcycle. They heard the sound of the engine diminishing down the road, they listened, their breath held, until they heard no more. Susan sank into a chair and wept. Cook, her hands pressed over her mouth, went out to the kitchen. Emily stood where she was, old, stricken, following him, suffering doubly, with him and for him.

They were ignorant of the law, all of them. He thought he was going to certain prison sentence, to condemnation of manslaughter; so did they.

The clock in the hall struck three; three heavy strokes. On the table stood the glass of milk, its surface wrinkling and shivering as if a chill went over it, as over them.

'His clothes are wet,' wept Susan. 'He's wet through. We let him go in his wet clothes.'

Cook came into the dark hall and stood there, looking in at the dining room. Miss Emily still stood like a statue under the lights.

'Sit down, love,' said Cook, going in and guiding her to a chair. 'Sit there. I'm going to get your rugs, you're both cold.'

'Don't go, Cook,' Susan besought her. 'Stay with us. Stay here.'

'I will, Miss Susan dear. I'll bring something for myself too. We brought him up together and we'll wait together. I dare say it will be a long wait.'

It was a long wait. Time crawled, the fingers crawled over the face of the dining room clock. It was the thin hour when human life and hope is at its lowest ebb. Despair filled the three stricken women sitting in the dining room. What was happening to him now, facing his ordeal on the deserted road, showing what he had done to his brother and the young girl? Those two poor young creatures, killed in their wild youth. . . . And that unknown man? They shuddered. They shuddered and prayed the hours away.

It was when daylight was showing greyly in the hall that Susan turned to Emily with a watery radiance in her face.

'I'm glad he didn't listen to me,' she said. 'I'm glad he went.'

'Yes,' said Emily, sighing. 'We were afraid of what was happening to him, but he was put to the test and he chose the right. All our hope for him was fulfilled tonight, though it has been in such a terrible way. Whatever happens, I don't think we need ever fear for him again.'

Cook gave a sob, but pressing her lips together she got up to draw back the curtains. The rain had stopped. The sun was rising, the birds were singing in the gardens.

The long night was over. They did not know it, but the worst was over too.

III

Wholly unlooked-for though it was, help began to come with the morning. During the night, they had seen none anywhere for Philip or themselves. The only light in the darkness was that he had overcome his own weakness and done what was right. They warmed themselves with that thought all the long night, but they did not hope for any relief from the terrible situation. They were so entirely ignorant of legal procedure that they expected only the inexorable closing in of the legal machinery on their boy. With him, they took the affair quite literally; he had killed three people and must suffer for it.

But even as they rose stiffly from their chairs and began to fold up the rugs they heard the sound of Philip's motorcycle in the road. They knew it too well to be deceived. They stared at one another, the rugs falling from their hands. Regardless of worn dressing gowns, lace caps and Cook's curlers, they hurried out into the drive, and stood, an odd group, with their eyes incredulously on the gate. He appeared. He brought the motorcycle to a standstill at the door and almost fell from the seat. Their shaking, eager hands were quick to help him, to take him into the house. Miss Susan looked back, expecting a policeman to appear in custody; but there was no one.

'They haven't arrested you,' she said in astonishment.

'No,' said Philip in a hoarse voice, his eyelids drooping from fatigue. 'No arrest. They say it's an accident. But I killed them. They're dead. All of them are dead. The man in the road too.'

'Come upstairs, dear,' said Miss Emily. 'Don't try to talk now.'

They found unutterable relief in looking after him, getting a hot bath ready, getting his breakfast. Hot milk, not coffee, Susan decreed. He must sleep. To make sure he should, she crushed sedative tablets into the milk.

When they had done all they could, they drew the curtains and left him lying in his bed, his dark head turned away, one hand clenched at the length of his arm outside the covers. They felt their hearts breaking with love and pity, but they blinked back the tears and went downstairs to tell Cook that they thought he would sleep now.

'He's been to see Gwen already,' they told her. 'And the girl's mother too. He's facing up to everything, you see.'

Cook had made tea for them, and they drank it at the kitchen table, their lips trembling so that the cup was unsteady against them.

'We must dress now,' said Emily. 'We must be ready to face the day.'

Cook was already her usual trim figure in print, her crimped hair concealed under a starched cap. Her heart had almost broken in the night, but her hair had gone on crimping itself in the curlers. She had wondered vaguely, as she unwound it, how it dared come out like this, as if nothing had happened.

The Miss Tophams stole upstairs again. Quietly passing from bathroom to bedroom, quietly opening wardrobe doors, they dressed. But as Miss Emily stood at her dressing table pinning on her jabot of fine lace, her nervous apprehension, calmed by Philip's return, leaped into violent activity again. She saw a policeman coming up the drive. She steadied herself against the table. It had been too good to be true, then? He was coming to arrest Philip. The dread Law had taken, among its inexplicable turns and twists, another turn.

'Susan,' she said, appearing at her sister's door. 'A policeman is here.'

Susan turned and put her hand, too, to her heart.

'A policeman! Emily – don't faint. Sit on the bed. See, I'll get you the sal volatile. Hold up, dear. See, this is nearly ready.'

But as she put the glass into her sister's hand, Cook came up the stairs and into the room, her face all smiles and tears.

'Oh, Miss Emily,' she said. 'It's Tom Holt. He said I was to say that. It seems you got his father a job a long time ago when he'd been out of work for months, and Tom – a very well-set-up-fellow,' said Cook, garrulous with relief. 'He was in the station last night when Philip went in, and he's heard something that'll relieve your mind since Philip left the station, so he's come round to tell you on his way home, because he knew you'd be in great trouble today.'

'Oh, Cook,' breathed Miss Emily. 'God is so good. I thought they'd come to take Philip away.'

They hurried down the stairs, and there in the kitchen was Tom Holt, large, healthy, reassuring, kind – the Law on their side, not against them.

'Good morning, Miss,' he said. 'You don't remember me, of course, seeing I was only a little shaver when you used to come to our house in Sale Street. You got my father a job as water-meter inspector, you remember?'

'Oh, you're Fred Holt's son,' said Miss Emily, taking his hand. 'Your father was such a nice man. I only went to see the Water Engineer once or twice; he got the job himself.'

'No, it was you told him about it. He'd never have thought of it, or thought he could get it, Miss, but you encouraged him and gave him confidence at a time when he'd lost it. He spoke about you many and many a time. In fact, that much, that we grew up thinking we owed about everything we'd got to you.'

'Sit down, Tom Holt, do please sit down,' said Emily. 'See, Cook's bringing you a cup of coffee. Cook says you've some good news for us, even on this awful day.'

'Well, it's like this, Miss,' said Tom Holt, sitting down and putting his peaked hat on the table. 'I don't know as I really ought to divulge it, but I just got to know, when I was going off home to my breakfast, that that man in the road had been dead for several hours before your boy had his accident. It was a dead body in the road, Miss – perhaps more's the pity he tried to avoid it, because if he'd run over it the two young 'uns might have been alive now. But it makes one less he has to blame himself for, doesn't it? Yes, the man had been killed by something heavier than a car – probably a lorry – several hours previous.'

'Oh, Tom, bless you for coming to tell us,' said Miss Emily, sinking into the chair Cook put for her. 'Bless you for your kindness. If I ever did anything for your father you've more than repaid me now,' she said, wiping her eyes.

'But the other two. He'll be judged for manslaughter, won't he?' said Susan, leaning forward to look into Tom Holt's face as if the answer to every legal question could be found there.

'No, no, Miss,' he said, throwing back his head in protest against such an idea. 'Not manslaughter. It was an accident. A dreadful accident, I know, and one that he'll never forget, judging by the way he's taken it. But it wasn't even negligent driving. He tried to avoid a man lying in the road – drunk, probably he thought – the road was wet, he skidded and ran up a bank. That's an accident.'

'But he'll be committed to the Assizes at the inquest, won't he?' asked Susan.

'I don't think so for a minute,' said Tom Holt. They stared at him incredulously. 'Mind you, all this is going to cost you a pretty penny. It wasn't him that took that car in the first place; somebody's come forward already and said they saw that other young chap come out of the car-park with it. My hat,' said Tom with feeling. 'I wouldn't like to be that chap at the car park! Well, as I was saying, your young man didn't take it, but he was driving it, and seeing he's only got a motorcycle licence he's not insured against car accident. You'll have to pay for that car, and it's a Rolls. Might cost you anything up to two thousand pounds, and I dare say the parents of the girl will try to get compensation out of you. Yes, last night's work will cost you a lot of money, I'm afraid.'

'Eh, dear,' said Cook with a heavy sigh. She knew how much money had gone already, one way and another.

But the Miss Tophams were not only undismayed, they were radiant. If only Philip could be saved from a charge of manslaughter, from the agonising wait for trial, from a prison sentence, they would pour out every penny they had and think nothing of it. The house could go – and probably would in any case, now – everything could go.

'Oh, the relief it is to hear you say these things, Tom,' said Miss Emily, wiping her eyes again.

'What you want to do,' counselled Tom Holt, picking up his hat, pulling down his tunic and preparing to go home to breakfast, 'is to get on to your own lawyer right away. I've only given you my opinion for what it's worth, but that's the way I think it will come out!'

He was right. That was precisely the way it came out. But there was much that was painful to be gone through first.

That afternoon the Miss Tophams, though by this time exhausted with fatigue, age, the effects of shock, went to see Gwen. They shrank from the visit, they would have given anything not to go, they confessed to each other, but it must be done. If their boy could face it, they could, and it had been so very much worse for him, they said to each other as they climbed the stairs to the flat door.

Ken admitted them. He did not look at them any more openly than he had ever done, but they saw his grief. He had loved and admired his son, who was endowed with all the dash and courage he himself had never had. Ronald did shady things without a vestige of shadiness, which is how his father would have liked to do them. He did wrong openly and cheerfully, above all cheerfully. He hadn't given a damn for anything, and he had been the pride of his father's heart. His death had shattered Ken.

Preceding Ken down the dark passage was like going through a tunnel with Gwen looming, in the lighter sitting room, at the end of it. She sat on a small chair in a short tight skirt, her feet planted apart, one hand doubled into a menacing fist on one knee, the other holding a glass of whisky on the other. She looked awful, and the Miss Tophams were appalled.

She received their expressions of sorrow and sympathy with a snarl.

'Oh, cut it out. It's done, isn't it? You won't bring him back. Twenty – and dead. A smart boy like that . . . could have done anything. Laughing here at this time yesterday, drinking out of that bottle of whisky with us, as a matter of fact. And he's dead now. Here, Ken,' she said, holding out her glass, 'give me another drink. And don't you look at me like that, you,' she said, thrusting her chin out at the Miss Tophams. 'I shall drink if I like. What can you do but drink when things like this get you? I got blind when Bern died. Absolutely blind. Or I'd have thrown myself over Brooklyn Bridge. And I'll drink now until I forget what I saw at the mortuary today. So you'd better go. Go away, you only upset me,' she said, turning her back on them. 'Show them out, Ken. I'd rather be left.'

But the Miss Tophams stood there, murmuring, full of pity and helplessness.

'Ken, pull that bloody blind up,' shouted Gwen, waving her glass to the high window where a white linen blind diffused the strong sunlight without keeping it out. 'He will have it down, God knows what for. No one can see,' she hissed at him. 'The body's not here. You're superstitious, that's what you are. Pull it up, or I'll tear it down.'

Ken passed noiselessly to the wall and pulled at the long cord. The blind went up. His son was dead and there was nothing to show it. The world went on just the same; traffic pouring down the street, the bread arriving, the meat, the milk, the hall would open tonight as usual, the partner wouldn't agree to closing it down, all the young people would crowd in, those tunes would pound out till midnight – all, all as usual. But Ron would not be there. He was amazed, wounded, that everything should go on in the same way, with no sign. So he drew the blind. It was the only thing he had been able to do to mark the difference of this day, and somehow it meant something to him. And now Gwen made him pull it up.

The rasp of her voice worked on his nerves like a saw. She had chivvied him all day, do this, do that, go there, come here . . . as if she were the only one who suffered, who mattered. To be left alone with Gwen, without Ronnie, who had made everything tolerable. . . . Ken put his hand over his mouth in a distracted gesture. But she was telling him to do something else. He took his hand away to give her his attention, his eyes wild.

'Show them out, for God's sake, Ken. Tell them to go, or I'll scream.'

'Better go,' he murmured, motioning them to the passage.

'You'll have to pay for that car,' Gwen shouted after them as they reached the stairs. 'It's your responsibility. Philip was driving. Oh, shut the door, Ken, and come in, for God's sake.'

And as the Miss Tophams went out into the streets, the posters were out round the doorways of small stationers' shops, and the newsboys calling: 'Fatal Joyride', 'Midnight Accident. Two Dead.' 'Adopted Son Wrecks Borrowed Rolls.'

'"Adopted Son,"' said Susan in bitter disgust. 'What's that got to do with it?'

'My dear,' said Emily, taking her sister's arm as much to get as to give comfort and support, 'this is only the beginning of a great deal of disagreeable publicity, so we might as well face it.'

Shaken from their visit to Gwen, straining to escape from the scream of posters and the interested or compassionate glances that seemed to meet them wherever they looked, the Miss Tophams reached home with relief, only to be met by Cook in the hall with the news that James was in the drawing room.

'Our bird of ill-omen,' sighed Susan. 'Let there be trouble and James comes to gloat and say "I told you so."'

This time she misjudged her brother. When the family lawyer telephoned to him in the morning, James had taken it as a matter of course that he should come at once to his sisters' help. In these cases blood is usually thicker than water, and James had set off with a genuine desire to support. But so strong was habit that, when Emily and Susan came into the room, instead of coming forward with sympathy as he had intended, James rose from the sofa with an accusing expression and said: 'This is a nice how-d'you-do, I must say.'

'There's no must about it,' said Emily wearily. 'But I'm sure you will.' Last straw though he seemed, she went to kiss him. 'Have you had tea?'

'No, I told Cook I'd wait for you.'

The Miss Tophams were sorry. They had hoped to be able to gain the refuge of their own rooms, but now they had to sit with him.

'Well,' said James, beginning again, 'I once read somewhere that 'Every Good Deed Brings its Evil Return', and by Jove, it's true.'

Cook turned from putting down the tray and stared stonily at him.

'If you're referring to our adoption of Philip as a good deed, James, though the good has come to us, since he's brought us happiness we should never otherwise have known,' said Susan stiffly, 'I prefer "Cast thy bread upon the waters and it shall return to thee after many days."'

'Gone pretty mouldy in this case,' said James.

'You know nothing about it,' said Emily. 'But you can take our word for it that Philip has justified all our faith in him by his behaviour in this terrible affair.'

'He's coming downstairs,' warned Cook, going out.

Philip came into the room. He went straight to his aunts, inclining his head to James in passing.

'I've been asleep far too long,' he said. 'Have you had to see anybody for me? Has anybody been?'

Susan drew him down into a chair beside her, and Emily hastened to pour out tea for him.

'Nobody's been but Tom Holt, a friend of mine, a policeman, who came to tell us that the man in the road had been dead for hours. You didn't kill him.'

Philip put his hands over his face. 'Then I needn't have tried to avoid him. I killed the other two to save a dead man.'

'Drink your tea, dear,' urged Susan helplessly.

James moved restlessly on the sofa.

'You'd better pull yourself together, young man,' he said. 'Newton's waiting at his office. I called to see him on my way up and arranged to have you down there before five.'

The Miss Tophams turned in sharp interrogation.

'The inquest is on Friday,' said James, and at that they

shrank. They looked stricken, as if everything were suddenly too much for them.

Philip stood up. 'I'm ready,' he said.

'But he's had nothing to eat all day,' protested Susan.

'Can't help that,' said James. 'Newton can't wait.'

His sisters looked at him. They deeply disliked James in this hectoring mood.

'I'm not hungry,' said Philip. 'I'll drink this tea.'

He smiled to reassure them, and followed James from the room.

James had looked forward for a long time to telling this young man what he thought of him. He had relished the idea of making it plain what disaster, financial and otherwise, he and his mother had brought upon the innocent and benevolent sisters. With the aid of the family lawyer, he set about doing it at last, showing the boy that not only had he disgraced the family name which, said James, they had been rash enough to give him, but that the cost of this accident would complete the near ruin of the Miss Tophams' affairs. The home they loved and had lived in from childhood, said James, piling it on, must be sold. The Miss Tophams must move out, they must deprive themselves of the comfort they had always been used to at an age when they most needed it. In future they must exercise the strictest economy. It was when James reached this point in his planned exposition that he realised to his dismay that he wasn't enjoying himself.

The boy sat, white and strained, his eyes fixed steadily on James's face, driven deeper and deeper into distress, but uttering no word in self-defence.

James had not reckoned with the fact that most people when faced with genuine suffering are sorry for the sufferer. James found himself invaded by wholly unexpected compunctious visitings of nature. He felt he was taking part in the baiting of an already wounded young creature, who took revilement with such touching acceptance and dignity that James was compelled into admiration, also reluctant. He was bound to admit, though only to himself, that the boy had something in him after all. That perhaps he had been, after all, worth saving.

James transferred himself from the offensive to the defensive side, thereby much puzzling Mr Newton, who began to feel James was as incalculable as his sisters. When he called in the afternoon, the man had been in a towering rage, and here he was, in the evening, laying a hand on the boy's shoulder and saying he must take him home to get something to eat.

'He's had nothing to eat all day,' said James, unconsciously echoing Susan.

All the same, when he got back to The Willows, James was careful to disguise the mollification of his feelings. It was not befitting to his dignity, he considered, to show such a complete, and to his sisters gratifying, change of front. It wasn't difficult to keep it from them. They were so taken up with looking after Philip that they did not concern themselves with James.

The next morning, Thursday, the Miss Tophams and James, coming down to breakfast, were astonished to find Philip leaving the house.

'Where are you going, dear?' asked Miss Emily.

'To work,' said Philip, turning at the front door.

'Oh, I'm sure they'll excuse you today,' said Emily. 'They won't expect you. Not before the inquest.'

'I must go,' said Philip.

He was in a fever to get to Fell and Brownings, to make sure of the job that meant so much to him now and of which he had hitherto been so careless. He must work hard now and try to keep the house together. He had depended on his aunts long enough; now they should depend upon him. He would work with all his might for them.

But in half an hour he was back at the house. He had been paid off. His work had never been satisfactory, they said. He had never applied himself, and now this disgraceful affair was the last straw. They had no room for playboys of his sort.

'Never mind, dear,' said his aunts. 'You never liked the work. Something better will turn up. Don't worry.'

But to Philip it was a bad blow. During the long night, the only way he had been able to fight off the nightmare memory of his dead brother and the girl, the only hope he had been able to fasten on after last night's disclosures at the lawyer's office, the only factor that could be used to redeem the rest had been his determination to work as he had never worked before, to save the situation for his aunts. And now the chance was gone.

James alone knew what he felt and why, and James was very uneasy about his part in the boy's despair. He felt he had hit Philip when he was down, and was ashamed. And once more he was compelled to admiration. The boy, though obviously strained almost beyond bearing, kept with his aunts, trying to help them through the long day. James, in his turn, hung helplessly about Philip, trying to help Philip through.

'Play something, Aunt Susan,' urged Philip from time to time, and Susan played. And though he had vowed he would never touch the piano again, when Susan asked him to play, Philip took her place without demur. He would do anything they asked.

So he played. Not jazz or swing; for the time being he was sickened of that. He played what he knew they liked best, pouring balm over their jangled nerves and apprehensions. James, laved in lovely sound, felt sadly that he had not had half enough music in his life. Doreen used to play to him, but she was far away in India now with her husband, and when she had gone his wife got rid of the piano because, she said, it took up too much room. His sisters had been wise in one thing, at any rate; they had held to music and taught this boy to do the same.

'Isn't it wonderful,' said Susan dreamily, 'that however bad things are, there's always music.'

Cook, busy in the kitchen with the door open – she said the time went better when she worked – listened to Philip's playing and kept putting up petitions for him: 'Please God, let it be all right tomorrow. I know they say it's going to be, but please make sure of it.'

At the inquest next morning everything happened as Tom Holt had said, except for one unforeseen incident. Miss Emily brought the Coroner's peroration to a close. As he was lashing unmercifully at great length at Philip, Miss Emily, unable to bear it any longer, called out: 'He knows. He feels it all.' The

Coroner was so taken aback by the interruption that he could not, or at any rate did not, pick up the thread of his discourse again, and the inquest came sooner to an end.

But Philip's ordeal was not over. When he said he was going straight on to the funeral of his brother and the girl, his aunts were aghast. The town was buzzing with the sensation of the double funeral of the young victims. There was no need for Philip to expose himself to the morbid curiosity of the crowds. He mustn't go, they said. He had been under too long a strain already. They besought him to let the affair end now, as he was certainly entitled to do.

'You'll not move him,' said Cook. 'He's punishing himself. He feels he ought to pay for being alive when they're dead.'

James too tried to dissuade Philip, but when he found he could not, he electrified his sisters by going with him. That the fastidious James should submit himself to the proximity of Gwen and Ken and the excited crowds was almost as much a moral victory for James as the determination to be with his mother was for Philip.

James and Philip left the house together, and the Miss Tophams and Cook stayed at home to suffer for their boy, seeing in imagination his white face above the tossing crowds.

At last he came back with James, and they were able to close the door on the dreadful day. At last they were able to make him eat and go to bed, and at last they were able to go to bed themselves.

'But somehow,' said Susan uneasily, as she kissed her sister good night, 'it doesn't feel *over*, does it?'

'I'm afraid that's because Philip doesn't feel it's over,' said Emily.

'It feels more as if there is something hanging over us still,' said Susan. 'But I don't know what it is.'

'Perhaps we'll all feel better after a night's rest,' comforted Emily.

They set the communicating door open between their rooms. Each, though neither said so, feared for the other after the events of the day. Each wanted to be within call of the other.

So that when Emily said quietly in the middle of the night: 'Susan,' Susan replied at once: 'Yes, dear?'

'D'you hear James's voice?' asked Emily.

Susan listened.

'Yes, I think I do,' said Susan, reaching for her dressing gown and joining her sister.

'He sounds as if he doesn't want us to hear. He sounds as if he's trying to be quiet, though James never could, could he? Let's put out the light and open the door carefully.'

They opened the door. Across the landing, in Philip's brilliantly lit room, was James, his grey hair in a cockatoo crest, his hand on Philip's shoulder. Emily gripped Susan's arm. Philip had his overcoat on and there was a suitcase at his feet. He had very obviously been on the point of running away. Susan made as if to dart forward, but Emily kept her back.

'You musn't go,' said James, in what he meant for a whisper. 'You'll break their hearts.'

Philip tried to remove James's hand. 'They'll be better

without me. If I clear out, *you'll* do something for them, sir. You won't if I'm here, and no wonder. . . .'

'Oh, yes I will,' said James, forgetting to whisper. 'I've been thinking about it all day. This house has to go, they know that. You'll all be better away from the town now. I shall propose that you all come to live in London. I need someone to follow me at the works and if it's one of the family, so much the better. . . .'

Emily drew Susan into the room and closed the door.

'Susan, he said *one of the family!*'

'I can't believe my ears,' said Susan. 'To think that all this time James has been all right underneath and we've never suspected it!'

'It's incredible,' breathed Emily. 'Poor James. I've said the most awful things to him at times.'

'We'll go to London, won't we?' said Susan.

'We'll go anywhere where Philip can work and be happy. Cook won't object to London either. I'm rather nervous, though, about living near James's wife, Susan.'

'London's a big place,' said Susan. 'Besides, I'm so happy about Philip's prospects that I'd put up with more than James's wife.'

'And there's another thing, dear,' said Emily. 'I don't think Gwen will dare to pester us with James at hand.'

'You don't think Philip will run away now, do you?' asked Susan anxiously.

Emily shook her head. In their worn gowns and lace-frilled caps they went to the door again, turned out the light and looked across the landing.

Philip had taken off his coat and jacket and was preparing to take off his collar and tie. He looked different already; he was smiling at James, and James was smiling at him.

Emily closed the door.

'Leave them to it,' she said. 'James can tell us all about it in the morning.'

MISS PRATT DISAPPEARS

I

'I think I'll go and pack now,' said Miss Pratt. She said it as if she hoped they would protest. She thought it would be very nice if one of them said: 'It *is* a pity you're leaving us!'

But neither spoke. Dolly in one armchair went on turning the pages of her film-news, and Jim, in the other armchair, continued to frown over the sports page. Miss Pratt, between them on a chair without arms, waited a little while before she said again:

'I think I'll go and pack now.'

'Righty-ho,' said Dolly negligently.

Dolly, Miss Pratt's sister-in-law, was always in the fashion, and as it was the fashion for young women of Dolly's sort in Bendle to say 'Righty-ho,' Dolly said it, and continued to gaze at a close-up of a celebrated girl kissing an equally celebrated young man. Dolly was very interested in the films and always implied that she herself could have been a star if she had not married into the Pratt family. She was certainly rather like a film-star, Miss Pratt admitted. Her hair was very blonde sometimes, and her eyelashes were stiffened and blackened; although when the stuff had been on for a time, it seemed to come off, Miss Pratt noticed.

Miss Pratt sat on in her place, and kept thinking she must go and pack. She did not want to pack. It was not that she was reluctant to leave Dolly's, only that she was reluctant to go to Maud's tomorrow. She should have gone today; the three months for which she was obliged to inflict herself on Dolly were up today. But Maud had sent a postcard from Blackpool to say she was staying on.

'Tell Annie not to come until after tea on Friday,' wrote Maud on the back of the view of the Tower.

'The dirty dog!' said Dolly, throwing down the card. 'She swore she'd be home on Wednesday so you could go on Thursday. She knows we're going away on Saturday, and there'll be all to straighten up when you've gone.'

Dolly always spoke as if her sister-in-law left chaos behind her, whereas Miss Pratt was as neat as the proverbial new pin in all her ways, and asked nothing better than to be allowed to clean the whole house from top to bottom every week. Her trouble was that neither Dolly nor Maud would let her do it; Dolly because she saw no use, she said, in turning things upside down to put them to rights again, and Maud because she was convinced that no one could do anything properly except herself.

'Anyway,' resumed Dolly, 'Maud or no Maud, I'm having this house to myself after Friday tea time, and that's flat!'

Miss Pratt had winced inwardly, but outwardly she had

kept the half-smiling diffidence that had come upon her since she had lived with relations.

She rose now and went out of the room quietly so as not to disturb them. Her very closing of the door was an apology for being there at all, but it only served to fan Dolly's irritation.

'Creeping about!' she said pettishly. 'My goodness, I shall be glad when she takes herself off tomorrow! I didn't bargain for this when I married you, Jim Pratt. An old maid relation for three months twice a year! My hat, it's enough to drive a girl out of her senses! Pansy Shaw says she doesn't know how I stand it.'

'Cheer up, darling,' said Jim. 'There's a good time coming! She's off tomorrow and we're going to the Hydro for the weekend. You'll be able to show off all your new frocks, and what with dancing and the band and a few cocktails, you'll soon forget you've had to put up with poor old Annie!'

Dolly recovered her good humour at the prospect of a gay weekend and went to sit on Jim's knee.

In the back bedroom, Miss Pratt took her fibre suitcase from under the bed. It would hold all she needed for a three months' visit to Maud, and had the advantage of being able to be carried to the tram and from the tram by Miss Pratt herself. Fortunately for Miss Pratt, who had no money for taxis, Dolly lived within reasonable distance of the tram terminus at one end, and Maud, although right at the other end of the town almost three miles away, within an equally reasonable distance of the terminus at the other.

When Miss Pratt had packed, she sat on the bed, unwilling to go down to Jim and Dolly. The wardrobe door was open, and Miss Pratt found herself wondering vaguely who was the plain, middle-aged woman she could see reflected in the unusual position of the long mirror. With something of a start she realised that it was herself. How old she was getting! There was hardly any colour left in her cheeks or any flesh on her bones. She looked insignificant – drab – defeated. And yet once she had been quite good-looking! She even suspected that Father, dead when she was a girl, had left the money to Herbert and Jim because he was sure that she, with her looks, would marry and have a husband to keep her.

Anyway, Father had been wrong. She had never married. Arthur Bell had turned queer when she had pointed out that Mother would have to live with them when they were married. He had wanted to know why she could not live with Herbert and Maud; Jim was not married then. But Miss Pratt would not hear of her invalid mother being handed over to the tender mercies of Maud. So Arthur Bell had broken it off, and Miss Pratt had gone on nursing Mother. She had been quite happy too, and never grudged a minute of it. It was only when Mother died, leaving her daughter with nothing but the sofa, now in Maud's parlour, and the best pink tea set, now displayed in Dolly's drawing room cabinet, that Miss Pratt discovered what a desolate place the world can be for a poor relation.

She wanted to 'take a situation'. But her brothers scoffed.

'What could you do?' they asked her. 'You're not trained for anything. In these days everyone is trained. Besides, you know, you're getting on, Annie. Nobody wants untrained, middle-aged women. It's hard enough for able-bodied men to get jobs. No, you're all right where you are. You'll shake down after a bit. Maud and Dolly will get used to it.'

That, and ten pounds a year 'spending money', was their interpretation of their father's injunction to 'look after Annie'.

'Oh, well,' sighed Miss Pratt, rising from the bed.

She went downstairs and found Dolly sitting on Jim's knee. She prepared to withdraw again instantly.

'I think I'll go to bed now,' she said, smiling at them in embarrassment from the door.

'Righty-ho!' said Dolly.

'Good night,' said Miss Pratt.

'Good night,' they replied.

At Maud's and at Dolly's, Miss Pratt went to bed early to get out of the way. She occupied the bathroom for as short a time as possible, always ready, if anybody tried the door, to fly out and cry: 'It's only me! I've finished.'

The next day, Miss Pratt was quite happy because Dolly allowed her to make some pastry. But she made the pastry only. Dolly filled the pies herself, so that she could ask Jim how he liked her pie. And when he said: 'Jolly good, darling,' she could take all the praise. He did not seem to notice there were no pies when Miss Pratt was not there.

II

Before he left the house that day, Jim gave Miss Pratt her half-yearly allowance, five pounds, for which she thanked him profusely.

Dolly fidgeted through the afternoon, looking frequently at the clock.

'Look here,' she said at last. 'I want to run down to Jim's office. I've got an idea about something. But I'll see you off first.'

Miss Pratt hastened to take the hint. She got through her tea very quickly and hurried to put on her hat and coat.

'Goodbye, Dolly,' she said when she was ready. 'Thank you for having me. I do hope I haven't been very much in the way.'

'Oh, it's all right,' said Dolly, holding down her permanent waves because the wind was blowing in at the door that Miss Pratt was keeping open.

Miss Pratt took her heavy suitcase in one hand, her mackintosh, umbrella and hand-bag in the other.

'Goodbye, Dolly,' she cried again at the gate.

'Cheerio,' said Dolly indifferently, and banged the door.

Miss Pratt went to the tram terminus. The conductor lifted her case to the platform and stowed it away. He was a nice young man, reflected Miss Pratt. When people were not relations they were often very nice.

She sat in the corner by the door so that she could keep an eye on her case all the way. When she arrived at the other end, the conductor lifted it down again for her, and she carried it, with many pauses to change hands, up the hill to Maud's.

Maud's house was one of a row, but was divided from its neighbours on either side by a high privet hedge. Maud was not one to encourage curiosity. The whole row had a dank, unwelcoming look, but as Miss Pratt approached, she saw that

Maud's house was particularly unwelcoming; all the blinds were down.

'Dear me,' said Miss Pratt, resting again from the case. 'They can't have got back yet.'

She went on, nevertheless, and turned in at Maud's iron gate. How soon, she thought, an empty house takes on a lost, deserted look! The privet hedges almost met across the garden, the grass was ragged, the faded yellow blinds showed fly-marked behind the dirty windows. Miss Pratt's steps rang on the flagged path. Although she knew it was useless, she knocked at the door. She peeped into the letter box; the stale breath of the house met her, and the silence and the sight of the stairs reaching upwards mysteriously almost frightened her.

She let the flap of the letter box fall, and stood disconsolately on the step.

'I shall have to wait,' she said.

She was glad the hedges were high; she didn't want anyone to see her waiting to be let in; it looked as if she was not wanted, which was true.

She turned her suitcase end up and sat on it very lightly so as not to strain it; but by and by she grew tired and sat on it more heavily. The April evening was chilly, and now and then Miss Pratt walked up and down the path to keep warm, peering frequently over the iron spikes of the gate to see if her relations were coming.

If only Maud had sent her the key, she could have had a fire going and bottles in their beds and a meal ready. But Maud would not let anyone do anything; she liked to do it all herself and then grumble because she had it to do. That was Maud all over.

'What's she going to do about buying in?' Miss Pratt wondered after a time. 'The shops will be shut in another few minutes. I think I'd better go and get some bread and milk. Though perhaps she will bring something with her and only be cross if I do. . . .' She wavered uncertainly. It was always difficult to know what to do for the best with Maud.

'Still, perhaps it would be better to be on the safe side,' she decided at last. 'If I pay for them myself she can't say much.'

She hid her case behind a bush and hurried to the grocer's at the corner. She was just in time; a clock in the town struck eight while she was in the shop. She almost ran back with her purchases, feeling sure they must have arrived by now. Once inside the house she would soon help to get things warm and ship-shape, in spite of Maud. She imagined herself dealing quite boldly, for once, with Maud.

But when she reached the gate, she saw that no one had come. She put her purchases on the step and took her case from behind the bush. She sat down again to wait, wrapping her coat round her legs. It was quite dark now and very cold. She wished very much that Maud would come. She might at least have said definitely what time she would be home. 'After tea' was too vague. Although Miss Pratt knew that Maud did not care how long her sister-in-law waited on the doorstep.

She went on waiting.

III

Suddenly a bright shaft of light shot out of the dark and hit her in the face. She fell back, blinking.

'What are you doing there?' asked a stern, male voice.

Miss Pratt realised that it belonged to a policeman.

'I'm waiting for my brother and his family to come home. They're coming home tonight. They're expecting me,' she faltered.

The policeman ran his torch over Miss Pratt, the suitcase, the loaf and the bottle of milk on the step. The mildness of all these must have reassured him.

'Cold job, isn't it?' he asked.

'It is indeed,' agreed Miss Pratt. 'I wish they'd come.'

'Been here long?'

'Since about six o'clock.'

'And it's gone nine now,' said the policeman. 'Well, I wouldn't wait for them any longer if I was you. I'd be off.'

Miss Pratt gave a short, mirthless laugh. She could not explain that she had nowhere to be off to.

'I shall have to wait,' she said.

'Well, I'll be off myself then. Good night to you.'

'Good night,' said Miss Pratt.

IV

The stars glimmered faintly in the sky, and the bottle of milk and the loaf in its white wrapping on the step. Miss Pratt looked from one to the other and was appalled. What a long way from the stars to the step! How vast, dark, mysterious this life, this world was! It was enough to frighten anybody, thought Miss Pratt – at least, anyone so alone as she was. She was suddenly panic-stricken and ran into the next garden. There was a light in the upper rooms of the house. The people were going to bed, but she knocked on the door and brought them down.

'Excuse me,' she said breathlessly, when a woman opened the door a little way and looked through the gap. 'Excuse me . . . but could you tell me what time it is?'

It was all she could think of to say, but it annoyed the woman.

'Good heavens!' she burst out. 'Fancy coming to ask that, at this time of night!' She looked back into the hall without opening the door any wider, and said crossly: 'It's ten to eleven, if you must know, and I was just going to bed.'

'I'm sorry to trouble you,' said Miss Pratt humbly. 'I've been waiting for them to come home next door. I expected them hours ago, but they haven't come yet.'

'Oh,' said the woman. She did not like her neighbour, and had no wish to put herself out for anyone belonging to her. 'Well . . .' she added reluctantly, 'I'm just going to bed, or I'd have asked you in.'

'Oh, thank you,' said Miss Pratt. 'But I don't think they can be coming tonight. I'd better go and catch the last tram to my other sister-in-law's, where I've been staying. Perhaps you'll tell Mrs Pratt I went back, will you? In case she is anxious.'

'Well, I'm not exactly on those terms with her,' said the woman, bridling.

'Never mind then,' said Miss Pratt, turning away. More unkindness coming to light, more bitterness . . . it made her want to weep. 'I dare say she won't be anxious at all. Good night.'

Miss Pratt went into Maud's garden and fumbled in the dark for her case. Fancy having to go back! After all these hours of waiting to have to go back to Dolly's!

At the bottom of the hill, the last tram was waiting, like an illuminated box. By chance it was the same conductor. His hat was on the back of his head, his collar undone. One permitted oneself these liberties on the last tram.

Miss Pratt was the only passenger.

'Going home now, I suppose?' said the conductor, when he came for her fare.

Miss Pratt smiled as cheerfully as she could by way of an answer meaning neither yes nor no.

'Well, it's nice to get home,' said the conductor, stretching his arms and thinking of his supper and his bed. He went back to the platform and whistled.

The car careered through the night. Miss Pratt sat in her corner, wondering how she was going to face Dolly. She felt she could not bear much tonight. The waiting and the cold had worn her out. She was afraid of breaking down and crying before Dolly and Jim, and that would look so silly at her age, thought Miss Pratt.

'Here we are!' cried the conductor. He jumped out and lifted down her case. 'Family plate, I suppose,' he said. 'It's heavy enough. You've not far to go with this, I hope?'

'No,' said Miss Pratt, all unsuspecting. 'Not far.'

'Well, good night,' he cried, leaping on the tram again. 'Fire away, Johnny!' Ping, ping-ping-ping, Pong, Pong! he played on the bell and away they went, the car to its home in Bartongate, the driver to his home, the conductor to his, and Miss Pratt to Dolly's.

She reached Dolly's gate at last, and stood stock still. This house was in darkness, too. Miss Pratt reminded herself, however, that it was long past eleven, and they must have gone to bed.

'Oh, dear,' said Miss Pratt, stealing fearfully up the garden path, 'fancy having to bring them out of bed! I don't know that I dare do it.'

She stood at the door and stared at the electric bell, which she could see faintly through the darkness.

'Oh, dear me,' she said, putting up her hand and withdrawing it again. She looked round at the almost impenetrable darkness. There was nowhere at all for her to put herself for the night, without disturbing them. The bell must be rung.

V

She pressed it slightly and waited, her heart beating hard. There was no response of light or movement in the house. Miss Pratt had hardly expected any. She had made only a tentative attack on the bell so far. Now she pressed a little harder and waited again. Silence and darkness still. She rang again; and then again, and kept her finger on the button. Nothing.

Miss Pratt stood there, the closed door before her, the black night behind. Fatigue, cold and some dreadful desolation of the spirit made her desperate. She felt that if she did not get in now, she never would get in – never get in anywhere. She rang the bell again and again. She bruised her knuckles with knocking on the door.

'Rap, rap, rap!' She waited, holding her breath. 'Rap, rap, rap!' She waited again. How they slept.

Suddenly she stepped back and peered upwards at the bedroom windows. Usually they jutted out hygienically into the night. Now they were closed. With a chill of the spine, Miss Pratt realised that this house was empty, too. Jim and Dolly had gone for their weekend today instead of tomorrow. That was what Dolly's idea had been about.

The house was empty. They had left her nowhere to spend the night. They just turned her off one to the other and did not care what became of her. Miss Pratt burst into tears. Sobbing, distraught, she dragged at her case, dragged it down the garden, down the unmade road. She was possessed by a frantic desire to end this night, end everything, by ending herself – in the canal. It was the only means she could think of. Weeping violently, she persisted towards it.

But when she reached it, it smelled, as usual, extremely unpleasant, and Miss Pratt, holding her tears to peer through the darkness at its sluggish surface, could not bring herself to enter it. The smell of the canal brought Miss Pratt abruptly to her natural senses; it was the turning point of that black night.

'Oh, how,' whispered Miss Pratt, in horror, 'did I come to think of this?'

She stood on the sticky cobbles of the canalside and shuddered at herself.

'I must have been mad,' she said.

Shocked to the depths of her respectable soul, she said:

'Fancy me coming to this!'

Then she laughed with relief as her eyes fell on the bulk of her suitcase beside her on the cobbles.

'Oh, I didn't mean it,' cried Miss Pratt. 'I couldn't have meant it, because I brought my case with me! I wasn't going to let go my case, that's plain to see!'

She laughed again and felt much less afraid of herself.

'Come on,' she said to her case, picking it up once more. 'I don't know where we're going to, but we're getting away from here before you can say knife.'

She made her way back to the streets, which were now dark, deserted, strung with sparse lights. At any other time, Miss Pratt would have been afraid of the town at dead of night; but she was not afraid now. She had gone too far for that. She had gone to some perilous edge and looked over. Now she was walking away from it to safety. The statue of Mr Gladstone on the Avenue, and the façade of the Town Hall, where the pigeons slept on the ledges, were the mute witnesses of Miss Pratt's return.

It had occurred to her that the station would be open all night, and that there might be a waiting room where she could sit until morning.

She made for the station, the case dragging cruelly at her arm.

VI

As she approached the goal where she would at last be able to rest from this weary night wandering, she saw a bus drawn up at the edge of the pavement. It was empty, dimly lighted, and on its front it bore the word:

MUNTHORPE

'Munthorpe!'

Miss Pratt came to a halt. She put down her case and gazed in fascination at the bus.

'Munthorpe!'

Why, she had once been there! She had spent one of her rare holidays at Munthorpe, staying at the cottage of a Mrs Bates. Miss Pratt remembered the kindness of Mrs Bates and the friendship that had sprung up between them. For years Miss Pratt had written to Mrs Bates at Christmastime, without getting much in the way of replies, for Mrs Bates was no letter writer. The one-sided correspondence had finally fallen off, but Miss Pratt had never forgotten Mrs Bates, and the name of Munthorpe on the front of the bus was a miraculous reminder that she had still one friend in the world.

'Should I go?' Miss Pratt asked herself excitedly. 'Should I go and see her again? I've got five pounds. I could pay for my board for a little while, and she could perhaps tell me what to do. . . .'

Her speculations were here interrupted by the arrival of the driver out of the dark. He prepared to climb into his seat.

Miss Pratt was galvanised into action. He must not go off and take with him her unique chance of getting to Mrs Bates.

'Wait a minute!' she called out. 'I want to go to Munthorpe! How much would it cost?'

She advanced into the headlights so that the driver could see her.

'You give me a start!' he said reproachfully. 'I didn't expect a passenger at this time of the night.'

'No,' said Miss Pratt. 'Naturally.'

'This 'ere bus was 'ired private. I'm just getting back now,' said the driver, with suspicion in his voice.

'Well, could you take me, please?' implored Miss Pratt. 'I want to get there as soon as possible – and I don't suppose there's a train till morning.'

The driver looked Miss Pratt over in the light from the lamps and came to the conclusion, as the policeman had done, that there was no harm in her.

'Ten bob's the fare,' he said.

'Very well,' said Miss Pratt recklessly. Ten shillings of her precious store going on a wild-goose chase! 'Never mind,' said Miss Pratt to herself. 'Nothing venture, nothing have!' She had never said such a thing to herself before. . . .

VII

Miss Pratt arrived at Munthorpe towards seven o'clock in the morning, and found it changed almost beyond recognition. It had changed from a village to a resort. Munthorpe, during the past dozen years, had awakened to the fact that it was only three miles from the sea, and as the sea did not seem prepared to advance towards Munthorpe, Munthorpe advanced to the sea by means of long feelers in the shape of bungalows, shops, petrol pumps and tarred roads. At the inland end of these feelers, knotting them together, remained the old village itself, a cluster of cottages, cobbled streets, flowering bushes and the church. The church tower quietly dominated the resort as it had dominated, for centuries, the village. It made a landmark for Miss Pratt, who remembered that Mrs Bates's cottage was opposite the church.

But as soon as her eyes fell on the cottage, Miss Pratt knew without a doubt that Mrs Bates no longer lived there. The windows and the door were painted bright blue; there were small blue window boxes on the sills both upstairs and down, and a painted sign hung out to announce 'Teas. Luncheons. Homemade cakes.' Mrs Bates had made cakes, she had made teas, but luncheons she had never heard of, and blue paint would have given her a fright.

Miss Pratt gazed sadly at the little house where Mrs Bates used to live. Was she dead? Or had she only removed? There was no sign of life in the house yet; she would have to wait until she could inquire. She looked wearily round for a place to wait in, and found the church standing behind her. She went into the churchyard and sat on a coping in the sunshine.

The spring morning was soft, yet brilliant. The shapes of the trees were misted, but every young leaf shone. The trunks were wet as if newly washed. Miss Pratt felt, as she had never felt before, the strength and promise of a newborn day.

She was tired from the night, she was middle-aged, without money, without prospect, and yet she was hopeful. As the sun rose higher sending a blessed warmth through her, Miss Pratt became more and more hopeful, without, she kept telling herself, any reason for it at all.

Then she saw that the bright blue door of the cottage was open. She took up her case and went towards it.

As she reached the doorstep, she realised that Mrs Bates's cottage was not only modernised without, but also within. From the interior proceeded what Miss Pratt thought must be the very latest kind of voice and language.

'My dear ass, I see no fun at all in serving a lot of louts with meat teas. Besides, my stomach turns at the sight of washing-up. It didn't enter into my calculations when I agreed to run this place with you.'

During an inaudible reply from the back premises, Miss Platt, fearful of being regarded as an eavesdropper, knocked on the blue door. The voice continued.

'Well, my dear, if only the village emporium would open, I should depart. I tell you frankly I've had enough of this – place!' A word here that Miss Pratt only knew from blanks and dashes in print. She gasped and had not recovered when the same voice inquired, 'What do you want?' and a tall young woman with enormous earrings stood in the doorway. She was as swarthy as a pirate and kept a cigarette dangling on her lower lip.

'Oh,' said Miss Pratt, completely taken aback by this apparition. She looked helplessly round at the village street to see what she did want, and then stammered: 'Does Mrs Bates live here?'

'Not that I am aware of,' said the young woman. 'I live here – for the moment. Mary Summers lives here. But Mrs Bates – no! Mary!' she called out as if she were suddenly tired of dealing with Miss Pratt. 'Forward please! Inquiries for Mrs Bates.'

VIII

The strange young woman left the scene, and Miss Pratt peered anxiously through the doorway, wondering what second modernity would take her place. But as soon as she saw Mary coming Miss Pratt relaxed. Mary was very young and taking, with blue eyes and a blue print frock. She came wiping her hands on a towel and half-smiling at Miss Pratt before she reached her.

'Mrs Bates did live here once,' she said. 'But I think she died about a year ago. Was she a friend of yours?'

'Yes, she was a friend,' faltered Miss Pratt. 'I've come a long way to see her.'

'Have you?' said Mary, with sympathy.

Miss Pratt stood on the doorstep completely at a loss. What could she do now? It seemed as if she could only proceed by inches along this road of adventure she had taken to so late in life. She was at a full stop again. She turned her bewildered looks back to the young girl.

'Can I help you?' asked Mary.

'Well . . . is this a café?' ventured Miss Pratt. 'I hardly like to ask, but I've been travelling all night, and I would be very glad of a cup of tea.'

'No, by Jove!' cried the piratical young woman, appearing again with startling abruptness. 'I do draw the line at that. We don't open at this time in the morning. We haven't had our own breakfast yet. Nothing doing, my good body, nothing at all. Try the pub.'

'I thought you said you'd finished with this place, Zoe?' said Mary, with a flush of indignation.

'So I have,' said the other.

'Then you've no further say in the management. Come in, please,' she said to Miss Pratt. 'The fire isn't drawing very well, but I'll make you some tea as soon as the kettle boils.'

'If you let this person in at this time in the morning, I warn you, I'll go today!' cried Zoe, letting the cigarette fall out of her angry mouth.

'You'll go tomorrow, if you don't go today,' said Mary. 'Do come in,' she urged Miss Pratt.

'But I don't like to,' said Miss Pratt, 'if your friend doesn't want me to . . . if it will make trouble . . .'

'Please come in,' said Mary. 'I can see you are very tired.'

She took Miss Pratt by the arm and drew her in.

'That finishes it!' stamped Zoe. 'I really shall go now.'

'You'd have gone anyway.' Mary turned her back on the blazing girl. 'There's a cloakroom up those three steps if you would like to wash.'

Miss Pratt scurried up the steps and shut herself away from the quarrel. Perhaps the queer young woman would cool down when she removed herself from sight. But even through the sound of running water, Miss Pratt could hear her raging.

She waited until the storm moved out of range, and then she left the cloakroom and stole down to the café.

What a pretty place! Yellow walls, sprigged curtains, little old round tables, blue pots to match the paint, and country posies in jugs. Miss Pratt, who had spent all her life in the manufacturing town of Bendle, had never seen anything so charming before.

She sat down and waited in grateful anticipation of tea. The quarrel suddenly burst out again in the back premises, and Miss Pratt looked with anxiety towards the door. Ought she to have come in? Perhaps she ought to go and let the violent one have her way. She half rose, but sat down again as Mary appeared with a tray. Mary smiled reassuringly but her cheeks were scarlet and her hands trembled.

'I do hope it isn't all because of me,' ventured Miss Pratt. 'I feel very worried.'

'Oh, *no* – it isn't because of you,' Mary disclaimed with vehemence. 'Please don't think that. My partner doesn't like this work. She wants to go. Only it's very awkward at the beginning of the season. We've only just opened, and it means a lot to me. I've put all I've got into this place. Have you everything you want?' she asked, scrutinising the table. 'I thought you'd like an egg.' She smiled again, but went away distractedly in the middle of Miss Pratt's thanks.

'Poor young thing,' said Miss Pratt, pouring out the blessed tea. 'She's all upset. Though I think the sooner that queer creature goes the better. She must be bad for trade. Nobody could be comfortable having a bite of something to eat with her about.'

Miss Pratt ate her breakfast with greater relish than she ever remembered, but nevertheless kept an anxious eye on the door. She did not want Zoe to appear and spoil everything. But Zoe did not come; only Mary, once to inquire if she needed anything more, and again to present a bill that even Miss Pratt considered suspiciously 'reasonable'.

'You have been very kind to me,' said Miss Pratt, getting up from the table with reluctance. 'I only hope I haven't brought trouble on you.'

'Oh, please don't think about that any more,' begged Mary. 'It was bound to come. Would you like to leave that case here while you look round this morning?'

Miss Pratt jumped at the offer. It would provide her with an excuse for coming back to the café. She was strangely unprepared to leave this young girl.

'Some people you like as soon as you see them,' reflected Miss Pratt, as she returned to the churchyard to make up her mind what to do next. 'And she is one.'

She not only liked Mary, she also regarded her with something like awe.

'Fancy striking out for herself at her age and starting that place! And look at me, at mine, with no idea how to set about keeping myself! Oh, I've been a soft thing,' said Miss Pratt severely, 'to believe what other people said when they told me I was too old and too ignorant. I let them frighten me. I'm ashamed of myself,' said Miss Pratt sitting on the coping in the sunshine. 'But I don't know what to do next for all that.'

Nothing in her surroundings suggested any solution of her problem. All was peace. A child went past the lych-gate carrying a can of milk; a cart with red wheels lumbered comfortably up the street; the birds sang, the church clock told the quarters and the morning slipped away.

Miss Pratt's thoughts would stray.

'I should like to live here . . . a sweet place . . . what a pretty young girl Mary is . . . when they're so pretty, they're not usually so kind . . . but she is . . .!'

She pulled her thoughts back to business, drove them round in her head, made them bustle, kept presenting them with the problem: 'What am I going to do now?' But it was all to no purpose. Miss Pratt could not find an answer; she could not imagine what to do next.

IX

Hardly, however, had the last of twelve strokes quavered into silence, than Miss Pratt was jerked out of her vague plannings by the sudden appearance before the cottage opposite of a small, but dashing car. Miss Zoe, having added a minute cap to the top of her head without removing the cigarette from her lower lip, got out of the car, disappeared briefly into the cottage, returned with luggage, stowed it away and with a negligent wave of the hand, went.

'Well, I never,' gasped Miss Pratt. 'She's gone! I never thought she'd do it. Leaving the poor young thing in the lurch like that. . . .'

X

She was still standing on the church path when a party of people walked up the village street and disappeared into the café in search, presumably, of refreshment.

'Seven of them!' said Miss Pratt. 'She'll never manage.'

She darted across the road and made her way round to what had been Mrs Bates's back door.

'Can I help you?' she cried to Mary, who had just come into the kitchen with an air of being at her wits' end.

'Can I help you?' repeated Miss Pratt eagerly. 'I saw your friend go and I saw those people come in, and I suddenly thought you had no one to help you.'

'Oh,' said Mary, anxiety ebbing out of her face. 'Would you really?'

'With the greatest of pleasure,' cried Miss Pratt, snatching off her hat. 'I've nothing to do, and I'd be glad to help you. I'll just wash my hands under this tap. I've got an apron in my case. I've got everything in my case.' Miss Pratt's voice soared with exhilaration. 'Isn't it lucky?'

All Miss Pratt's efficiency, kept under for so long by Maud and Dolly, returned in a flash. What happiness to be handling pots and pans again, to be making coffee, slicing ham, bustling from table to cupboard, from cupboard to stove in the service of the new young friend who had been kind to her in the morning!

'Oh, dear,' cried Mary suddenly, when the party had paid and gone. 'I never got any scones made this morning! I was so worried I forgot them.'

'Never mind,' said Miss Pratt gaily. 'I'll make them. I'm a good hand at scones although I say it myself. How many do you want? I came across a good tip in a paper the other day. Dip a lump of sugar in orange juice, it said, and press it into the top of each scone. It makes a nice finish and a change. Shall I try a few?'

'Do!' cried Mary. 'It sounds delicious. Oh, Miss Pratt, you are a boon!'

It was a pleasant change for Miss Pratt to be called a boon. It warmed her heart, and she sang over the scone-making. She had not sung for so long that she did not know what to sing. All she could think of was 'Toil for the Brave', but she made it sound quite jolly.

All through the day, she and Mary worked together in complete accord. It was not until the last customer had gone, the blue door closed for the night, and everything tidied up, that a strangeness fell upon them.

Mary was wondering how to broach the subject of payment to Miss Pratt, and Miss Pratt was wondering how on earth Mary would manage tomorrow. She dared not offer her help again; she reminded herself that she was a complete stranger to Mary and must not impose herself.

Mary fiddled with the pots in the cupboard, trying to make up her mind to say, brightly: 'Now, Miss Pratt, I must settle my debts.' Mary, although courageous and capable, had bouts of youthful shyness which she found very difficult to overcome. She was such a long time with her head in the cupboard that Miss Pratt felt she must be waiting for her to go, and said lamely, in much the same tone she had used to Dolly:

'I think I'll be going now.'

'Must you go?' asked Mary from the cupboard.

'Yes, I think so,' said Miss Pratt, taking a long time to turn down her sleeves.

'Oh,' said Mary.

Then she knocked down a teapot lid, and they plunged simultaneously to recover it.

'It's not broken,' they both cried with relief.

The excitement of the incident loosed their tongues.

'I *have* enjoyed myself today,' said Miss Pratt heartily. 'How that young lady could leave this little place, I don't know.'

'I wish you weren't going,' said Mary. 'I wish you could stay here and help me. But I suppose you want to get back home now to your friends and everything.'

Miss Pratt stood with her hat in her hand and gazed at Mary, while a slow blush overspread her cheeks.

'But I've no home,' she said. 'And as for friends, Mrs Bates was the only friend I could think of when I tried to think of one.'

'Could you stay then?' asked Mary eagerly.

'Oh, if you'll have me,' breathed Miss Pratt. 'But you don't know anything about me . . . although I'm all right really. I mean, I'm genuine,' said Miss Pratt, wistfully. 'But I've no money. I've only somewhere about five pounds.'

'Put your hat down,' cried Mary, leaping towards her. 'Let's take that case upstairs to Zoe's room. Thank goodness she's gone! You and I will manage this place splendidly. Today showed me that. We'll work it all out.'

'Well,' said Miss Pratt, following Mary up the little old stairs. 'Who'd have thought . . . I never . . . it just shows,' she burst out as they reached Zoe's room, 'that it never does to despair, and last night, yes – only *last night*,' said Miss Pratt, with solemn emphasis, 'I despaired.'

She told Mary about Dolly and Maud, but not about the canal. The canal must never be mentioned, never remembered again.

'Won't they be in a stew now?' said Mary, not without glee. 'And it serves them jolly well right.'

Miss Pratt, however, was unwilling to believe that they would take any more notice of her absence than they had done of her presence. Besides she did not want to think about them any more. She was full of joy and relief at having found what she called a 'situation'. And such a situation!

She looked round the clear, white-washed room with its row of little windows through which blew the air from the sea. Here was a place where you could surely sleep soundly and wake happily! Miss Pratt's heart sang as she put away her things. Then she went downstairs to have her first business discussion over supper with Mary.

XI

Miss Pratt had stepped, with apprehension, out into the world and found the world kind. The work at the cottage was hard, but it was exactly the kind of work Miss Pratt liked and could do best. There were times when her unaccustomed legs almost gave way, but her heart bore her up. She was, perhaps by contrast with what had gone before, happier than she had ever been in her life. She was happy with work she enjoyed, a dear companion – for her affection for Mary grew every day – with the fun and interest provided by the café, into which she peeped whenever she had a moment to spare.

Every day when she awoke to the sight of the square church tower against the morning sky, Miss Pratt was moved afresh to feelings of joy and wonder at her good fortune, and also to a little apprehension in case it should be too good to continue. But it went on! And Miss Pratt's cheeks began to glow with the old colour, her step took on its former briskness, and a sense of humour, doused by Maud and Dolly, began to raise its head and tickle her and Mary into further enjoyment of the human comedy going on around them.

Mary and Miss Pratt worked together with astonishing smoothness. While Mary saw to appearance and the social amenities of the café, Miss Pratt in the back premises put into practice the lessons she had learned in a hard school where there had never been any too much money. She baked, she bought, she bottled, preserved, used up, sternly prevented waste and saved money for her young employer.

When the café was closed and preparations concluded for the next day, there was often no time left to do anything but go to bed, but sometimes she and Mary snatched a brief airing on the small grass plot at the back of the cottage, where three apple trees made what they proudly called an orchard. When it was wet, they sat in the kitchen with the wireless turned on.

This they were doing one night several weeks after Miss Pratt's arrival. Mary was adorning a menu card with a row of daisies; Miss Pratt was mending a tablecloth. Neither was paying much attention to the wireless, until Miss Pratt suddenly became aware that astonishing sounds were proceeding from the loud speaker.

'Missing from her home . . . Bendle . . . Annie Pratt, aged about fifty . . .'

'What!' whispered Miss Pratt. 'Is it me?'

Mary's eyes were round.

'Height five feet three inches . . . hair grey . . .

'Hair grey?' said Miss Pratt, raising her hand to it in surprise.

'Brown eyes . . .'

'Brown eyes!' cried Miss Pratt, turning a blue gaze on Mary.

'Feared she may be suffering from loss of memory . . .'

'Loss of memory!' repeated Miss Pratt bitterly. 'No, I'm not! Too much memory, you should say!'

'Communicate with . . . any police station!'

'Goodness me!' Miss Pratt leaped to her feet. 'No!'

'No, no!' said Mary soothingly. 'Don't worry. . . .'

The SOS gave way to news of more import to the world at large, but Miss Pratt did not hear it. She gazed at the loudspeaker as if she had realised suddenly and for the first time the amazing wonder of wireless telegraphy.

'Well . . .' she breathed. 'Well, I never . . .'

'Fancy them sending out an SOS for *me*!' she said to Mary. 'But you don't think anyone will go to the police about me, do you?'

'No, I don't,' Mary reassured her. 'People just think here

that you came to take Zoe's place. I'm the only one that knows about you, and I see no reason for running to the police station at the corner.'

Miss Pratt sat for a moment in silence, then burst out indignantly:

'You see – they've known me all those years and they didn't even know what colour of eyes I've got! Brown eyes!' she said indignantly. 'And aged fifty! Do they think I'd go back after that? They're wrong then. I was thinking of sending them a postcard, but now I'm blessed if I will.'

Mary laughed. She took Miss Pratt's disappearance as a huge joke.

'But I've bothered them, haven't I?' asked Miss Pratt with wicked glee. 'If they'll go so far as to send out an SOS. I've bothered them.'

'Serve them right,' said Mary.

'It does,' agreed Miss Pratt. 'Well, I'm not going to concern myself with them, not I! Shall I be making our cocoa?'

XII

But Miss Pratt was not to be allowed to turn her back thus lightly on Maud and Dolly and the past.

A few days later Miss Pratt, fearing a shortage of butter, had run out hastily for more when she saw a motor-coach from Bendle arrive in the village. Like a monstrous over-ripe seedpod, it burst its doors and shed its occupants in all directions. While they clustered and scattered, Miss Pratt stood petrified. Suppose Dolly or Maud should be among them or someone who knew her and could tell them where she was! But she saw that neither Dolly nor Maud was there, and no one from Bendle seemed to be taking any notice of her. When the café emptied at night, however she found a Bendle paper adrift under a table. She seized it eagerly.

'My goodness!' she called to Mary. 'There's a piece about me!'

'Oh, what does it say?' asked Mary, running to see.

'Where are my glasses? You be reading it, love, will you?'

'"Disappearance of Bendle resident,"' read Mary, '"No trace has yet been discovered of Miss Annie Pratt who disappeared from her home . . ."'

'Home!' interrupted Miss Pratt, fumbling with her glasses. 'What do they call my home, I'd like to know.' She leaned over Mary's arm. 'Oh, Maud's was my home, was it? Well . . . go on, love.'

'"New facts have come to light. Mrs Maud Pratt admitted, when questioned by the police, that she had not informed her sister-in-law that she was not returning that night from Blackpool where she had been spending a holiday with her husband and little daughter. On the evidence of Mrs Brown, a neighbour, and PC Selby, Miss Pratt had waited many hours in the dark, in the garden of Mrs Maud Pratt's house."'

'Dear me!' exclaimed Miss Pratt. 'They've ferreted it all out, the police, haven't they? What's that about Dolly?'

'"Mrs Dolly Pratt told the police in an interview that she had left home with her husband unexpectedly on that evening, and that the house was, therefore, closed when Miss Pratt returned to it at half-past eleven at night."'

'Well, well,' said Miss Pratt uneasily. 'They are being shown up, aren't they? What shall I do?'

'Nothing,' said Mary. 'When in doubt, do nothing. You don't want to go back, do you?'

'Mercy, no!' cried Miss Pratt.

'And you don't want them coming down here unsettling you and worrying you, just when you've started so nicely. Wait until you can show them what you can do without them,' Mary advised.

'Yes, I will. I'll show them some day,' Miss Pratt vowed.

XIII

'I say,' cried Mary, coming in from the café some days later, 'there's an object lesson for you! Do go in and watch Auntie Dora – that's her name, it appears! You can be arranging the cake table. I'll cut up here for a while.'

Miss Pratt went into the café.

Auntie Dora sat in the place of honour behind the teapot, pouring out tea for her relatives: two brothers – Miss Pratt guessed it from their looks – their wives and three children to be distributed somehow between them. Auntie Dora was a bad hostess; she poured out the tea carelessly, and did not trouble to make any conversation. And yet, Miss Pratt observed while arranging puff-pastries on a plate, everything was passed first to Auntie Dora; she was obviously the most important person there.

'It's because she pays for them!' said Miss Pratt to herself.

The party kept on deferring to Auntie Dora. The sisters-in-law, although wives and mothers, which double status usually bestowed, Miss Pratt had observed, such immense superiority upon females, nevertheless talked all the time to the spinster. They asked her advice, and she gave it without appearing to care whether they took it or not.

Miss Pratt marvelled. Maud and Dolly had never asked her advice in anything, and she had never dared to offer it, not even in the matter of boiling a sixpence with the mushrooms to make sure they were not poisonous.

Observing Auntie Dora, Miss Pratt was envious. How fine it would be if she could one day entertain her relations in such a way! Treat them to tea and the pictures and that kind of thing, and have a place of her own where she could show them what hospitality was – not a chair without arms and the place farthest from the fire, crusts no one else would eat and glances to see how much butter was taken, and one lump of sugar put into tea when she really liked two.

Here the last cake at Auntie Dora's table was about to be taken by the youngest boy, when his mother snatched the plate from him and offered it to Auntie Dora.

'My goodness, she's taken it!' said Miss Pratt, holding a gingerbread poised in the air from shock. 'Well, that's going too far!'

She thought how, if she had been in Auntie Dora's place, she would have given the cake to Herbert's little Elsie.

'If that's what money makes of you,' thought Miss Pratt sternly. 'You're better without it.'

Nevertheless, Miss Pratt began to acquire money. The season progressed, the café flourished like a green bay tree, and Miss Pratt was increasingly staggered by her share of the profits.

'I didn't know money *could* be made like this,' she said in awestruck tones to Mary.

'Oh, give the public what it wants and it will pay for it,' said Mary gaily. 'But remember, we've got to earn enough to enable us to live on here during the winter when not a soul will come.'

'You don't mean to say,' said Miss Pratt, 'that you are going to keep me on during the winter?'

'It's not a question of keeping on,' said Mary. 'When this season is over, I shall see about a deed of partnership being drawn up, and then you can sign it, if you approve.'

'Oh, love,' said Miss Pratt with sudden gravity, 'it's too much. I'll stay on here and help you as long as you want me, because I've never been so happy in my life. But deeds of partnership and all that – they're unnecessary.'

'Oh no they're not,' cried Mary. 'Business is business! Besides, I know a good thing when I see it.'

XIV

'Do go into the café,' said Mary. 'And look at those dismal holidaymakers by the door. They can't make up their minds what to eat. They don't seem to have the heart for anything.'

Miss Pratt wiped her hands and went into the café smiling with the usual anticipation of fun. Then she backed slowly out as she had come. The party by the door consisted of Maud and Herbert and Elsie, Jim and Dolly.

'Whatever's the matter?' asked Mary.

'They've found me!' breathed Miss Pratt, as white as flour.

'Who?'

'Maud and the rest . . .'

'Good heavens! Are you sure?'

'Quite sure,' whispered Miss Pratt, sinking on to a kitchen chair. 'They're by the door.'

'The dismal ones I sent you to look at?'

Miss Pratt nodded, unable to speak.

'Good heavens,' said Mary again, beginning to laugh. 'No wonder you left them! I must go and have another look at them.'

'No, don't . . .' besought Miss Pratt. 'Leave them alone. Let sleeping dogs lie!'

'But I can't, even if I wanted to. They must be served. Unless you'd like to go and take the order yourself.'

'Oh, no,' wailed Miss Pratt. 'I'm all of a tremble.'

'Goose!' said Mary, whisking off with a tray.

Miss Pratt waited breathlessly.

'Well?' she asked, as soon as Mary reappeared.

'Tea, scones, cakes and jam for five,' rattled Mary. 'But cheer up, they've not seen you! It strikes me they've not seen anyone or anything for weeks! They're all slumped in their chairs, not taking any interest in anything. I should think, Pratty dear, you've knocked the stuffing out of them completely.'

'Oh, dear, have I?' said Miss Pratt, trying to butter scones with shaking hands. 'It is queer for them to be together,' she marvelled. 'Maud and Dolly were at daggers drawn.'

'Ah,' said Mary, with a wise nod of her head, 'but a common crime has drawn them together. They behaved badly to you, and everybody knows it, so they go about together for protection.'

'Do you think so, poor, things!' said Miss Pratt. 'But what on earth made them come here?' she burst out again, pouring boiling water on the tea.

'Everybody comes to Munthorpe sooner or later, of course,' said Mary. 'Oh, this *is* a nice situation! I am enjoying it!'

She went off again with the tray, and Miss Pratt so far ventured as to peep through a crack of the door at her relations.

Mary was right; they looked depressed. Maud even smiled deprecatingly at Mary when she reached them with the tray, and Dolly did not seem to have taken half so much pains with her appearance as of yore. Jim and Herbert looked permanently worried, with their eyebrows raised into their hair. Only Elsie was bright.

'How she's grown!' thought Miss Pratt, with sudden warmth.

Mary was coming back.

'Have they any appetite?' asked Miss Pratt anxiously.

'We shall have to wait and see,' said Mary.

'I wonder what they'd think if they knew I'd made those scones,' said Miss Pratt.

'Be a sport and go in and tell them,' suggested Mary.

'Oh . . . do you think I ought to?' she asked.

'Well, I think perhaps they've been left in suspense long enough,' said Mary. 'And besides, I should want to show myself if I were you. You look so much better since you came here; different altogether. In fact, I don't think they'll know you.'

Miss Pratt, thus bolstered, rose from the kitchen chair on to which she had again sunk.

'Oh, dear,' she moaned softly, 'I hardly like to face them.'

'Go on!' urged Mary. 'How many times have you said you'd face them any day?'

'I was boasting,' admitted Miss Pratt.

XV

She turned herself round for Mary's inspection.

'Will I do?' she asked with anxiety.

''Course you'll do,' said Mary, giving her a sudden hug on her way to the larder. 'Go on; I'm coming in behind you. I wouldn't miss this reunion for worlds.'

Miss Pratt, looking both excited and guilty, went through the door into the café. She threaded her way through the tables and chairs, mercifully, for the moment, empty. Maud, in the act of passing scones to Elsie, looked up and saw her coming. Her mouth fell open; she held the plate in the air and said nothing until Miss Pratt was almost on them. Then she poured the scones on to the floor and cried, 'Annie!'

'Well, Maud,' said Miss Pratt breathlessly.

Dolly stood up hurriedly, and knocked her tea over.

'Annie!' she cried in her turn.

The sight of the tea dripping from the table dispelled Miss Pratt's nervousness in a trice. She was used to dealing at once with such events.

'Wait a minute, I'll get a cloth,' she said.

This enabled her to return to the kitchen and still further pull herself together. She came back into the café complete mistress of the situation.

'Now, then, I'll just mop this up,' she said, proceeding to the task.

'Well, Annie,' said Maud, wiping her face which was all bedewed with the perspiration of surprise, 'you have given us a turn!'

Her sister-in-law rose from the floor.

Jim was the first to recover himself.

'Where on earth have you been?' he burst out.

'Why did you go off like that, Annie?' asked Herbert. 'You frightened us to death.'

'People have been treating us as if we'd driven you to suicide,' Jim blustered. 'And you all right all the time, and flourishing too, by the look of you!'

'You seem disappointed about that, Jim,' said Miss Pratt. 'Perhaps you'd rather I had committed suicide?'

'Oh, don't talk like that,' said Jim harshly, who had evidently not recovered from the fear that she had done so.

'You played a nice trick on us, Annie,' said Herbert indignantly.

'You played the first trick,' said Miss Pratt calmly.

'You've ruined us with all our friends,' said Maud.

'Nay, you've ruined yourselves. It only came out into the light,' said Miss Pratt.

But she was sorry for them.

'It will be all right when they know I'm found,' she assured them.

'You'd better pay us a visit,' said Herbert, 'and show yourself.'

'You can come to me, Annie,' said Dolly eagerly. 'I'd be delighted.'

'No, it's my turn,' said Maud.

Miss Pratt shook her head.

'Thank you all, but I wouldn't dream of leaving my work or my partner. Yes, I'm a partner here – or shall be when the deed is drawn up. We're very busy. The place is a little gold-mine. You'd be surprised, Herbert, you so interested in money!'

She casually mentioned profits that made Maud gape.

'Can't you come back with us, Annie?' begged Jim, who had always been her favourite. 'I'm sick of being asked about you. That blooming tram-conductor asks me every day. I'm driven to walking a mile and a half each way when I see him on the tram.'

'I thought you were thinner,' murmured Miss Pratt. 'But then you *were* too fat.'

'And that Mrs Brown next door has made such bad feeling in the neighbourhood,' complained Maud, 'we're thinking of moving, aren't we, Herbert?'

'A good thing, too,' said Miss Pratt, speaking her mind for the first time about Maud's house. She felt a little nervous when she had said it, but Maud said nothing but: 'Won't you come back, Annie?'

'No,' said Miss Pratt briskly. 'I'm sorry, but I can't come back. I might come and see you for a day or two when the season's over, just to collect my sofa and the tea set – but I won't promise anything. In the meantime, you'd better put a piece in the paper. Not under the Births, Marriages and Deaths – but somewhere about there. Oh, Lost and Found, of course. Well, your tea's gone cold. I'll get some more, and take a cup with you myself. And, Elsie,' she said, leaning towards the little girl with a benevolent smile, 'you can eat as many cakes as you like for once, because your auntie's going to pay for them!'

XVI

She went off with the teapot, leaving her relatives to stare after her with mixed feelings.

'Well?' asked Mary, in the kitchen.

'Come along,' said Miss Pratt, with a chuckle, 'and watch me being Auntie Dora! I've never played the part before, but you'd think I was born to it!'

SUSAN

Susan was making the bed in the room with handsome crimson roses on the wallpaper. Her mistress did not help with the beds; she attended to the aspidistras on the wire stand in the porch first thing every morning. So Susan was alone, and she was glad. She was glad to be able to walk heavily, to turn the mattress slowly, not with a great throw as she used to, and pause for breath a moment at the open window.

There was a little ring of snowdrops in the side bed; your eyes flew to them every time you passed the windows, so white and pretty they were in the muddy garden where everything else was still dead. The snowdrops would have smuts on them, she knew, when you bent down close, but from a distance they looked very pure.

She raised her eyes from the garden, and took in all that the window looked out on: the black ribbon of road, threaded with two narrow ribbons of tramlines; the few bare trees, whose trunks gleamed from the night's rain; the spaces between the houses, and on the hill behind, the Union, square, bare, cruelly clean, surrounded by pale grass cut up by asphalt paths. In the morning sun, its windows glittered like sword-blades.

Susan stared, as if fascinated, at the Union buildings. Once she had been very afraid she was going to end up – not there – but in one of those places. Not there. She would never have disgraced her mistress by going there, so near, if Tom hadn't acted properly by her. Mrs Shaw was a good mistress; very kind, considerate, and childless. And that last was a good thing, otherwise she would have noticed something long ago.

Susan left the window and returned to her bed-making. There was only today and tomorrow to go now. On Thursday she would take an hour's tram-ride into Manchester and be married to Tom.

A trembling joy filled her at the thought. Her child would be born respectable, would have a home and a father! They would all live together, a family, in a house, and the child would go to school and be happy with other children. No one would point at it and call it dreadful names, or tell it about its mother, and ask who its father was. Oh, God was so good to her, so much better than she ever deserved! She wiped her eyes on the corner of her mistress's sheet, then dropped it hurriedly and applied her own apron to her tears. She shouldn't have done that with the sheet, she remembered. If her mistress had been there, she wouldn't have done it; well, then, she mustn't do it when she wasn't there. Susan's maxim, as applied to mistresses, had once been: 'What the eye doesn't see, the heart doesn't grieve for.' But now all that was changed. Susan must be purified, because Tom was going to marry her, and let her child be born legitimate. They were so good, God and Tom.

She walked heavily round to the other side of the bed to arrange the master's pillow. The master and the mistress slept in the two little places they had worn for themselves in the big bed; side by side, every night. And it was all right for them. But all wrong for her and Tom. If only she had been able to remember that, to think of the wrong in it that time, so long ago now, and remote, when Tom had wept, and she, in an exaltation of love, had comforted him.

The exaltation had not lasted. It had soon become a nightmare in which she struggled alone. There was so much to face: Tom's anger, her own ill-health, the fear of her mistress finding out and turning her away, the fear of not being able to do her work. But now the long wait, the long agony of mind was almost over. Tom had promised to marry her on Thursday.

'Oh, I'll be a good wife to him,' she whispered, smoothing the bedspread. 'I'll never forget what he's done for me.'

She would get up at half-past four in the morning when he was on early shift. He was a tram-conductor on the route she travelled to see her friend in Manchester, and she had fallen in love with him for the way he smiled when he said 'Than*kew*' to her fare. They had got to passing the time of day, and at last he had asked her to go to the pictures when he came off his shift.

She had got off at the terminus with him, and waited happily in the street while he changed his clothes. He told her he lived with his mother; she was a widow and he her only son.

'A bit of a tartar,' he said, by way of excuse for not asking Susan in.

She had looked at the outside of the house with great interest; a little, low, shut-up looking house it was, with lace curtains as yellow as yolk of egg. And now that was where she was to live!

There was the sound of someone arriving at the back door. Susan went out on to the landing.

'Susan,' called Mrs Shaw in a mildly excited voice. 'Your wedding present has come.'

'Oh, 'm,' cried Susan.

Her heart gave a leap of joy. A wedding present made it all seem so true.

'Wait a minute,' called Mrs Shaw again. 'I'm going to spread it out. Don't you come.'

'No, 'm.'

Mrs Shaw came upstairs and went into the spare room. There was a hollow sound of strong paper being unwrapped, and then silence. Susan wondered what her mistress could be doing. As a matter of fact, Mrs Shaw was being dazzled by the splendour of her present to Susan. It really was a good one; satin on one side. She wondered if she should keep it for the spare bed, and give Susan something not quite so . . . but, no, Susan had been a very good maid, and after all, four years' service . . .

'Susan,' she called, 'you can come now.'

Susan came diffidently round the spare room door, and gasped with delight. On the spare bed was laid, like a coil of monstrous satin sausages, a magnificent and highly floral eiderdown.

'Oh, 'm,' breathed Susan, 'is it really for me?'

'With the master's and my best wishes for future happiness,' said Mrs Shaw in a wedding-card manner. Then she became entirely human and put her hand on Susan's strong arm. 'You've been a very good girl, Susan, and if you make your Tom as comfortable as you've made us, he's a very lucky man. I've never seen him,' she finished anxiously, 'but I hope he's all right?'

'Oh, yes, 'm, Tom's all right,' said Susan fervently. He was. He had turned out to be.

'Well, now, how are you going to get this eiderdown away on Thursday morning?' asked Mrs Shaw, dismissing Tom. She did not feel too amiable towards him, he was taking the best maid she had ever had. 'It will never go into your box.'

'No, 'm, that it won't. It's such a grand big one. Fancy me with an eiderdown like that!' She thought, fleetingly, how impressed Tom's mother would be, perhaps welcome her more for it. 'I shall carry it, 'm,' she decided. 'I'll make it up into the parcel again. It'll be safer with me, and not get crushed. It's too lovely to let out of my sight, 'm. Eh, it is bonny. . . .' She stroked it, but her rough fingers rasped the satin and she ceased.

'I hope you get some nice useful presents,' said Mrs Shaw.

'Oh, no, 'm, only this,' said Susan. 'But this is all as I want. This does for all, this does.'

'Well,' said Mrs Shaw, 'I shouldn't have thought so, I must say. What about your sisters? What about Tom? You're taking this wedding very quietly, Susan. I should have thought you'd have gone in for a new dress at least.'

'Well, I always used to think I'd have white satin and a piece of veiling,' admitted Susan, with a smile backwards at her dreams. 'But I've changed my mind now as it's come to it, you see, 'm.'

'You're very sensible about the white satin,' said Mrs Shaw on her way to the door. 'What's the good of white satin afterwards, I'd like to know?'

No good, thought Susan, folding the eiderdown, no good, but it would have been lovely. Just for one day to be all in white and carry a bunch of roses. And have nothing to hide; to marry Tom as if there was nothing behind it; to be all jolly together like those weddings in Cumberland she remembered when she used to live in a cottage with a white step and a bush of lavender by the door. She would have invited Elsie if it could have been a wedding like that, and Willy too, perhaps. But none of that now. Let her get into safety as quietly as possible. She felt she must make herself unnoticeable and slip past something that was waiting to pounce on her and drive her out into . . . into a Home for Bad Girls, or one of those Union places. She waited for Thursday. She waited with bated breath for Thursday.

In the meantime, there was the bathroom to be done. All the other spring-cleaning was finished long before its time, so that everything should be tidy for the new girl, who was to come in on Thursday afternoon when Susan had gone. Gone to be married. Married by then. Her heart suddenly lifted within her. She wanted to sing. But it was a hymn that rose unbidden to her lips:

'Can a woman's tender care
Cease toward the child she bare?'

It turned a knife in her heart. She closed her eyes with pain. Clasping the billowing eiderdown, she prayed that God would make it all right for her baby.

'Now, Susan,' called her mistress, with mild remontrance at the time Susan was wasting in the spare room.

'Yes, 'm, I'm coming, 'm,' called Susan, hurrying into the bathroom.

All that day she scrubbed and wiped and polished, labouring through the hours with relentless determination. She was very tired, but she kept on. It wouldn't be for long now. And if Tom's mother turned out to be a kind woman, she would let her rest a little after Thursday.

She kept wondering what Tom's mother would be like. She only knew she was a bit of a tartar, and kept Tom tight for money, taking his wages at the week's end, and giving him some for spending. She saved for him because she said he would never save for himself.

Tom would have told her about marrying Susan by now. She might take it badly, being her only son. Tom seemed to think there would be a row about it; but he had promised it wouldn't make any difference what sort of a row there was. That was so good of him.

Susan made up her mind to efface herself as much as possible in the household, to cause as little trouble as possible, and if Tom's mother couldn't love her, she would be sure to love her grandchild when it came. That sort always do, thought Susan.

On Wednesday, she worked very hard, putting the house entirely straight, and when that was done, she was free to wash her best blouse, and take her marabou neck-piece out of tissue paper. She hung it up behind her bedroom door to get the smell of moth-balls out of it. Towards evening, a feeling of security began to grow, like a tremulous flower, so she took the silk rose out of her black hat and dyed it a blush pink with a penny packet of dye from the shop at the back of the house. She tried the hat on before the looking-glass on the yellow-painted chest of drawers, and smiled diffidently. She was pale and hollow-eyed, but the pink rose brightened her up wonderfully. She hoped Tom would like it.

She pulled out the little tin trunk, yellow like the chest of drawers, and in it she packed her clean, strong clothes; her blue prints and her aprons to wear when she did the work for Tom's mother, her flannelette nightgowns with the feather-stitching, her best handkerchiefs with the butterflies worked in pink and green silk, her workbasket and the Bible the Vicar had given her when she left the Cumberland village, her best stays, and two silk petticoats she had made for her bottom drawer when she first started walking out with Tom. She packed them all and tied up the trunk with a length of stiff, hairy rope she had bought with the dye from the shop at the back of the house.

She wrote the address of Tom's mother on a piece of paper and stuck it with stamp paper to the yellow trunk. When she was gone in the morning her mistress would give it to Barton the carrier, and he would deliver it later in the day.

All was ready for Thursday now.

She went downstairs to take the hot milk into the drawing-room.

'Well, Susan,' said Mrs Shaw, looking up from her book, 'you won't be here tomorrow at this time.'

'No, 'm,' agreed Susan reluctantly. She did wish her mistress, though she meant it kindly, would not keep talking in this way. Susan felt as if Something might overhear, and laugh in its sleeve.

'Good night, Susan.'

'Good night, 'm.'

She climbed the stairs again. She would be glad not to have to go up so many stairs. There couldn't be many in Tom's mother's house. That little low house with the yellow curtains was her haven, her port; like a ship in a dangerous sea, she strained towards it. Surely she was getting nearer now. She got into bed and fell asleep at once from sheer fatigue.

She woke to the trill of the alarm clock that had ticked reverberantly throughout the night on the chair by the bed. She put out a hand and turned the alarm off. When the bell ceased, she could hear a thrush singing in the garden. It sang: 'Pretty girl, pretty girl, pretty girl,' just like the thrushes in Cumberland. It was a hopeful sound to hear first thing this morning. To-day the nightmare would be over. This afternoon.

She got up and dressed. Her fingers trembled and were cold. She longed for a cup of tea.

'Then I'll be all right,' she told herself.

She went down through the silent house, down two flights of stairs, the polished rail slipping through her nerveless hand. As she turned to begin the third flight, her eyes went straight to the tiles inside the front door. But of course, she told herself, drawing a steadying breath, the post hadn't been yet. Too early.

She put the kettle on the gas stove, and set herself to rake out the rusty ash from the kitchen grate. But many a time she had to rest. Her heart fluttered like a trapped bird in her breast. When she had drunk the tea, she was calmer. She went to do the 'room' fires, and cast another glance at the front door. Perhaps there were no letters for them at all today. She breathed more easily at the idea, although she knew it was still too early for the post.

She did the fires and the rooms. She came back into the kitchen and made the tea for upstairs. She went up into the darkened bedroom where her master and mistress still slept. As soon as she drew back the curtains, the Union leapt into her view. There was no getting away from it.

'Is it a fine morning, Susan?' asked Mrs Shaw, waking at the light.

Susan looked to see.

'Yes, 'm.'

'Fine for your wedding day,' said Mrs Shaw, raising herself to pour out the tea.

But Susan could not speak. She had seen the postman coming up the garden path. She got herself out of the room, to the top of the stairs. She looked over. One letter lay on the tiles inside the door. Pressing her hand to her heart, she went down, her eyes fixed on the letter.

She reached it. It lay wrong side up, but she knew it was for her. A greyish-white envelope thumbed down by Tom. For a moment, she stooped over it, breathing heavily. Then she picked it up and took it to the kitchen. Her shaking fingers prised open the envelope, and unfolded the sheet of paper. She didn't seem to be able to see. Her heart was beating in her eyes. She held the paper nearer, and read it at last. There was not much to read:

Dear Susan,

    Sorry to say we can't be married after all. Mother takes it very bad and says she won't have you here so what can I do. There is nowhere else for us besides she is my mother and I can't go against her. No more at present.

    Yours truly,

Tom

The letter dropped to the kitchen table and Susan remained leaning over it, her hands pressing down against the table, her head sunk between her shoulders.

The bedroom bell rang in the little glass case above the door. She did not hear it. It rang again. She raised her head in bewilderment. What was it? Slowly she returned to her environment. The shaving water. Mechanically she lifted a jug from a hook and filled it at the kettle.

'I thought you'd forgotten me, Susan,' said the master, waiting on the landing.

'Yes, sir,' she said, forcing her stiff lips into a servant's smile.

'But on your wedding day,' he said kindly, 'you can't be expected to think of shaving water.'

'No, sir,' said Susan, turning away.

She went downstairs again. Into the kitchen. The letter was still there, balancing itself on the table.

'Dear Susan,
Sorry to say we can't be married after all. . . .'

She closed her eyes at it. She sank into the rocking chair and drifted off into a strange daze, lying inert while the letter, which seemed to have taken on a life of its own, cried out from the table: 'Mother takes it very bad . . . very bad . . . we can't be married after all . . . yours truly, Tom . . . she won't have you here so what can I do. . . .'

'What can I do?' She came to herself at that and sat up, staring about her.

The kitchen clock struck eight.

Breakfast. There was breakfast to get. She took the letter from the table and threw it into the fire. She seized the poker and pushed it down into the flames. Now perhaps it would be quiet.

She straightened her cap with incompetent fingers. There was breakfast to get; and although she had been getting breakfast for more than eight years, she didn't know how to begin. She had to think, slowly, painfully, what to do. You made the coffee and put it by the fire to brew; you cut bread for toast; you fried the bacon . . . that was it. But first the coffee. . . .

'We can't be married after all.'

Oh, God, what was she going to do now?

'Susan, Susan,' said Mrs Shaw, coming into the kitchen. 'You haven't even set the table and it's nearly half-past eight.'

'I'm just coming, 'm,' said Susan desperately.

'Now don't flurry yourself. You look very pale. It's the excitement, I suppose.'

'Yes, 'm.'

She went away with the tray and habit enabled her to set the table blindly.

They were shut into the dining room at last with their breakfast, and she could sit down again in the rocking chair. But as soon as she sat down, the letter began again. 'We can't be married . . .'

She got up and pressed her hands to her eyes. She was lost in desolation. She was alone, and there was no one she dared ask for help.

A bell rang in the little glass case again. What was it this time? To clear away. She rubbed her cheeks with her apron to make the colour come, so that they should not remark again on her pallor.

She cleared the table and washed the pots, leaning on her hands in the sink to listen to the letter. 'She won't have you here.'

Nobody would have her anywhere. She was an outcast; she and the child. It didn't matter for her now, but it was wrong that the baby should suffer all its life for what its mother had done. They would point at it now when it went to school. They would take it from her if they could. In those places, they took the child away so that the mother could work. She knew. Well, they wouldn't get her child away from her, she determined, setting her lips in a pale line. She would die first.

Perhaps she would die anyway. If the time came before she could get to one of those places. Better if she did. But the child might live, and what would happen to it then? She must hurry to give herself up.

She was spurred to dry the pots with haste and put them away.

'I've washed out the towels, 'm, for the new girl,' she said.

'That's right, Susan. Everything looks very nice and tidy.'

'I'll go and do upstairs and it will be finished.'

Mechanically she swept and dusted. She scrubbed out her own room and removed every trace of herself from it.

'Now, Susan, you haven't too much time,' called Mrs Shaw.

Time enough, thought Susan, but she called back:

'No, 'm, thank you.'

She took up the hat with the fresh pink rose. They'd think she was a brazen piece going to one of those places with a rose in her hat like that. But she must go out of the house as if she were going to her wedding. Her mistress must never know; never know the dreadful truth.

She put on the hat and hung the marabou round her neck; she forced her hands into the new kid gloves and cast a wild glance round the room. She was leaving her only refuge.

Her eyes fell on the tin trunk and the eiderdown. Well, the thing must be played out. Leave the trunk and take the eiderdown. She lifted the ballooning parcel by the criss-cross of string. They'd think she'd stolen it where she was going, likely. That somehow was the last straw. She had to stand behind the door and squeeze the tears back into her eyes. A thief, a bad lot; that's what everybody would take her for now.

She mastered the tears and went downstairs.

'I'm ready now, 'm,' she said, presenting herself in the porch where her mistress was doing the plants.

'You're ready, are you, Susan?' said Mrs Shaw, retreating into the hall with her. 'Well, you look very nice, but rather too frightened. Cheer up, it's not so bad as all that.' She laughed. 'What a big parcel the eiderdown makes, doesn't it? But you are very wise to take it with you. Now, here's your last week's money.'

She took fifteen shillings from her purse, and Susan put it carefully into hers. If she hadn't paid off the instalments on Tom's motorcycle, she'd have had far more than that now. What a fool I've been, she thought, bowing her head over the worn purse, what a fool, what a fool!

'Well, goodbye, Susan, and I wish you much happiness,' said Mrs Shaw, taking Susan's hand, which resembled a large brown shrimp in the tight glove.

'Goodbye, 'm, and I'm sure I thank you kindly for all as you've been so good to me,' said Susan brokenly. For one wild moment, she felt she was going to blurt out all the truth, but with pressed lips, the moment passed in silence.

'Goodbye, 'm,' she said again.

'Goodbye, Susan, and let me know how the wedding goes off. Come and see me very soon.'

'Nay, I'll never see you again,' thought Susan, turning away with another goodbye.

Her mistress watched her go, crunching the little stones of the path under her imitation skin shoes, the pink rose nodding insecurely in her hat, the eiderdown swinging round her legs, first to the front, then to the back. Mrs Shaw waited to wave her hand when Susan should look round at the gate. But she did not look round. She stood a moment as if in uncertainty, then crossed the road and disappeared from view.

BITTER SAUCE

The grey blinds monogrammed in silver were down, but the door of the shop opened under his hand.

'Has Mrs Catlow gone?'

'Not yet,' said a young girl, smiling up from putting things away in drawers.

Robert Pentland went silently and eagerly over the expanse of jade carpet and knocked on a silvered door.

'Come in,' said a voice, which changed from weariness to joy at the sight of him. 'Oh, Robert, how nice! I was just feeling so dull and done up. What inspired you to come round tonight?'

She swung round in the revolving chair and held up her face to be kissed. She was too tired to stand up and be folded in his arms. Besides, someone might come in.

'Can we talk?' he asked, drawing up a chair so that he could still hold her hand.

'In a moment. There's only Miss Potter left. She'll be gone soon. Have a cigarette.'

Waiting, he looked round the room sacred to the proprietor of 'Rose, Modes et Robes.' It was a model of efficiency and good taste. She was jolly clever, he thought, to manage all this. Would she leave it? Though after all, she wouldn't leave as much as he would. She was free; a widow. She had no ties.

He looked at her as she swung and smiled in her chair. She, too, was a model of efficiency and good taste. Her clothes were wonderful, her hair was dark and smooth as satin, her lips were full and delicious, her hands lovely – but her eyes were tired. This fatigue only added to her charm, he felt. She didn't get tired in the ugly way Amy got tired. When Amy was tired, which was pretty nearly always now, although he couldn't for the life of him see why – Amy's face went red and her hair came down. He had been married to Amy for thirteen years and always when she was tired her face got red and her hair came down. It exasperated him to think of it. But when Rose was tired he was touched.

'I rang up to say I wouldn't be home until the nine-thirty,' he said, to make conversation until Miss Potter should be gone.

'Good,' said Rose.

There was a knock at the door.

'Have you finished, Miss Potter?' called Rose. 'Very well. Turn out the lights there, and lock that door. I'll see to the rest. Good night.'

'There,' she said, turning her chair to Robert. 'Now we're alone. Go ahead.'

'Wait a moment,' he said, pressing out his cigarette and getting up to kiss her.

He was rather slow in his movements, but his deliberation thrilled her. She put her arms round his neck as he leaned over her.

'Oh, Robert, I'm so tired,' she complained, relaxing deliciously from the efficiency of the day and becoming a spoiled child in his arms. 'I'm so tired.'

'Are you, darling? So am I. That's what I've come about. I wrote to you last night.'

'Did you? But I've had no letter,' she said, freeing herself to look at him.

He returned to his chair, drawing it still closer to hers.

'No, because I didn't get it posted. The cistern chose last night to overflow, and there was such an upset that I couldn't get out with your letter.'

'Where is it? Have you brought it?' asked Rose, who never liked to be done out of a demonstration of love on Robert's part.

'No, I haven't brought it,' he said. 'As a matter of fact, I left it in the pocket of the old Trinity blazer I wear in the house.'

'Robert!' cried Rose in alarm. 'How appalling! How could you be so careless?'

'My dear, I absolutely forgot it this morning. I was thinking so hard about ways and means and you that I quite forgot the letter.'

'But suppose your wife finds it?' she cried.

'Well – does it really matter?' asked Robert. 'That's what I wrote about. It's what I've come about. I couldn't wait even until tomorrow to talk it over with you.'

He took the hand she had removed, and stroked it with his own, which was thick and blunt.

'Rose, darling,' he said, 'hasn't the time come for us to cut loose? Let's go away and get out of this. I'm absolutely sick of my life as it is, and so are you. Let's go.'

Rose Catlow's eyes widened as she stared at him. Her breath came quickly, but she did not speak. She was thinking. It was true that she was tired; tired of the shop, the bills, the buying, the customers, the hours; tired of looking after herself, of earning her own living, of being alone. Besides, trade was bad and might soon be worse; it would be wise to sell out while selling was good. She was, moreover, in love with Robert.

'What about – er – your wife?' This was awkward to say. 'And your three boys?' she added with another effort.

'I've worked it all out many a time,' said Robert eagerly. 'Ever since I knew you I've been working it out. As I said in my letter, I can leave them quite comfortably off; not rolling in money, you know, but quite comfortable. Amy will manage on it. And there'll be quite enough for us for two or three years until I get another job. A civil engineer can always get another job, you know.'

'Can he?' asked Rose.

'Oh, yes,' said Robert airily, 'I've no fear about that. We could go abroad, darling,' he went on in a rather cosy voice. 'Until Amy divorces me. She'll divorce me, I know, because she's always said an unhappy marriage should be ended. There's nothing between Amy and me any more, as you know,' he said, with the customary euphemism. He went on stroking her hand.

'And anyway,' he burst out, 'I can't stand it any longer. Everything in that house gets on my nerves so badly that I behave like a perfect brute all the time I'm in it. Amy, the boys, the meals, the rooms – everything gets on my nerves now. If things had been different . . .' Robert Pentland was always saying that. 'If things had been different – I mean, if I hadn't been in love with you, I'd have stuck it out. As it is, I can't. After all, as I said in my letter, a man surely has some right to his own life. Why should he be a mere domestic appendage? I grub for the money; they spend it. That's my life. As I said, a man surely has some right to – er – to beauty and – er . . .' He stammered a little. It had been easier to write all this than to say it; and it looked much better on paper too.

'Let's go, Rose,' he urged, 'you know how I love you. Let's go!'

She tapped on her desk with a pencil and looked at him with bright, amused eyes.

'Well,' she said, 'I'm ready when you are. Where shall we go to?'

'Italy,' he said promptly. 'To the sun.'

It had been very dull weather in London lately, but when he got away with Rose, the sun, he felt, would always shine.

'Italy,' repeated Rose. 'It sounds all right, doesn't it?'

'Oh, Rose,' he cried, plunging towards her. 'It will be wonderful . . . wonderful! Oh, how happy you make me. You're marvellous! No fuss, or anything . . .' he was incoherent with joy.

They talked on and on. Robert walked about the room, explaining and expounding. Rose swung in her chair, her brain busy, her heart light. A fresh start, a fresh love – how alluring, how wonderful! And, though neither of them said so, what an escape! What an escape from the life they had made for themselves so far!

'But, Robert,' said Rose, returning to the only thing that worried her, 'it was a frightful mistake to leave that letter at home. Suppose your wife finds it, addressed to me?'

'It wasn't addressed to you. It wasn't in an envelope. But what does it matter if she does find it? She'll have to know some time. She'll take it quite well. She knows I don't love her. I must say Amy is very sensible in her way; never asks for anything you don't want to give her. Rather wonderful, really,' he said, looking a little startled for a moment by the merits of Amy. But that, he knew, was only because he was leaving her.

'I'd hate her to find that letter,' said Rose, fearing a scandal before she could get away. Once gone, she did not care what happened.

'Don't worry, Rose, darling. It will be all right.'

Robert always felt things would be all right.

'Post it to me tonight, then,' begged Rose, who loved Love and felt this letter should be rather marvellous.

'Do you really want it?' he asked.

'Yes, I do.'

He consented to post it, as if to humour her whim, but, secretly, he wanted her to see how well he had put it; how he was ready to leave his wife, his sons, his home, his work, his reputation – all for her.

'I shall begin to wind up my affairs at once, and you'll do the same, won't you?' he said.

'I'll do the same,' promised Rose. 'If you're going to catch that train, you must be going.'

They parted, full of love and eager anticipation. Rose went home to her town flat, and Robert took the train for his half-hour journey to the suburbs. He hated this twice-daily journey, and was elated to remember, suddenly, that it was one of the things he would consign to the rag-bag of the life he was leaving behind.

In the corner of the compartment he closed his eyes and went over it all again.

Amy and the boys would be all right. Of course he would see that they were all right. He would give them all he could from generosity and – well – relief. There was no baulking the fact that they were too much for him.

He opened his eyes briefly to stare in surprise at himself. He must be without paternal feeling, he thought. The boys had been jolly little chaps enough as babies, but they had come too quickly one after the other to retain their novelty. And now they had got to the stage when they broke everything they laid their hands on, they kicked the stair rods when they went upstairs, they were clumsy and unattractive, with stubbly hair and dirty hands, they got hot and fought incessantly and made an appalling row from morning till night. Three boys of almost the same age were more than he had bargained for when he married. If only there had been a girl among them, it would have been different. A man always likes to have a daughter. It was like Amy to be monotonous even in her children.

He shuffled with exasperation in his corner. The noise, the bills, the bother . . . always something: tonsils or holidays, letters to Headmasters or from Headmasters, maids leaving, cisterns overflowing, and no peace, no privacy, no place to himself; even his dressing room would have to go soon to make a bedroom for one boy, because they made such an unholy row morning and night when they were all together in the attic. By Jove, there wasn't a corner in the whole of that house – *his* house – where he could keep anything private. There was something terribly wrong with a manner of living that caged human beings up like fowls in a pen. At any rate, it wouldn't do for a man like him. He would free himself.

His thoughts leaped forward to his new life with Rose. He had a vision of Italy in spring, the little trees like pink and white coral in the valleys, the young vines taking hands to dance, the small, exquisite cloisters in Rome and Florence; and in summer, Brittany, perhaps, and in winter, Switzerland; and Rose, in her lovely clothes, always pretty, amusing, efficient, yet feminine, modern and wonderful!

Oh, they must go quickly! He had never been so excited about anything in his life before.

He got out of the train and walked up the hill towards home. The light from the street lamp shone on the house, showing its ugly bay windows wreathed in dusty ivy. Soon, soon this place would know him no more! He and Rose would have a villa – a small one, though Rose had made quite a lot of money really – a villa above some lake, and there, when it was dark, the nightingales would sing, and rose and jasmine scent the air. He sniffed ecstatically, and drew in a fugitive smell from a distant but pungent gasometer.

'Pah!' he grimaced.

He went into the house and stood for a moment in the

hall. The boys were thundering about in their bedroom. They were supposed to be in bed long ago, but they enlivened the nights occasionally by pillow and other fights. He thought irritably that Amy might at least see they were quiet by the time he came home.

He was glad, all the same, that Amy had evidently not heard him come in. It gave him the chance to retrieve the letter from his blazer pocket and go out again to post it in the pillar box at the corner. He went upstairs, springing easily and lightly from very buoyancy up two steps at a time.

As he went into his dressing room, a loud yell from the boys' room made him pause.

'Oh, Peter's knocked a tooth out! Peter's knocked a tooth out! Oh, help – somebody!'

Confound it, something was wrong again! Well, Amy would deal with it.

He went to his wardrobe and took his blazer from its accustomed peg. Was his letter there? Yes, it was there. He drew it out, and another letter with it.

His heart turned over with a curious movement, and the hand holding the letters trembled suddenly.

Amy knew.

He drew a long, wavering breath. She knew; and there would be a scene tonight, just when he didn't feel ready for it. Unless she had written what she wanted to say to him, and would make no scene? She had done that once before; written to him and never spoken at all. A good way of doing things; it made him grateful towards her. But it wouldn't help her this time; his mind was made up. He was going with Rose.

The yells continued upstairs. Amy would be kept up there for some time. He could read her letter, and compose himself before he saw her.

He unfolded the sheet of paper and began to read.

'You had forgotten that we arranged to send this blazer to the cleaners . . .'

Yes, by Jove, so he had.

'I did not hesitate to read this letter, because I have known for a long time that something was wrong, and I wanted to know what it was.'

Oh, she had, had she? Well, that would make it easier.

As he read on, his brows drew together in bewilderment.

'The boys need a father more than a mother. If anyone has to go, it must be me. . . .'

What in the world . . .?

'It isn't fair that you should be forced to leave your sons, your home, your work, your reputation, because I have been a failure. For a long time now I have felt a terrible failure . . .'

The words danced before his eyes. He held the paper nearer and concentrated his gaze.

'I don't blame you at all. I haven't been able to do my job. It has beaten me . . .'

The bawlings upstairs increased and made a hideous background to the turmoil in Robert's head.

'Don't worry about me,' went on the letter. 'I earned my living before I married you. I can earn it again. I'll find some way of freeing you, never fear. Then you can marry this girl you love and bring her here. I am going now – today – to make things easier for you. Goodbye.'

She'd gone! She'd left him with the boys! And Rose would never . . . Oh, it wasn't fair! It wasn't *fair*. . . .

He rushed out on to the landing, where the boys swarmed, all blood and tears.

'Amy!' he shouted furiously, above the din of the battle. 'AMY . . .!!'

EXIT

The black-out was up. In the starched caps, like globe arti-
chokes in linen, which they had unresentfully worn in the
afternoons for twenty years in the service of their Miss
Florence, the two maids sat by the fire, Minnie with her
knitting, Alice with a back number of *Christian Novels* passed on
to her by a friend. The kitchen was warm, quiet and very tidy.
On the table, also dressed for the afternoon in a red cloth,
was a folded board inscribed in silver with the word: 'LUDO'.
The clock wagged its pendulum against the wall and Alice
whipped round again to look at it.

'Quarter to seven now,' she announced in a sharp voice.

'Well, did you ever,' said Minnie, turning her needles.
'After I heard Miss Florence meself say half-past five. 'Ow she
'as the cheek . . .'

'She's cheek enough for anything, if you ask me,' said
Alice.

'It's pouring with rain too. She'll be coming in wet
through, messing up my floor just when I've given it a good
polish,' said Minnie, casting a proud proprietory glance at the
brown linoleum which shone like caramel toffee.

'Whatever does she want to go traipsing two miles to the town every day for, specially in this weather?' asked Alice.

'To look at the shops,' said Minnie. 'She says she must have something to look at. She said to me this morning, she said: "'Ave you been looking at nothing but them two trees from this 'ere window for twenty years?" she said. "I should go barmy," she said. Of course she put it different, but I'm not going to repeat it. I don't like her langwidge, you know, Alice.'

'No more do I,' said Alice censoriously. 'It's not fit for decent girls like us to listen to.'

They always spoke and thought of themselves as girls though they were both over forty.

'Hark!' Alice raised a hand. They listened intently. There were steps on the gravel. They turned their heads with the posed caps to the back door, waiting with a gleam in their eyes.

The door opened briskly and a young woman came through, slamming it behind her.

'Quiet, Lily, please. Miss Florence is in,' said Alice.

Lily advanced into the kitchen. She was wet through, her bush of blonde hair dark with rain, her woollen cap sodden, her coat dripping to the floor.

'Here, mind my floor,' complained Minnie, getting up at once for a cloth.

'Well, I've got to come in, 'aven't I?' said the girl with loud determined cheerfulness.

'In weather like this, you've no need to go out, Lily,' said Alice.

'Haven't I?' said Lily, wringing out her cap over the sink. 'That's all you know then.'

She hung her coat behind the door.

'Here,' said Minnie again. 'Not there, thank you. In the wash-house.'

'Right you are,' said Lily. 'Anything to oblige.'

She came back squeezing the hem of her draggled skirt in her hands as she came. She went to the table to get the short-legged stool from beneath it and bringing her chin low over the game-board, she laughed:

'Heh! Ludo!'

She planted the stool between Alice and the mantelpiece and sat down.

'Cripes, but I'm wet,' she said.

The others followed with fascinated gaze the movements of the hands struggling with the knots of the wet shoelaces. The middle finger of Lily's right hand was a limp stump, sewn up at the top. It was like a little roly-poly pudding, Minnie often said, and it gave her the creeps to look at it.

Lily had been employed at a laundry to put the pins in the parcels. The finger that pushed pins so incessantly became septic; the bone had to be taken out. Lily, ill and out of work, found herself suddenly without a home. It was destroyed by a bomb; and Miss Florence had selected Lily from evacuees assembled in the village hall after arrival.

Lily pulled off her shoes and then, to the amazement of the others, peeled off her stockings. At the sight of Lily's feet, bright pink from the wet and the cold and none too clean, Alice and Minnie audibly drew in their breath. Outraged, they gazed at Lily's feet and then at each other. But Lily, unaware of the sensation she was causing, stood up to hang her stockings from the mantelpiece, putting the tea-caddy on one to keep it up, the string-box on the other.

'There,' she said, sitting down and extending her feet to the fire. 'That's better.'

It was Alice who spoke.

'Lily,' she said. 'We're not used to this, you know.'

'You're not used to what?' asked Lily.

'We're not used to people taking their stockings off in our kitchen!'

Lily stared at her.

'Why? What's up with taking your stockings off?' she asked.

'You ought to know,' said Minnie, looking deeply at her. 'Showing your feet.'

'What's up with me feet?' asked Lily loudly.

They didn't say. They looked across at each other, their lips compressed.

'Aw, go on,' said Lily giving them up. 'You're barmy. If you don't like me feet, you can lump them.'

She clapped them against the mantelpiece, and folding her damaged hand over the other in her lap, swayed herself to and fro.

'Take your feet off our mantelpiece, Lily,' commanded Alice. 'You're making a mark.'

'I'm making no mark that won't come off when I put me feet down,' said Lily, keeping them where they were.

Alice and Minnie looked at each other. Then Alice got up and went out of the kitchen. She went to Miss Florence, who was sitting among the ranged china in the drawing room.

'Well, Alice,' said Miss Florence, raising her head from her book. 'What is it?'

'I'm sorry to disturb you, Miss Florence, but that girl's sitting in the kitchen in her bare feet and me and Minnie don't like it. We've always kept things nice, Miss Florence, and we're not used to other people's bare feet in our kitchen.'

'No, Alice, I'm sure you're not,' said Miss Florence sympathetically. 'Dear me. What can we do about it? Have you put it to her?'

'We have, Miss Florence, and met with nothing but abuse.'

'You see, Alice,' said Miss Florence, 'the point is that we might get someone so much *worse*. An expectant mother or several rough children. That would be dreadful, wouldn't it? You see, if we've got to have somebody, we might as well have this girl. That's how I look at it and that's why I chose her.'

'Yes, I know, Miss Florence, and I wouldn't complain, but bare feet, you know, and not clean at that. It's not right. And she seems that bored with 'erself. Minnie and me has always been contented in our nice kitchen, but she doesn't seem to know what to do with 'erself.'

Miss Florence pondered on this, looking into the fire.

'I think I'll have to take her with me to the Mothers' Union on Thursday,' she said. 'She's not qualified to go, of course – at least we hope not. But I can explain to them. We must help her to settle, if we can, for our sakes as well as for her own.'

'Well, I'm sure me and Minnie's done everything we could to make her feel at home, Miss Florence,' said Alice self-righteously.

'I'm sure you have, Alice,' said her mistress.

'We've never asked her to help with the work,' said Alice. 'Minnie's offered to show her how to knit. We've played Ludo with 'er every night. Some lovely games of Ludo we've had. We were all ready to play with 'er now before supper, but she never come in, you know.'

'Well, Alice, we must just persevere,' said Miss Florence. 'I'm sure it's a case for perseverance. We must just go on setting our good example and trust that she will follow it in the end. You go back now and perhaps you can very tactfully get her to put a pair of bedroom slippers on. There's that old pair we were going to give to the Jumble Sale. And you and Minnie have a game of Ludo with her. I don't mind waiting another half-hour for my supper. After all, in these times, we all have to make concessions, Alice,' said Miss Florence, pointing the moral.

'All right, Miss Florence,' said Alice, mollified and uplifted by this talk with her mistress. 'I'll go and have another try at getting on with her.'

'That's a good girl, Alice,' said Miss Florence, returning to her book.

But when Alice reached the kitchen there was only Minnie there.

'Oooh, you should have shut the drawing room door properly while you was talking,' said Minnie, her chin sunk dramatically on the bib of her apron. 'She went and listened in the passage and she 'eard what you was saying.'

'Well, what were we saying?' challenged Alice. 'Nothing as wouldn't do her good to hear. Where is she?'

'She came and got her shoes and stockings and went

upstairs. I don't know what she's doing, but she's banging about a lot in 'er room.'

'Let 'er bang,' said Alice, sitting down before the fire and taking up *Christian Novels*.

'Listening in the passage,' she smouldered.

She turned over the pages of her book, but she couldn't read. Her ears, like Minnie's, were straining at the sounds above. When steps began to descend the stairs, the eyes of both slid sideways to the passage door and, tense, they waited.

Lily appeared, dressed again in her wet cap and coat. She carried the cardboard case she had arrived with and walked through the kitchen to the back door, followed by the eyes of the others, by this time round and aghast.

'You're not going, Lily, are you?' quavered Alice.

'Yes, I'm going,' said Lily. 'Thanks for everything, but I'm fed up. You can say thanks to the old girl for me. I don't want an interview.'

Alice rose warily to her feet.

'Stop where you are,' said Lily. 'I'd be out of the gate before you got to her.'

She leaned against the door, smiling at them.

'You do look a scream in them caps,' she remarked.

Hypnotised, they gazed at her.

'Well,' she said. 'Ta-ta.'

Her smile, at once belittling and benevolent, roamed the kitchen and broadened as it fell on the game-board.

'No more Ludo,' she said, and, tapping the crown of her woollen cap, she raised her damaged hand in mocking salute and was gone.

BOARDING-HOUSE

It was their first season, Mrs Pink explained to everybody.

'Is everything all right?' she would ask anxiously, a small woman with a thin face, generally red from cooking and the excitement of running a boarding house.

'You see it's our first season,' she would say, with a mixture of pride and apology.

She said it to all the visitors in turn. To Mr Bagshaw, the cheerful bachelor who stipulated for a bedroom with a sea-view and a table in the window of the dining room. Mr Bagshaw liked the best for himself, but Mrs Pink was very willing to give it to him.

She said it to Mrs Walton who, it seemed, had travelled across England simply to sit at Mrs Pink's front door. She was moored there, too fat to get any farther. But she got the benefit of the air, sitting there, she said, and she was sympathetic about its being the Pinks' first season and often called out advice from where she sat to Mrs Pink, scurrying about the inside of the house in the mornings when everybody was out on the beach.

Mrs Pink said the same thing to Miss Porter, who had come with her fiancé.

'Oh, that's all right,' said Miss Porter, a smart young woman with glasses and prominent teeth. 'We're not hard to please, are we, Alfred? Too much in love,' she said, taking Alfred's arm. 'We've got it badly, haven't we, Alfred?' She sent an amorous look, much magnified by her glasses, at Alfred, who looked sheepish and in a moment disengaged himself.

Mrs Pink said the same thing to the Burton family, father, mother and three little boys, and she said it again to the two young girls from Nottingham, friends who worked in the same office, it appeared. Two pretty slender young things, so pleased with the sea. Kathleen Hill and Phœbe Wood, their names were. It was a pleasure to see them about, said Mr and Mrs Pink to each other.

Mrs Pink having explained that it was their first season and the visitors having suitably and reassuringly responded, the atmosphere was cleared beforehand at 'Rosedene' and all seemed set fair.

The Pinks had gone into the boarding house business like nervous bathers entering a rough sea. They went in inch by inch and would have turned back many a time, but Mr Spence wouldn't let them. With loud, coercive cries of encouragement, Mr Spence drove the Pinks on.

Mr Spence was the jolly, go-ahead builder from East Bay. He had developed East Bay very successfully. That is, he had cut the fields to ribbons and run up a lot of little houses in fondant-coloured concrete, pinks, yellows, greens and blues. The Spence Park Estate, in a very short time after Mr Spence had finished with it, looked camouflaged ready for war; but that was not intentional, it was merely the blotchy action of damp on the concrete.

Having developed East Bay, Mr Spence turned his attention to West Bay.

'There's no accommodation for visitors, here,' he said to the Pinks. 'And lots of people want to come to a nice, quiet little place like this. You've only to put up a house in that field by the sea and you'll be full up every season. If you don't take the chance, somebody else will and I'd sooner you had it than anybody,' said Mr Spence, as if he had always had the welfare of the Pinks at heart.

The Pinks had lived contentedly for years in their cottage on the village street. Mr Pink had an allotment, sold his vegetables and put in two or three days a week in other people's gardens as required. Mrs Pink had been left a little money by some aunts. She added to this by putting a card in the parlour window, inscribed, first of all: 'Teas and Hot Water', extending later to: 'Bed and Breakfast', and later still to 'Apartments'.

Further than this she had no wish to go, she told Mr Spence. She didn't feel qualified to go, she told him, not having had the experience. Besides, she said, she didn't want to risk her bit of money, which just made all the difference between being anxious about their old age and not having to be anxious. But she showed, all the same, that she was fascinated by Mr Spence's proposals and that was fatal.

It wasn't done in one visit. Mr Spence worked hard at the Pinks and how they came to consent they never exactly knew. But consent they must have done, because the plans were got out and the house begun.

Arthur Pink then became a fatalist. He accepted the fact that, once begun, it had to be finished. But Mrs Pink was different. She kept trying to stem the flood of expenditure, to clutch back a bit here, a bit there.

'He's rushing us,' she said, keeping her husband awake at nights with her fears.

'It's much too big,' she would say, going to hang over the bricklayers. 'Stop it. It's much too big.'

And the bricklayers would down tools and hang about until Mr Spence came and told them to get on with the job.

Mrs Pink, at this stage, was beset with suspicion of Mr Spence. She was sure he was trying to ruin them.

'He's rushed us into letting him put that house up and as long as he gets the money out of us, that's all he's after,' she kept saying.

But she had to admit, later, that the money did not seem to be entirely all that Mr Spence was after. Having taken the Pinks up, he showed every desire to make a success of them. He helped them in every way. Not only did he show Mrs Pink how to get hold of her money, how to deal with the Building Society, how to buy furniture on the Hire Purchase System, but he also told them what papers to advertise in, how to word their advertisements and how to range their prices. He even gave the house its name. It was called 'Rosedene'. There were no roses, but these would come, he said, and in earnest of them put up a couple of gaunt rustic arches.

When 'Rosedene' was finished and they at last took possession, the Pinks could hardly believe it. There it was, this large fine house, with all those bedrooms, all theirs. They went over it in awe and pride, Mrs Pink laying her thin red hand with deep pleasure on the doors, on the furniture and saying 'Oh, Arthur,' with almost every breath. Arthur came behind, as moved as she was, but saying less. Long, thin, with his kind, quiet face, his back a little bowed from much stooping over vegetables, Arthur followed his wife over their new house.

Mrs Pink had provided for others as she had always provided for herself and Arthur. In consequence, the beds were thin, the blankets thin, the mats on the floor thin and the curtains at the windows mere strips that would never draw together. The wash on the walls was thin, pale mauve, pink, blue, different in every room, but the paint the same all over, a bluish-white. The linoleum on the landing was so highly varnished that your feet came up from it with a tearing sound, but Mrs Pink said that would go off in time.

Mr Spence, still helpful, suggested that Mrs Pink should go over and get some tips about running a boarding house from Mrs Cooper, who was doing very well with hers at East Bay. Mrs Pink went and Mrs Cooper told her so much, she had to buy a penny notebook and write down at once as much as she could remember on the way home in the bus. How many pints of custard, made with powder, to the dozen persons, how not to bother with fruit pies, but to serve stewed fruit with little squares of pastry made separate, what coffee essence to use and how to make a substitute for cream, and to put Arthur into a white jacket and send him into the rooms to empty the ashtrays and give tone to the place.

'Eh, I can't do that!' cried Arthur, horrified.

'Arthur,' said Mrs Pink solemnly, 'you'll have to. Now we're in it, we've got to make a go of this place or we'll lose it altogether. Remember that, now, and make up your mind to that white jacket. I shouldn't be surprised, either, but what you look very smart in it,' she said soothingly.

But Mr Pink was not soothed. He hadn't bargained for going in among strangers, dressed up in a white jacket, emptying ashtrays, he said. He had never emptied an ashtray in his life, he said, and he didn't think he could manage it. But in the end he admitted, heavily, that if the success of the boarding house depended upon the wearing of a white jacket, he supposed he'd have to wear it.

And now he was wearing it. Every afternoon towards five, he came in from the vegetables, wiped his boots, put on his jacket and went with his long, loping step about the rooms, carrying a little tray for cigarette ash and ends and being very careful not to look at anybody.

Incredible though it seemed to the Pinks, the boarding-house was an established fact. It stood in the field by the sea, very white and new, with coloured bathing suits hanging out of the windows and Mrs Walton sitting in a striped chair by the front door. Fourteen people were staying in the house, sleeping in the beds, sitting down to meals. Help was hard to get in the village, but Mrs Pink had secured Mrs Boxer to wash up and Maud Marsden to do the bedrooms and wait at table. Mrs Pink did the cooking herself.

'I think it's best to do my own cooking,' she confided. 'Just till we get our reputation.'

'That's right,' agreed Mrs Walton from the front door. 'If you want a thing done properly, do it yourself, I always say.'

So Mrs Pink served her rissoles, her stewed fruit with little squares of pastry cooked separate, her coffee essence and cream substitute, her packet blancmanges and tinned soups, and since that was what other boarding houses in other summers had served to them, the visitors made no complaints. It was what they were used to.

Mrs Pink liked her visitors. She liked having Mrs Walton at the front door. She loved the two pretty young girls, Kathleen Hill and Phœbe Wood, and always took their bathing suits to rinse in fresh water, wring out and dry by the fire so that they should be nice to put on for the next bathe.

She liked Mr Bagshaw, so smart in his gay pullovers, plus fours, bow ties and brown-and-white shoes. It took Arthur about half an hour to clean these shoes, keeping the white off the brown and the brown off the white. But it was worth it, Mrs Pink said, to keep Mr Bagshaw smart. It was a pleasure to see him coming in at their gate, she said. She liked to hear, from the kitchen, Mr Bagshaw talking in the dining room.

'I'll have another portion of jelly, Maud, if you please,' he would say.

'The bottle of sauce, Maud.'

'Are there any pickles, Maud?'

'The vinegar with this fried plaice, that's a good girl.'

Mr Bagshaw gave importance to the food. He made the dining room cosy and Mrs Pink was glad of him. On chilly mornings he was as good as a radiator.

They were all very friendly in the dining room, calling out from table to table and not minding if they had to wait sometimes between meat and sweet. Only Alfred, Miss Porter's fiancé, was quiet, in spite of Miss Porter's constant efforts to draw him into the general conversation and show him off. Mrs Pink was worried about Alfred. He didn't seem to be enjoying himself and she wanted people to enjoy themselves at 'Rosedene', not only because she hoped they would come again, but for their own sakes too.

Miss Porter played golf. 'Because she thinks it's smart,' remarked Mrs Walton, calling inwards to Mrs Pink from the front door. Alfred did not care for golf, but he had to play it. He would rather have bathed, but Miss Porter didn't bathe. 'Too skinny,' called Mrs Walton.

The sun shone, the sea beyond the garden wall was blue, the air was strong and pure. Things were going well at 'Rosedene', and Mr and Mrs Pink, when they went to bed at night, congratulated themselves on their ability to manage.

'We're managing, Arthur,' Mrs Pink would say exultantly. 'And you know I thought we never should.'

Then Mr Spence, still being helpful, called with the General.

The General was a familiar figure in West Bay. Not that he spoke much to people, but they were used to the sight of him. He had been a great man in the Army in his time, someone said, but now he was retired and lived in a little old house far out on the salt marshes. His passions, shared apparently by his wife, were birds and yachting, lonely passions both and ones that did not bring him into close contact with the villagers. They went rather in awe of him, Mrs Pink among them, and she was flustered when she saw him standing in the hall with Mr Spence.

She was still more flustered when she found he had come to see if she could take his sister from London as a boarder for a fortnight.

'Well,' said Mrs Pink uncertainly, looking, not at the General, but at Mr Spence. 'I could show you a room . . .'

'Oh, that'll be all right,' said the General dismissingly. A wind had sprung up and he wanted to be off to his yacht. 'I only wanted to know if you could take her. We can't put her up ourselves. Very cramped quarters, you know, and too far out and all that. She wouldn't like it. Right you are then, Mrs Pink, she'll be here on Tuesday night. She'll dine with us and I'll bring her in later. Denby-Moore, the name is. Got it? Very well. Good morning to you.'

Mr Spence conducted the General to his old car and returned to collect his due of thanks from Mrs Pink.

'I'm ever so grateful to you, Mr Spence,' said Mrs Pink, doing as she was expected. 'But I do hope I'll be able to manage.'

'You've been hoping that from the start,' said Mr Spence jovially. 'And you've managed, haven't you? Nice gentleman, the General, isn't he? But what a car! If I couldn't drive a better car than that,' said Mr Spence with feeling, 'by George, I wouldn't drive one at all.'

And he returned, with complacence, to his own superior automobile.

It was so late on Tuesday night when Mrs Denby-Moore was brought in by the General that Mrs Pink had no more than one awed glimpse of her before she went to bed. But early next morning, the trouble began.

It was Mrs Pink's innocent habit to send by Maud to each visitor in bed a cup of what she considered nice, hot, strong tea, with two lumps of sugar in the saucer. She didn't charge for this; it was something she liked to do for her visitors.

But Maud returned from Mrs Denby-Moore's room cup in hand.

'She doesn't want your tea,' she said, putting it down on the table. 'What is it, she says, looking into the cup as if she'd never seen nothing like it before. It's tea, I says. I don't drink tea like that, she says. I have China and I pour it out myself and have you no tray, girl? Of course we've got a tray, I says, but we haven't got *fourteen* trays, which is what we'd need if everybody in this house had to have a tray. But you don't need to drink the tea, I says, there's no obligation. It's only kindness on Mrs Pink's part, I says, sending it round. I told her straight,' said Maud, arranging her curls at the looking glass over the sink.

Mrs Pink wasn't listening to Maud. A slow blush had suffused her face. Wasn't it the thing to offer tea to the visitors? Was it presumption? Mrs Pink felt a deep shame at that thought. She mustn't send it round any more.

'She wants her breakfast in bed,' Maud was saying. 'You should see her. She's got her chin tied up like a corpse and diamond rings thrown about the dressing table. She's got a peach pink crêpe de chine nightdress on, all lace at the top.

My goodness, I wish it was mine! What good is it to her at her age?' asked Maud, admiring her young reflection in the glass.

'You'd better run out to the shop, Maud,' said Mrs Pink coming to herself. 'And see if they've got any China tea. Bring half a pound.'

But when she sent up China tea for Mrs Denby-Moore's breakfast, Mrs Denby-Moore sent it down again. She said she had coffee for breakfast. But when Mrs Pink sent up a jug of nice hot coffee essence, Mrs Moore sent it down, saying not that sort of coffee, and demanding China tea again.

'If she thinks I'm going to spend my time running up and down with what she wants and doesn't want,' said Maud indignantly, 'she's mistaken, that's all.'

Mrs Denby-Moore also rejected the kipper Mrs Pink had carefully cooked for her and Mrs Pink began to feel doubtful about her menus for the rest of the day. Would the mince do for lunch? She feared it wouldn't. She rushed out to the butcher's and against her better judgment bought two legs of lamb, too fresh, she knew, to eat anything but tough.

The unprofitable purchase lay heavy on her mind as she made the beds with Maud. She herself tiptoed carefully about, but Maud wouldn't. The linoleum on the landing made its usual tearing protest every time Maud crossed it, which was often. And then the thing that Mrs Pink had dreaded happened: Mrs Denby-Moore rang her bell.

Across Mr Bagshaw's denuded bed, Mrs Pink and Maud looked at each other.

'You'd better go, Maud,' said Mrs Pink.

'I'm not going,' said Maud, setting her mouth. 'I've answered that bell often enough this morning and if it means my notice I'm not answering it again.'

Mrs Pink's heart, already beating too fast from the ring of the bell, beat faster still at Maud's impertinence. She ought to rebuke Maud, she knew, but for the moment, she couldn't. She would deal with Maud, she hoped, later. Nervously smoothing her apron and putting back a strand of hair, she crossed the landing.

'What is that extraordinary noise?' asked Mrs Denby-Moore, sitting up in bed in a cape of pink feathers. 'That incessant tearing sound?'

'It's the linoleum,' faltered Mrs Pink. 'It's new. You see this is our first season . . .' But her voice tailed away. It was no use, she could see, saying anything like that to Mrs Denby-Moore.

'I can't stand noise of any kind,' said Mrs Moore. 'Certainly not an absurd noise like that. Do something about it, please. And somebody must do something about these curtains,' she said, turning her beautiful, tired, bored eyes to the window. 'They don't meet. What was the good of putting up such curtains, Mrs Pink? They're neither useful nor ornamental. I don't like light in the mornings. And I like an eiderdown on my bed.' She dropped her eyes to her book to show that the conversation was finished. Mrs Pink stood there humbly for a moment and then went out. An eiderdown! There wasn't one in the house. She would have to go to East Bay and buy one. But what an expense!

Mrs Pink went back to finish the beds with Maud. It was well known in the village that Maud was difficult. Maud could afford to be difficult; the demand for her services exceeded by far the supply and Mrs Pink had thought herself very lucky to get her. She had always got on well with Maud, but now, she felt, the trouble was beginning. She and Maud finished the beds in awkward silence.

And soon another awkward situation developed. Mrs Walton started calling out from the front door. More noise, thought Mrs Pink in a panic, and ran to answer Mrs Walton at close quarters in a low voice. But Mrs Walton kept on calling out and Mrs Pink had to keep running out to answer her and the morning was flying away with no work done. At last she had to tell Mrs Walton that she hadn't time to keep leaving her work to run out to the front and she daren't shout in answer from wherever she happened to be, because Mrs Denby-Moore had already complained about noise. But she saw at once that she had mortally offended Mrs Walton.

'So I suppose this Mrs Denby-Moore, as you call her,' said Mrs Walton witheringly and with injustice, since Mrs Pink had no choice but to call Mrs Denby-Moore by her name, 'I suppose she's the only person to be considered?' finished Mrs Walton.

Nobody likes being asked not to shout, and Mrs Walton liked it no better than another. Mrs Pink returned, wretched, to the kitchen. Everything was going wrong.

It continued to go wrong. She cooked the legs of lamb, as she considered, to a turn, but Mrs Denby-Moore did not come down to the dining room until everyone, except the two young girls, had left it.

The girls had come in late from the beach, and apologising to Maud, who surprised them by tossing her head, they sat down to gobble their lunch and get out of Maud's way as quickly as possible. But before they could finish, Mrs Denby-Moore came in, with Mrs Pink hovering behind her.

'I'll sit here,' said Mrs Moore, going to the window.

'Well,' said Mrs Pink nervously, 'that's Mr Bagshaw's table, but I daresay, being a gentleman, he'll let you have it.'

Mrs Denby-Moore sat down and Mrs Pink withdrew to send in her lunch. The girls were gaping. They had never seen anyone like Mrs Moore before, never seen such beautiful grey hair – who would have thought grey hair could be beautiful? – never seen such a linen coat and skirt before, such a pearl necklace, such hands, such an expression of sad ennui anywhere. Compassion and admiration showed in their eyes. For one who had been so beautiful to be old, their eyes said.

'I'm late,' said Mrs Moore, from Mr Bagshaw's table.

The girls were startled. They had not expected her to speak to them. They smiled diffidently and put their curls back.

'It takes me a long time to dress myself,' said Mrs Moore bitterly. 'I'm not used to it.'

Phœbe stared. Not used to dressing herself?

Maud now laid a plate of roast lamb before Mrs Moore.

'What is it?' asked that lady.

'It's best leg of lamb,' said Maud pertly.

'I don't want it,' said Mrs Moore. 'Tell Mrs Pink I'd like salad and brown bread and butter and cheese.'

She sighed, waiting, and rubbed her wrist.

'My arms ache abominably when I put my own hair up,' she said to the girls. 'I hate it.'

Phœbe continued to stare. Did she go to a hairdresser, then, every single morning?

But Kathleen, swiftly adapting herself to a mode of life she had only read of, suggested diffidently:

'Perhaps you miss your maid?'

Phœbe turned her stare from Mrs Moore to her friend. How did Kathleen know about ladies' maids? How did she know Mrs Moore had one? Kathleen seemed suddenly experienced, worldly, and swept far away from Phœbe.

'I certainly miss my maid,' said Mrs Moore. 'She had to have her holiday, I suppose, but it meant my taking a holiday too. I couldn't manage in London without her, though God knows I go out little enough nowadays.'

She sighed heavily and looked unseeingly out of the window, crushed with the boredom of being where she was, of being a widow, of not being invited anywhere for this fortnight. 'It's cutlet for cutlet,' she thought bitterly. 'I can't entertain, so no one entertains me now. To think that I should have to come to a place like this. After the life,' she thought, 'I've lived.'

She closed her eyes against the dining room, but opened them again on being addressed by Maud.

'D'you want the mayonnaise?' asked Maud truculently, bringing it.

'Out of a bottle?' said Mrs Moore. 'No.'

Maud went out of the dining room, but spoke in a loud voice in the passage outside.

'It's a quarter-past two and my afternoon off,' she said. 'I'm not going to stand this, so you know, Mrs Pink. I've no need to.'

'What an ill-mannered girl,' said Mrs Moore, eating her salad. 'I'm surprised Mrs Pink keeps her.'

'She's not always like that,' ventured Phœbe defendingly, and blushed.

Mrs Moore seemed not to hear. She was looking out of the window again as if she were alone.

The girls laid down their spoons with as little noise as possible. They had finished and Phœbe thought they could now go. But Kathleen with a frown signalled that they must remain in their places. Phœbe stared again. Until now, Kathleen had been as eager as she had to get back to the beach. What was the fun of spending this splendid afternoon sitting on at the table when they had finished, asked Phœbe's blue eyes? But Kathleen ignored the question.

Outside the dining room door, Mrs Pink waited with a serving of bluish blancmange in her hand ready to bring on, since Maud wouldn't. After a while she went to stand uncertainly in the kitchen. If she couldn't get the tables cleared soon, she'd never get through her work today, she grieved. She went to look through the crack of the door again, but Mrs Moore was, as Mrs Pink put it, still at it, her salad unfinished on her plate.

At last, plucking up her courage, Mrs Pink advanced with the blancmange.

'No, thank you,' said Mrs Moore rising. 'Will someone put a chair for me in the garden?'

But when Mrs Pink had placed the chair, Mrs Moore, after one look about her, followed Mrs Pink back into the house.

'Does that enormous woman sit there all the time?' she
asked in her cool, carrying voice.

'Well, generally,' admitted Mrs Pink.

'Then I shall sit indoors,' said Mrs Moore. 'Where is
there?'

Mrs Pink led the way to the drawing room, to the best
three-piece suite, the pampas grass in the Japanese vases, the
looking glass screen painted with bulrushes in the hearth.
Mrs Moore closed her eyes on entering, but turned to smile
charmingly over her shoulder to the girls who hovered in the
hall, Phœbe because Kathleen detained her by the hand.

'Are you coming in here?' she said. 'It is at least cool.'

Kathleen drew Phœbe after her and they sat side by side
on the sofa, their young backs rounded, their curls falling
forward, Phœbe's toes turned in. Mrs Moore sat in a hard
high chair like a queen.

Mrs Pink went back to the kitchen. She was filled with
nervous trepidation lest Mrs Walton should have overheard
herself being called an enormous woman. But Mrs Walton's
manner had been so cold since morning that Mrs Pink,
though she went specially round by the front door, could not
tell whether there had been an increase of offence or not. She
worried about it all afternoon and forgot the baking powder in
the scones for tea.

In the drawing room, Mrs Moore was talking to the girls.
Phœbe felt resentfully that she only talked to them because
she had nothing else to do. She kept them with her to beguile
the time that hung so heavy on her hands, but time, for
Phœbe, went so fast during the holidays. It was so precious

and yet here they had to sit with this bored person while the tide was going out leaving long stretches of cool sand over which Phœbe loved to pad in her bare feet. It was too bad, thought Phœbe, shuffling on the sofa, but Kathleen, with a pinch, quelled her. The wistful expression of Phœbe's face increased; she was too young to dare to be rude enough to get up and go.

'How pretty you are, my dear child,' said Mrs Moore graciously to Kathleen. 'Now that I come to look at you, I find you remind me of Princess Amelie when she was a young girl.'

Kathleen had never heard of Princess Amelie, but she blushed with pleasure. This was a compliment she would never forget.

'I once had my room directly under Princess Amelie's,' said Mrs Moore, brightening in reminiscence. 'She used to do gymnastic exercises at six o'clock in the morning over my head. I had to send up in the end to tell her she mustn't start until after seven-thirty.'

Kathleen almost gasped. Fancy telling Princesses what they mustn't do.

'Of course, they were very keen on keeping their figures,' said Mrs Moore. 'Princess Elizabeth, you know, used to sleep wrapped from head to foot in cold-water bandages. No pillow. Blankets to cover her. *Il faut souffrir pour être belle.* No one knew that better than she did.'

To Kathleen this was the most entrancing conversation she had ever heard in her life. She drank it in. But Phœbe looked through the window at the sky. Oh, to be out, to be able to go! A whole afternoon wasted, and they had so few.

'The Grand Duke asked to be presented,' Mrs Moore was saying when Phœbe brought her attention into the room again. 'He said: *"Voulez-vous me faire l'honneur de me présenter à Madame?"*'

'What does that mean?' asked Phœbe in a flat voice, but Kathleen pinched her.

'I was the only one,' said Mrs Moore, smiling reminiscently.

Although Mrs Moore had come to West Bay because her brother lived here, she would not, it appeared, be going much to his house.

'His wife's such a tiresome woman,' said Mrs Moore.

Phœbe was dumbfounded. Fancy saying a thing like that. Why, Phœbe didn't like her brother's wife either, not really, nobody in the family did, but no one would dream of saying so, even to each other, let alone to people never seen before.

And in a moment, Mrs Moore shocked Phœbe again.

'I'm so *poor* now,' said Mrs Moore in disgust.

Fancy talking about being poor, thought Phœbe in astonishment, a thing surely everybody tried to hide. Besides, how could she be poor with a maid and a pearl necklace and diamond rings? Phœbe stared in bewilderment, but Kathleen was sympathetic. 'Smarmy,' Phœbe thought, suddenly.

It was tea time before Phœbe got away and even then Kathleen remained behind with Mrs Moore.

Dinner that night was an uncomfortable affair. Maud's report of Mr Bagshaw's displeasure at being deprived of his table threw Mrs Pink into such distress that she burnt the gravy at the last moment.

'Oh, Arthur,' she said to Mr Pink standing by in helpless concern. 'I feel at my wits' end.'

In the dining room, in the elegant presence of Mrs Moore, sitting with an absent expression at Mr Bagshaw's table, there was silence instead of the usual cheerful hubbub. The dispossessed Mr Bagshaw sulked on the side; he didn't even ask for the sauce. Mrs Walton sat in heavy displeasure. Miss Porter did not hold Alfred's hand, holding it *down* on the table as she usually did. She confined herself to sending him fond glances through the sweet peas. Mrs Burton corrected her little boys frequently, but in whispers, motioning with her head towards Mrs Moore as if she were using that lady as a bogey to frighten them into good behaviour.

Mrs Moore herself broke the silence.

'What is it?' she asked, as Maud proffered a dish.

'It's custard,' said Maud in a highly dangerous tone.

'Custard?' said Mrs Moore. The aqueous yellow blobs trembled beneath her gaze.

'No thank you,' she said.

Maud controlled herself until she reached the kitchen, but she burst out there.

'If she asks me again what anything is, I'm leaving, so you know,' she shouted. 'Making a fool of me in front of everybody.'

And the next day she left. She marched into the kitchen after lunch and took her apron off.

'You can keep this week's money,' she said. 'I can make it up somewhere else.'

Mrs Pink sat down and cried.

* * *

'I can't imagine,' Mrs Moore was saying with a shudder in the dining room, 'how I'm going to survive a fortnight in this dreadful place. But I can't get away from it. I shall have to stay until my maid comes to fetch me. She'll pack for me. It's so dreadful for me, getting about nowadays,' she sighed. 'My husband was such a perfect courier.'

'Does that mean he was in a Travel Agency?' asked Phœbe afterwards.

'Oh, Phœbe, don't be so stupid,' cried Kathleen. 'Her husband was an ambassador.'

She was horrified by Phœbe's ignorance. She hadn't realised until now how little Phœbe knew. In Mrs Moore's presence, Kathleen was painfully conscious of Phœbe's shortcomings. She was ashamed of her, she was ashamed of everybody in the house. Mr Bagshaw seemed so common, she winced whenever Miss Porter opened her mouth, Mrs Walton's size was so vulgar, it overflowed all bounds, it shouldn't *be*, thought Kathleen. The difference, thought Kathleen, between Princess Elizabeth wrapped from head to foot in cold-water bandages and Mrs Walton: nobody in Mrs Moore's world would ever let themselves get so fat, Kathleen was filled with critical dissatisfaction. She spent a great deal of time looking at herself in the glass thinking of the Princess she was said to resemble, thinking of the worlds she might conquer if only she could get out of the one she was in.

That night, the visitors were astonished to see Mr Pink, in his white jacket, come in to wait on them at dinner. He had to;

there was no one else. Their eyes followed him about. Phœbe saw how his hands trembled as he proffered the potatoes.

'It makes me kind of uncomfortable to see him doing this,' she said uneasily to Kathleen.

But in a cool voice copied from Mrs Moore, Kathleen said that was because he did it so badly; and the rift between the friends widened.

Across the room, Phœbe met Alfred's eyes and saw that he felt as she did about Mr Pink. Miss Porter caught them looking at each other and put her hand over Alfred's on the table to show that he was hers.

The visitors had been submerged, as it were, under the constraint of Mrs Moore's presence; now they were coming up again, but changed. Mr Bagshaw was asking for things again, but differently.

'The sauce, Pink.'

'This meat needs pickles, Pink. Where are they?'

'I like vinegar with my fried plaice, *as I've said before*.'

The eyes of the Pinks as they tried to cope with their boarders were wild, like the eyes of cattle crossing a deep river.

Disaffection, started by Mrs Moore, set in and there were many complaints. To make things worse for the Pinks, the weather changed. The wind blew in all day from the sea and dimmed the windows with a fine cold mist. Everybody stayed in the house.

'We tried to play golf,' said Miss Porter, coming in with Alfred behind her. 'But it was *that* muddy . . .'

Alfred looked at Phœbe and his look was desperate.

Mrs Walton could no longer sit at the front door, and she would not sit in the same room as Mrs Moore. For a day or two she sat in the hall, but at the end of the week she announced that she would finish her holiday at Mrs Cooper's at East Bay, where there was a sun porch and nobody who considered themselves too good for other people. When Mr Bagshaw heard this, and that he would be given proper consideration, he said he would go too. Mrs Burton could not keep her little boys, confined to the house, quiet enough for Mrs Moore, and her temper and theirs suffered in consequence.

Then Mr Pink fell with the potatoes at dinner. His white jacket caught on the back of a chair and he fell headlong, the potatoes rolling in all directions. The visitors sprang to their feet, but it was Phœbe and Alfred who reached him. They helped him up with murmurs of compassion. They retrieved the potatoes from under the chairs and put them back into the dish for him. With bowed back and shamefaced eyes, Mr Pink went out of the dining room. Nobody spoke, but Phœbe and Alfred in the middle of the room looked at each other. There were tears in Phœbe's eyes.

Mr Pink did not reappear. After a long pause, Mrs Pink brought in more potatoes.

'You must help yourselves,' she said, putting the dishes on the sideboard.

After dinner, when Alfred went out into the garden, Miss Porter went after him and they had a dreadful quarrel. Miss Porter broke off the engagement.

In the kitchen, Mrs Pink was weeping among the after-dinner chaos.

'I can't go on, Arthur,' she wept. 'I can't.'

'No,' said Arthur, standing beside her in distress.

They were too timid and too proud for such a life. They could not expose themselves any more.

'It would have been all right if the General's sister hadn't come,' wept Mrs Pink. 'I was getting on all right until she came. Places like this aren't for people like that, Arthur. They should keep out.'

'Aye,' said Arthur heavily. 'They should.'

They talked late into the night and came to their decision.

In the morning, after breakfast, Mrs Pink asked everybody to go. Miss Porter had already gone, by the early train. Mrs Walton and Mr Bagshaw were going, so there were not many left to dismiss.

'We're closing down,' said Mrs Pink. 'So you must please make your arrangements. There's plenty of room at East Bay. We've made out your bills up to today, charging half-price this week for inconvenience caused. We're very sorry,' finished Mrs Pink. 'But it can't be helped.'

The sensation died down. It died quickly because war was declared soon afterwards. The declaration of war was, so to speak, useful to the Pinks.

'The war came, you know,' Mrs Pink used to explain later when they were back, minus Mrs Pink's money, in their cottage. 'So we gave up "Rosedene."'

She should have said: 'Mrs Moore came.' But perhaps nobody would have recognised that as a reason.

ONE DARK NIGHT

Mrs Mason was horrified when she came out of the pictures. It was pitch dark. She stood on the rubberoid steps of the Smart Cinema and looked, appalled, into the night. However was she going to manage?

She hadn't expected this, she told herself. By going to the cinema so early in the afternoon, she thought she had given herself plenty of time to get to the bus station in daylight, but here it was – pitch dark. The programme must have been much longer than she realised. The Smart Cinema, she decided, gave you far too much for your money. While she had been watching the screen, night had been creeping over the town, deepening and deepening until now it was inky black and she couldn't see a thing before her. Whatever was she going to do?

While Mrs Mason stood on the steps, asking herself these questions at some length, the rest of the audience had streamed away from her and now that she came to look round for help, for someone who might be going to the bus station too, everybody had gone. She was alone. And even as she stood, the doors of the cinema, being shut after the matinée, rattled across so close behind her that Mrs Mason, who projected rather a long way at the back, was propelled brusquely off the step and sent at a run into the street.

'Here!' cried Mrs Mason indignantly, straightening her hat.

'Sorry, lady,' said the attendant, unperturbed, putting his head through the gap between the doors. 'But how did I know you was there?'

'You should look,' said Mrs Mason.

'What's the good of looking?' said the attendant cheerfully. 'You can't see anything.'

He drew the doors still nearer together.

'What's the time?' called Mrs Mason despairingly, as he was about to disappear behind them altogether.

'Ten-past five,' he called from within and his voice echoed in the empty hall behind the doors as if it came from the other side of the world. He slammed the doors together, shot the bolts and went off, heartlessly, to his tea.

There was absolute silence, absolute darkness in the street. Mrs Mason stood in it, clutching her bag.

When Phœbe, her maid, had told her how dreadful the blackout was, Mrs Mason hadn't believed her. She thought Phœbe was exaggerating, dramatising, as usual. But she had been wrong. The blackout was every bit as bad as Phœbe had made out. It was worse. The town had obeyed orders far too thoroughly. There wasn't a guiding gleam anywhere. Not one.

'Well, it's no good standing here,' said Mrs Mason, talking aloud to herself. 'I shall have to make a move some time.'

But which way? The Smart Cinema was in a remote part of the town, a part she wasn't used to at all. Why had she ever come to it? Why hadn't she gone to the Regal or the Carlton? Why hadn't she provided herself with a torch? Why hadn't she brought Phœbe with her? Why – oh, why had she ever quarrelled with her sister Polly? If she hadn't quarrelled with Polly, she might have had someone to go about with now, instead of having to go to the pictures alone and get herself lost in the dark.

Mrs Mason was very sorry for herself. She thought, fleetingly, that if Polly, who could not be very far distant, could only know of her sister Jenny's plight, she would, in spite of the quarrel, be sorry for her too and would come out to help her home, for Polly was braver than she was, always had been.

Polly was too brave; she was reckless. Polly was the one who wanted to try everything and Jenny the one who tried to hold her back. She hadn't been able to hold Polly back when, left a widow soon after Jenny herself had been widowed, Polly, instead of coming to live with her sister as invited, decided to set herself up in a wool shop on Barton Street. Jenny hadn't been able to understand this at all. Unlike Polly's husband, Albert had left her very well off. It hurt her to find that Polly didn't want to live on her money. Polly wanted a wool shop. She wanted to make and sell knitted things. Polly had always been good at knitting, though Jenny couldn't follow the simplest pattern and hadn't been able to complete so much as a pair of bedsocks since they quarrelled.

In spite of all her arguments, she could not change Polly's mind, but she could refuse to lend Polly the money for such a foolish enterprise and refuse it she did. That did not deter Polly. She risked the whole of her small substance, borrowed the rest elsewhere and got the shop. Mrs Mason had never set foot in it. She had never seen her sister since; and that was eighteen months ago.

Each week she secretly expected that Polly would come and ask for help, but each week went by and Polly did not come. Well, thought Mrs Mason, sitting alone in her comfortable house, Polly should see that she could hold out as long as Polly could. After all, thought Mrs Mason, she was the one who had everything; money, maids, position, everything. Polly was the loser, said Mrs Mason, bridling alone in her drawing room.

But standing in the dark, no farther yet than five yards from the Cinema, Mrs Mason admitted that Polly had something she herself had not. Polly had courage. She was able to look after herself. Polly would have made short work of this darkness, Jenny knew.

'I think,' said Mrs Mason dubiously, faltering forward in the dark. 'I must have come up this way.'

Ten-past five, she thought. The bus had gone. There wasn't another till six o'clock. Mrs Mason lived on the outskirts of the town and buses going as far as that were infrequent. But if once I get to the bus station, thought Mrs Mason, I don't care how long I have to wait.

She lurched suddenly down a step she hadn't expected and bit her tongue hard.

'Oh, dear . . .' she cried painfully. 'Oh . . .'

She leaned against an invisible wall, with her hand pressed to her mouth. That she, the highly-respected Mrs Mason, living in the best part of the town and all that, should have to stumble about in the dark and bite her tongue and keep knocking her hat crooked. It was so undignified. She wasn't *used* to it, she complained.

As she stood there, a faint light began to bloom along the lowest bricks of the wall, a faint furtive noise approached. Mrs Mason was rooted in fear. What was it? What was coming? A car crept up, with shrouded lights, crept past, crept on. The blackout made even a passing car sinister and menacing, thought Mrs Mason.

'Help!' she cried, realising too late that the car had not proceeded of its own volition but must have contained a fellow human being who might have taken pity on her and borne her to the bus station. 'Help! Help!'

But darkness reigned again. The car was swallowed up in the night. Its lights, feeble though they were, had been sufficient to show Mrs Mason that she was in a street of warehouses. No help to be got here. She must move on.

It was only ten-past five. The shops must still be open, if only she could get to them. She could telephone from a shop for a taxi. Encouraged by this thought of escape from the dark, she plunged forward, forgetting that as there had been a step down there must sooner or later be a step up. She fell to her knees this time, her hat slipping to her nose, her bag dropping from under her arm. Kneeling where she was, she groaningly put her hat back and scraped about the pavement in her good gloves for several minutes before she found her bag. Then, very shaken, she got to her feet and set off again. She didn't lift her feet from the pavement now; she shuffled.

Feeling well beforehand for steps up and steps down, she shuffled.

She hadn't realised until now how helpless she had grown. She was nothing but a large, overweight woman, getting old, her eyes, her ears, no longer to be relied on. Ah, she made a good enough show in the daytime, she told herself, but in the dark what a pitiful creature she was. In the daytime, she could walk about with a firm step, giving orders, impressing people with her money and her expensive clothes; in the daytime, she was all right. But in the dark she shuffled along like an old beggar, terrified, alone and in danger.

Yes, she was in danger, she thought. She might fall and stun herself at any minute. An unseen assailant might grab her bag and fell her from behind. She might be knocked down and killed as she was crossing the road, because she had to cross the road in a moment.

At least, she hoped so. At the end of this street there should be a Belisha crossing. If there wasn't, it meant that she had come the wrong way and goodness only knew what she would do in that case. When she reached what she thought must be the end of the street, she peered anxiously into the roadway. Sure enough there were the faintly gleaming studs of the Belisha crossing.

'God bless that man' said Mrs Mason fervently, crossing.

She stood at the corner.

'Now it should be Green Street this way and Gas Street that,' she said. 'At least I think so. If I go down Gas Street and take the second turning on the left I ought to get to High Street and the shops.'

The Belisha crossing having given her confidence, she went along her chosen street quite briskly until confidence and breath were knocked out of her by collision with a post, a short post that caught her most unexpectedly in her middle.

'What on earth is it?' she gasped in pain and irritation. 'I didn't think there were any things that height about.'

After that collision, she not only shuffled with her feet, she kept her hands extended before her, feeling for other possible posts. She was tired of straightening her hat and retrieving the head of her fur from the middle of her back now. She let them dangle as they would.

'A nice way for a woman like me to go along,' she thought, shuffling and groping.

'Second to the left. I turn here,' she told herself.

At last she reached the end of the street and came into a wider thoroughfare. A few cars were stealing about with lowered lamps, as if in shame at being out at all.

'Now here I am,' said Mrs Mason in relief. 'In High Street.'

But which part of High Street? She wanted to know, because looking as she felt she must look, quite wild, she feared, she preferred to go into a shop where she was known. If she could only locate Woolworth's. she would know where she was. But even in this street, there was no glimmer of light to indicate Woolworth's. She knew the shops must be there, behind this wall of night, carrying on their business as usual, but they were entirely invisible and no one could possibly tell one from another.

But someone was coming. Someone was actually out in this pitchy dark besides herself. She could ask her way now.

'Excuse me,' she said, stepping forward and colliding, again with some violence, with the oncomer. 'Excuse me, but can you tell me where Woolworth's is please?'

'Ah,' said a guttural female voice. 'Je no speak English.'

'Oh,' murmured Mrs Mason, abashed.

A foreigner. An evacuee. Or perhaps a spy. But in any case, no help.

'I must go into a shop,' decided Mrs Mason, making sundry passes at her hat and hair with dirty gloves.

She fumbled along by what seemed a hoarding and came into what seemed to be a short passage.

'I don't remember a passage in High Street,' she thought.

But there was a faint red light showing at the end of the passage and Mrs Mason was so glad to see any light at all that she went towards it. In small letters illuminated blood-red on the darkness, stood the word: 'Dentist.'

Mrs Mason turned and fumbled her way back to the street.

Reckless now, she seized the first door handle she came to and turned it. The door opened. A smothering thick curtain hung inside, obstructing the light and Mrs Mason. She thrust it aside and found herself in a sort of maze constructed of black plywood. She wound her way through that and emerged into a well-lighted shop, a shop hung about with soft things in white and pink and pale blue, a wool shop. There was one person in the shop, a woman bending over a cash-desk in the distance. Polly.

Polly! Mrs Mason gave one gasp and turned. She rushed at the plywood maze and in her haste to negotiate it, she knocked it down and trampled on it. With a sound of rending wood, she extricated her feet, fought with the velvet curtain, and got out into the street leaving the door ajar and a great square of light pouring out into the night from Polly's shop. She ran into the dentist's passage and hid at the far end. She cowered there, her face covered, her heart beating madly. Polly!

She could hear Polly's voice in the street.

'Special!' Polly was calling. 'ARP! Anybody! Come! Constable, are you there?'

Feet came running. Mrs Mason cowered closer into her corner. The street had seemed empty to her, but now a crowd was springing up from nowhere to hunt her down, to expose her and bring her out.

'Somebody broke into my shop!' Polly was crying excitedly. 'To rob me, most likely, but when they saw I was at the cash-desk myself, they rushed out again. It must have been a disreputable character, constable, because they were in such a hurry to get out again, they broke down my screen – shattered it to pieces.'

'Did you see the person?' asked the deep voice of a policeman.

'It was a woman,' said Polly. 'A powerful woman. Big build you know, and very untidy. Proper old tramp, she looked to me from the back, which was all I got sight of.'

'Let's have a look down here,' said the constable, flashing a powerful torch to the very end of the dentist's passage.

'There she is!' cried Polly, rushing down the passage at the head of a small army of people. Mrs Mason groaned.

'That's her, constable!' cried Polly.

Cleaving the crowd, the constable put a hand on Mrs Mason's sinking shoulder and turned her to the light of his torch. Hat askew, hair straggling, face begrimed from her dirty gloves, nothing to be seen of her fur but the chain under her chin, Mrs Mason blinked shamefacedly not at the constable, but at Polly.

'Why,' cried Polly in a loud astonished voice. 'It's Jenny!'

'It's who?' asked the policeman.

'Who? Who did she say?' the crowd asked each other. 'Who?'

'It's Jenny. It's my sister. Why, Jenny love . . .' said Polly, 'whatever were you doing?'

'I got into your shop by mistake,' mumbled Mrs Mason. 'And I was trying to get out again, that's all.'

'Oh, Jenny, I'm so sorry,' said Polly contritely, putting her arms round her sister. 'To think I've been waiting for you to come every single day and then for me to set the police on you like this. But oh, Jenny love, what have you been doing to yourself? Your face is all dirty and your hair's coming down.'

'It's the blackout,' whimpered Mrs Mason. 'I've run into everything you could think of and I've fallen down twice.'

The crowd was very interested, but Polly thrust them aside.

'Let us pass, please,' she said, guiding her sister through. 'It's all right, constable. It was all a mistake. I'm sorry to have troubled you.'

She piloted Jenny into the shop and locked the door.

'Closing time,' she said. 'Another minute and you wouldn't have got in, by mistake or otherwise, love, and then we should have wasted another day in our silly quarrelling. Oh, Jenny,

I'm so glad you've come,' she cried, throwing her arms round her sister's substantial, dishevelled form.

'Yes, I'm glad I've come too,' said Mrs Mason, clasping Polly. 'Though I must admit it was quite involuntary on my part.'

And at that she began to laugh as she hadn't laughed for eighteen months, as she never laughed with anyone but Polly.

TEA AT THE RECTORY

It was Christmas Eve and, at four o'clock in the afternoon, almost dark. The Miss Whartons, at their gate, hesitated which way to go to the Rectory, whether by the field path or the road. Their grand-nephew Richard waited for them to make up their minds, which always took time.

He sighed and was ashamed of himself. In the desert, in Italy, in Normandy, he had thought of his great-aunts with much affection. Since his parents had been killed and his home destroyed in the Blitz, his thoughts had no one to turn to but his aunts. All the time he was in hospital he had longed to get home to them, remembering their kindness, their endearing oddity. Why then, now that he was with them, was he so often exasperated, and not only with them but with all of life, with everything, big and little? Why did going to tea at the Rectory seem the last straw, seem so unbearable? He told himself it must be because he wasn't well yet, but he really felt that things would never be right again. Never. How could they be in this war-shattered world?

He waited, looking at his aunts. In the last wild light from the winter sky, or any light at all for that matter, they were an odd-looking pair only to be met with, surely, in the English countryside. Two maiden ladies in tweeds and felt hats, unfashionable, indefatigable in spite of their seventy-odd years, voluble, argumentative, and much given to erratic and frequently startling gestures. They were pointing vigorously with their stout sticks, now to the field, now to the road, and now for some unexplained reason to the whole sweep of the sky, arguing meanwhile.

Richard, listening – he tried nowadays to listen closely to keep his mind from his dark thoughts – wondered why so many people of his aunts' class and generation had such difficulty with their *r*'s. Had it been a fashion in their youth, was it a pose, or was it a real speech defect? There was nothing else posey about the Miss Whartons, but to roll an *r* was beyond either.

'My dear,' one would say to the other, 'I'm afwaid I shall have to wepwimand Wose.' Rose was the small maid, frequently in trouble, at Rambler Cottage. The aunts were now taking Wichard to tea with the dear Wector. 'If only they would make up their minds which way to go!' he thought, standing there with his fists doubled on his hips, tall, thin – far too thin – and still, after the interminable years of war, only twenty-six.

The argument came to a sudden end. The sisters had decided upon the field path. They never went this way after nightfall, they explained, because of the darkness under the elms, but since Richard was with them, it would be all right. Everything seemed all right to the Miss Whartons when Richard was with them.

He helped them over the high stile; first Aunt Emmy, then Aunt Jemmy. Their baptismal names, Emmeline and Jemima, had very early in life been thus shortened. They hurried down the field path now, brandishing their sticks so wildly that Richard often flinched as if about to be hit. Once he would have called out 'Hi!' in laughing protest, but now he said nothing.

Volubly, the Miss Whartons conjectured who would be at the Rectory for tea. Mrs Ware, Mrs Burton, Miss Pike were sure to be there, because they always were. They hoped Pamela Lane was home for Christmas; if so, she would also be there and she was such a dear girl, they assured Richard.

'But if Miss Pike awwives with a bag today,' cried Miss Emmy, raising her stick in a threatening manner, 'you can expect twouble. Because I shall tell her what I think of her and her kettle-holders. There's no social gathewing of any kind in this village any longer but Miss Pike is there to thwust her kettle-holders upon the guests. Well, I've had enough, and today I shall tell her so.'

'You have my full permission, dear,' said Miss Jemmy.

Hurrying over the rough path, they chattered on, but they were not so inconsequent and unobservant as Richard thought and hoped. Their chatter was partly designed to cover his silence, to enable him to be silent. The hearts of the two old ladies yearned over the war-torn boy. They wanted desperately to heal and help him, but feared they did not know how. They feared too that they had annoyed him by that foolish argument at the gate. At least, it appeared foolish in retrospect, because the Rectory was only a quarter of a mile away and what could it matter which way they went?

The Miss Whartons almost always came to this conclusion about their arguments, and would make the warmest amends and apologies to each other, each laughingly protesting that the other was right, or even if she wasn't, it didn't matter.

'It does *matter*, my dear,' one would say, and the other would say, 'No, of course it doesn't.' And they would both laugh heartily. Outsiders were frequently bewildered by this rapid change of front, but the sisters understood each other very well.

They felt, however, that Richard, since he had come home from the war, found them exasperating. They wanted to reform their ways, but they kept forgetting, and behaved as they had behaved for the last seventy years. They were remorseful now and hoped there would be a nice tea at the Rectory, that Miss Pike would not be too tiresome, that Pamela would be there, that the Rector would be able to do something for Richard. They didn't know what, but something. That somebody would do something, since they couldn't. If only they had a piano. It was a dreadful thing to be without a piano for Richard, who was so musical. But there was no room at Rambler Cottage that a piano could have been got into; they were all far too small. Everybody had been so kind, putting their pianos at Richard's disposal, but he wouldn't go and play on any of them. Poor boy – how long would it be before he was healed of the terrible years of war?

Richard strode beside his aunts. 'Why am I going to this place?' he asked himself. 'Why do I drag about like this? I'm crushed. Crushed. Ye gods, what am I doing – going to tea at the Rectory!' He felt, like one about to be given an anaesthetic, a fear of what he might say. He felt he might break out with all his savage, bitter thoughts this afternoon. He felt that the very mildness of the company might provoke an outburst that would hurt his aunts and do what he hated most: draw attention to himself and his suffering.

The bare branches of the elms reached up into the night sky. The little church lay at the foot of the grassy hill. Above it shone a single star. The star of Bethlehem, perhaps. How often he had thought, abroad, of Christmas in England. In the heat of the desert, tormented by dust and flies, he had kept himself sane by thinking of the Pastorale he would write for Christmas when he was home once more. But now that Christmas was here, and he was here, he couldn't do it. He never would do it, he told himself.

They went through the wicket gate, through the church-yard where the old stones leaned peacefully under the yews. In the Rectory drive, Richard halted. He wanted to say, 'I'm not coming in. You shouldn't expect it of me. Damn it all, what do I want with tea at the Rectory?' But when his Aunt Jemmy said, 'Come along, dear,' he went forward obediently.

II

Miss Jemmy rapped with the brass knocker on the white Georgian door. The ladies stood with their muzzles lifted like two dogs waiting to be let in, Richard as if he would bolt at any minute. An ancient maid, far too old ever to have been called up, admitted them to the panelled hall. The Miss Whartons surrendered their sticks as if entering a museum – and a museum this place probably was, reflected Richard, following his aunts up three shallow steps to the drawing room.

When the door was opened, such a rush of heat and noise was let out that he fell back. The room seemed to be full of women and shrieking birds. It was a second or two before he realised that the birds were on the wallpaper and quite silent. It must be the women who were shrieking. Certainly they seemed to be rising at him from all sides, taking him by the hand, saying how d'you do, lovely for you to be home for Christmas, it *is* so nice, are you better, I'm so glad, you're not quite well yet are you, sit here, nearer the fire, have some tea, sugar, muffin, or sandwich.

He answered at random and, sitting down at last, found himself almost at floor level on a plush chair without sides. Queer what a chair can do to you. This one gave him an inferiority complex. It also embarrassed him. When he stretched out his legs, he appeared to be lying at full length; so he drew them up and let his knees poke above his head, since that was the only alternative. His cup shuddered on its fluted saucer, betraying the trembling of his hands. He was annoyed; this wretched tea party had set his hands off again just when he had thought they were cured.

He bit into his muffin. It was cold and damp like a piece of felt left out all night. He put it down and looked round the lofty room. A period piece. Victorian, with the life of the prime mover of that age portrayed in huge engravings round the walls. The Coronation of Victoria, the Marriage of the

Queen, the Christening of the Prince of Wales, the Marriage of the Prince of Wales, August, very tidy assemblies such as we shall not see again. Under them stood a full-sized grand piano. He dared bet, he told himself, that no one ever touched it.

He took up his muffin again, since he had to. If he didn't dispose of it, it would hold everything up. With this piece of muffin, he could prolong tea indefinitely. He thought of doing it, in revenge for having come. But he took another bite and looked round at the company.

Among the collection of felt hats, bobbing in animated conversation, his host's bald head was conspicuous and his hostess's snow-white hair. Also the scarlet cap of a girl at the other side of the room. Not a bad-looking girl either, though he felt no interest in her. He supposed he must have been introduced, but hadn't noticed it.

He located his aunts. Miss Emmy was at some distance. Beside her was a middle-aged woman at whose feet, leaning trustfully like a dog, was a large American-cloth bag, stuffed to capacity. In every pause of the conversation, Miss Pike laid a hand tentatively on this bag, but under Miss Emmy's threatening eye she withdrew it.

In the circle of chairs, Miss Jemmy was next but one to her nephew. Mrs Ware was between them. Richard, having disposed of his muffin and refused all else, now became aware that she was telling him how much money she had made for the Red Cross from the sale of her raffia baskets.

He murmured in congratulation. 'This room,' he thought, 'is frightfully hot,' and wrenched at his collar. Miss Jemmy glanced at him with anxiety.

'That is one of my wastepaper baskets,' said Mrs Ware, indicating a sort of Leaning Tower of Pisa in straw beside the mantelpiece. It was ornamented, though that is not the word, by the usual female figure in a crinoline and poke bonnet. The bonnet hid the face, which was convenient because Mrs Ware was not good at faces. 'I sometimes put a row of delphiniums instead of hollyhocks,' said Mrs Ware, 'and I *sometimes* put my lady the other way round.'

'Really?' said Richard, looking wild.

'Of course, I don't only make wastepaper baskets. I make shopping and garden baskets. In fact, every conceivable kind of basket, and I do so enjoy it. It is my way of expressing myself, you know. The Rector and dear Mrs Kenworthy have always been so encouraging. They have one of my baskets in every room, and since there are twenty-four rooms in the Rectory – a William and Mary house, you know – you will understand that they have been very good customers of mine. Of course, you know,' said Mrs Ware confidentially, 'I made them one for nothing. One for the Rector's study. I left the lady out on that one – just put extra flahs. I thought it was more suitable.'

'Wichard!' cried Miss Jemmy, making everybody jump. 'Piano! Play something while you have the chance, dear boy. Play. Play.'

'Please do,' invited the hostess, rising at once to open the piano. 'I'm afraid no one has played on this piano for quite some time. But we keep it tuned, you know. Mr Wharton, do give us the pleasure of some music.'

III

Richard, looking hunted, went to the piano. He wasn't fond of performing in public, but anything would be better than sitting on that chair, by that furnace of a fire, at the mercy of Mrs Ware and her raffia baskets. He sat down and touched the keys. The piano was all right. What of the audience? The faces, all turned towards him from the circle round the fire, irritated him. 'I wish I liked the human race,' he thought, his hands tentatively on the keys. 'I wish I liked its silly face. Bah!' he thought, crashing out a few of Henry Cowell's cluster chords. The felt hats jumped perceptibly. 'Yes, that makes them sit up,' he thought. But he hadn't made up his mind what to play, so he let them off for a few minutes, playing quietly.

One by one the hats turned inwards to the circle. They didn't know what he was playing. Something modern, they supposed. They tried to look as if they were listening, but they couldn't keep it up. Sitting silent, talk was collecting inside them. Talk is like love; the more it is suppressed, the more it must come out. It gathers force from hindrance. From nods and becks and an occasional whisper, they began to lean one towards the other and a hum arose.

Richard, hesitating, without ceasing to play, between Ornstein and Sorabji, crashed into more Henry Cowell. But they were beyond surprise. They were well away now, he noted, and had given up all pretence of listening.

Except the girl, Pamela Lane. She was directly opposite Richard at the piano and could watch him. 'These young men,' she thought. He wasn't much older than she was, but what he had gone through! He looked savage and bitter, and he played as if he meant to get his own back – possibly on the world. She saw him glance sideways at the company and burst into fresh discords. 'Why must they talk when he's playing?' she wondered. It was so rude. If they couldn't understand, at least they could keep quiet.

The music, though unheeded, was nevertheless having an effect on the company. The louder Richard played, the louder they talked. Pamela sat up straight on her chair, her lips parted in alarm. Richard looked across at her and smiled. He saw that she was in on the game. He burst into Rubinstein's Octave Study, and almost burst into laughter.

The talkers jerked like marionettes. The Rector so far forgot himself as to get up and shovel a lot of coal on the fire. The room and its occupants seemed bewitched. Richard wondered what on earth all the talk could be about. Fragments reached him 'That girl of Swinton's.' 'What – again?' 'Dear Mrs Burton, are you sure of your facts?' 'Those wretched goats – completely eaten the hedge –' 'They say, though of course I don't know –' And the tones of his Aunt Emmy, alas, as strident as anybody's. He looked at her. She had a hand on Miss Pike's bag. 'No, Miss Pike,' she was saying. 'No kettle-holders. I won't buy any of your kettle-holders and no one else wants to. You make a nuisance of yourself at every social gathewing, Miss Pike. Now do be sensible and give it up. Or make something else. Move with the times. Kettle-holders have gone out. All kettles have heat-pwoof handles nowadays.'

But Miss Pike, struggling indignantly, freed her bag and, in spite of Miss Emmy, brought out a bundle of velveteen squares. These she passed round the circle. But the company took no more notice of Miss Pike's kettle-holders than of Richard's music. Absently, talking hard, they passed the bundle on. Until, when it reached Miss Emmy, it remained on her knee, whether from malice or preoccupation Richard did not know. He caught Pamela's eye and laughed outright. Their young faces lit with laughter, they rocked in their places. Everything seemed deliberately funny. She was so glad he could laugh, and he thought she was lovely. That swinging hair, those dark eyes – were they blue? – and that lovely laughing mouth! Why hadn't he noticed when he came in that he was in the presence of a most beautiful girl?

And now an end to all this tomfoolery. 'This is what I wanted to play,' he told her mutely across the piano, beginning the Pastorale. 'This is what I wanted to write as soon as I came home. It's for Christmas. It was like this,' he thought, playing. The winter silence, the Mother and Child, the trustfulness of the animals, the star and the following men. It's old and always new. Simple and still a mystery, holy, homely. 'It was like this,' he thought, playing, listening both to himself and to what was beyond. 'It's like this,' he said to the girl, using no words, feeling his way on the keys. 'Listen. I only half hear it yet, but do you? Can you hear? It's like this,' he played. His face was happy. He looked at her and smiled.

He played as far as he heard. More would come. More would come, now that some strange terrible obstruction in his spirit had gone. His hands fell from the keys. He looked at the company. Everybody was quiet. The faces were all turned towards him, smiling. He smiled too, and getting up from the piano, he went over to Pamela and sat down beside her.

'It needed somebody of his own age,' thought Miss Emmy gratefully.

'Miss Pike,' she cried, startling that aggrieved lady. 'Give me some of your kettle-holders. I'll buy some after all. I'll stuff them and they'll do for the shoes. Now that *is* a good idea, Miss Pike. Stuff the things and sell them as shoe-polishers. They'll go like hot cakes.'

'I believe they would,' said Miss Pike, beaming happily. 'I'll take your excellent advice, Miss Emmy. You see,' she said confidentially, moving closer, 'I had only my old dining room curtains that I could use for the NSPCC and I simply didn't know what I could make from them but kettle-holders.'

'And your windows are *huge*. No wonder you made so many,' said Miss Emmy, now all sympathy. 'Well, I think you'll find shoe-polishers –'

'It feels like Christmas, doesn't it?' said Richard, lighting Pamela's cigarette with a steady hand. 'My first at home for five years.'

'I hope it will be a happy one,' she said.

'It is,' he said, smiling at her.

THE SWAN

Two swans on the water seemed merely part of the dreaming beauty of the Park, where people were allowed in by the Countess who owned it, but was not often there herself. I, for one, had never seen her, and, for most of the time, the Park might have been mine for all I saw of anyone else.

The two swans were usually in view; floating on a lake or drifting down one of the narrow streams, or grooming themselves on the grass. But they were absorbed in their own life; they didn't need or invite notice. There were two, always two.

Then one winter day I saw that there was only one. She was alone at the edge of a pool and there was something so yellowed and forlorn about her that I left the path and went towards her.

She startled me by rising out of the water and coming for me, hissing furiously. I backed away, but she didn't pursue me far. She went back to the water, where she brooded as before. Her neck was thin and her once snowy feathers were stained and bedraggled.

I wondered what was wrong. Had her mate flown away and left her? But swans, they say, are faithful to each other for life.

And if he had gone, why shouldn't she go too? Then I wondered if she was hungry. It was bitterly cold and the water was freezing over.

Glad to have thought of something to do for her – who wouldn't help a swan? I went back to the car at the park gates and hurried home.

When I came back with a bag of brown bread, I approached her cautiously. She rose out of the water at me again, but I stood my ground this time, and when she went back to the pool I threw bread into it and spoke soothingly to her.

I stood for a long time, coaxing. But she wouldn't eat and I had to leave her. Going away, I looked back. In the greyness and the freezing cold, she showed white, her neck curved sadly over the shrouded water.

The thought of her haunted me, and a few days later, as soon as I could, I went back to the park. She was exactly as before. It looked as if, in all that cold, she hadn't moved.

I began to talk to her from far away, to let her know I was coming and to get her used to me. But she came hissing out of the water again. Not for long, though. She soon gave up, as if she was too weak to bother with me.

I saw that the other bread was gone, though I didn't know whether she had eaten it or whether it had floated away. Careful to make no sudden movement, I threw bread into the water and waited.

She watched me with a wary eye for what seemed a very long time. Then suddenly she bent her head, took a piece of bread and sopped it in the water. Then she reached out for another piece and ate that. Soon the pool was clear of bread and she turned towards me, looking for more. I stood there, exulting, throwing bread while she ate it all.

That was the beginning of a friendship. Whenever I could, I went to feed her. She got very used to me. Sometimes she was waiting on the pool under the bridge, sometimes there was no sign of her and I had to call. I called her Beautiful, because that carried well and because it suited her.

The Park was threaded by waterways, branching in all directions. Some streams were clear, some choked with bulrushes, some fell into pools, others spread out into small lakes. I would call this way and that over the Park: 'Beautiful, Beautiful.'

Then far away, down one of the waterways, I would see her coming, small in the distance, growing larger and lovelier as she came, swimming strongly towards me. When she reached me, she made little hoarse sounds of pleasure and ate bread from my hand. I had to be careful she didn't take my fingers with it in her eager beak. I was proud to have made friends with her and naïvely thought I had consoled her for the loss of her mate.

I was wrong.

One day when lambs were frisking round their mothers in the park, I couldn't find her. I called in vain. She didn't come down any of the waterways. As I stood looking about on all sides, a raggle-taggle band of small boys appeared down the avenue. As they came up, I saw they were carrying glass jars containing tadpoles or unfortunate fish.

'Have you been frightening a swan from here?' I asked them.

They stood in a group, looking up at me.

'Oooh no,' they said. 'We durn't go near it. It's savage.'

'It's been savage ever since Jimmy Newth killed the other one with his catapult,' said one.

Shocked and revolted, I looked in silence at their dirty faces, their innocent eyes. This was it, then. This was why.

'Is Jimmy Newth here?' I said.

'Oooh no,' they said. 'He's older 'un us. But he durn't come neither. That swan went for him.'

'Serve him right,' I said. 'He ought to be hurt. He ought to be hurt hard for killing a swan. If the Countess knew, she'd see to it that Jimmy Newth got what he deserves. Where's the swan now? You're sure you haven't been teasing her? She's always been here and now I can't find her.'

'She's over there,' said one, pointing to a pool deep in bulrushes. 'She's making a nest on that there island.'

'Making a nest?' I said. 'She can't be. What makes you think she's there at all?'

'We sord her neck sticking up,' said one. 'You can see if you go round that side.'

I looked at them, marvelling. Why is it that small boys know and see everything?

'All right,' I said. 'I'll go when you've gone. She won't come out while you're here. She's had enough of boys. So be off with you.'

They trudged off with their jam-jars and I waited. Making a nest? She had no mate. She couldn't be making a nest.

But when I went to the pool and peered across the water, she had made a nest all right. Barely perceptible in the rushes, she was perched on a structure of reeds and sticks, and, as I watched, she picked here and there about herself, lifting twigs and leaves and tossing them over her back. She looked as mad as Ophelia. She took no notice of my calling. I had to go home in the end.

I went again and again. She wouldn't leave the nest. Her neck, I could see, was stringy and yellow again. She sat on and on, but no cygnets appeared. I had read up about swans and I knew the time of hatching was over. She was deluded. She was thinner and thinner and I was afraid she would die.

At last, one morning, I left everything and went to the Park. I was determined to lure her off that nest if I had to stop till nightfall. I posted myself on rising ground where I could see her head sticking up out of the reeds like a golf-club, and I began to call her.

I threw bread so that she should hear the plop as it fell into the water and be tempted. I talked to her. I called and called.

Her head was rigid. The water flowed, the birds sang, primroses bloomed under a hedge, daisies sprinkled the grass, lambs chased one another; in all the spring scene only she was out of key. I called and called. I was glad there was no one about. I must have seemed mad too, calling to apparently nothing.

I was tired and the bread was almost gone.

'Do come,' I besought her.

There was a movement. I held my breath. The golf-club head had gone. I saw a rippling line running over the rushes. They parted and in the parting she appeared. Yellow, draggled worse than when her mate died, she made her way through the impeding reeds towards me.

I had won, for the time being. But something would have to be done. I kept her company while she ate – she was ravenously hungry – then I went home to write a letter.

I wrote to the Countess. With no idea how she would manage it, but knowing that she had keepers, other estates and perhaps other swans, I asked her to get another swan to keep mine company. I told her about the catapult-killing and the false nest. I told her all about it and left it to her. I didn't sign the letter. I didn't need a reply, only a companion for the swan if that was possible.

I waited. I kept going to the Park. The swan didn't go back to the nest. She was as friendly as before, but she was obviously pining.

Then, reluctant though I was to go, I had to leave home for a time. As soon as I got back I hurried to the Park. On all the water there was no sign of her and I feared the worst. I felt she must have died in my absence.

But I began to call her. I turned in all directions, calling, making the Park ring.

Then far away, I saw her coming. Down a ribbon of water, she was coming and – I could hardly believe what I saw – she had another swan with her! There were two swans. She had him in tow. She was bringing him with her.

The Countess had done it. How she had done it, I don't know. But my swan had a mate again, and she has him still.

SUNDAY MORNING

At breakfast on this Sunday morning, John West propped up the paper and hid behind it. He didn't like doing it. Phyllis must think he was beginning to get like Robert already. Robert had been Phyllis's first husband and one of the things that had hurt her about him, she had confided, had been his habit of reading the papers throughout breakfast. During the six months of their pretty nearly blissful marriage, John had not once read the papers at breakfast.

But this morning he had to pretend to. He must screen his face from those wonderful blue eyes, or, such was Phyllis's power of intuition, she would divine that he was up to something. After that, it would only be a matter of time before she got it out of him that he was actually going to see Robert today. Then, naturally, she would be horrified. She would suspect him of disloyalty to her. She would prevent him from going. He didn't know how, but he knew she would do it. He could not withstand Phyllis. He was either too weak or he loved her too much. He preferred to think the latter.

So he kept out of sight behind his paper. He must see Robert today. He could bear the load of what he thought of as his own treachery no longer. When he came back from Malaya with no home and no job – the plantation had been ruined by terrorists – it was Robert, his friend from boyhood, who had taken him in. It had been wonderful for a time to live with Robert and Phyllis, but alas, he fell terribly, uncontrollably in love with Robert's wife. He left the flat and Phyllis followed him. John had never faced Robert again. After the divorce, John and Phyllis married and were ecstatically happy. Or would have been, John felt, but for the thought of his betrayal of Robert.

Phyllis didn't seem to mind about Robert. John couldn't understand it, but was glad. It was wonderful to have made her so happy that she regretted nothing.

'Have you really no regrets at all?' he fondly asked her once.

'Only for the dining room curtains,' she said, laughing.

He took it for a joke, but it wasn't. Phyllis was good at interior decoration and the material of her former dining room curtains was something quite special which she had been unable to get again.

Phyllis had thrown herself heart and soul into the furnishing of their present flat. After six months she was at it still. There were new purchases almost every day. John was finding it rather a strain on his finances. His new job in London was not half so well paid as his old one in Malaya. But he told himself he must make allowances for the first year of marriage. Once they were 'set up' as Phyllis called it, there would be no more to buy. They could economise then.

Once, when he diffidently disclosed the state of his bank balance, Phyllis suggested they should ask Robert for a few of the things she might have brought away with her, but had left behind. Such as the dining room curtains, for instance. John had been shocked, but she laughed at him.

'Robert doesn't care two pins for things like that, 'she told him. 'He never even sees them. He's not like you, darling. You do appreciate what I do. You do admit the rooms are beautiful, don't you? You do *like* them?'

John said he certainly did, but he could never take anything more from Robert.

'I took you,' he said. 'I took everything that made life worth living.'

And Phyllis kissed him and said he really was sweet.

But in spite of kisses and blandishments, remorse had worked so strongly in John that at last he rang Robert up to ask if he could see him. Robert's voice sounded just as usual. Just as friendly, just as if nothing had happened between them. John was moved almost to tears when Robert fixed Sunday morning.

'It's very good of you, Robert,' he said with emotion.

'Not at all,' said Robert.

And now Sunday morning was here. John's hand shook a little as he passed his cup round the paper for more coffee, but Phyllis was too engrossed in her own affairs to notice.

John needed no alibi for his visit. Phyllis rarely appeared in the public eye until after lunch and he usually went for a walk by himself in the Park on Sunday morning. When it was time, he sought her out where she was re-arranging the spare room – she was always re-arranging the rooms – kissed her and set out.

Robert still occupied the flat he had shared with Phyllis and as John walked down the familiar street, wide and empty in Sunday calm, he was overwhelmed with shame. What an appalling thing he had done to Robert! He could never make reparation, but he could at least let Robert see that his remorse was genuine. He could tell Robert that he had never meant to rob him of Phyllis. The whole thing had simply been too much for him. He had broken under it and betrayed his best friend.

He climbed the three steps and stood before the dark-blue door. The card above the bell of the ground-floor flat was a fresh reproach to him. Once it had been inscribed: 'Mr and Mrs Robert Mount.' Now someone had run a pencil through the 'Mrs'.

With bowed head, John rang and waited.

A pleasant, middle-aged housekeeper answered. His name could have conveyed nothing of his disgrace to her or she would not have smiled as she did. She took his hat and opened the sitting room door for him.

'Hello, old man,' said Robert, coming towards him.

With difficulty John controlled his emotion. It was too much – too magnanimous altogether. He grasped the offered hand convulsively and couldn't speak.

'Come and sit down,' said Robert, leading him to the fire and sitting down himself.

He reinstalled a cat he had evidently removed from his knee to greet his visitor. A cat was a new departure, thought John. Phyllis would never permit cats. She said they scratched the furniture. John was glad Robert had a cat. Though no substitute for Phyllis, a cat was at least something.

'Well, how are you?' said Robert cheerfully. 'Both all right? Good.'

He offered his tobacco pouch.

'You like this mixture,' he said.

'Er – no thanks,' said John taking a cigarette of his own.

'Oh, I forgot,' said Robert. 'Phyllis doesn't allow pipes, does she? So you've given yours up and I've gone back to mine.'

He smiled genially, filled and lit his pipe and propped his feet against the fireplace. Since there was a dark patch on the Adam mantelpiece which Phyllis had had stripped, pickled and put in, it was probably the usual place for his feet.

John was shocked. He couldn't keep his eyes away from the dark patch. Robert knew perfectly well that Phyllis wouldn't like it.

'Will you have a drink?' asked Robert.

'No thanks. Not in the middle of the morning,' said John with constraint. He would have welcomed some stiffness on Robert's part. This easy assumption that nothing out of the ordinary had happened between them made him feel worse than ever.

'I'll get Mrs Dobbs to make us some coffee then,' said Robert.

'Not for me, please.'

'Oh, do you good. You look cold or something.'

He rang and the pleasant housekeeper appeared.

'Could you produce some coffee, Mrs Dobbs, do you think?' and Robert.

'Certainly, sir,' she said smiling, and withdrew.

'Lot to be said for a housekeeper,' said Robert with an appreciative wag of the head.

'Robert,' John burst out miserably. 'I'm so sorry for what I did . . .'

Robert turned.

'Already?'

'What d'you mean – already?' said John. 'I was sorry all the time. To rob you of Phyllis, to abuse your hospitality . . .'

'Oh, I see,' said Robert. 'I thought . . . but never mind. Carry on, old chap. I see you want to get something off your chest. What is it?'

'What is it?' repeated John. 'What else could it be but to tell you how sorry I am?'

Robert puffed at his pipe and said nothing.

'I played the world's dirtiest trick on you,' said John with emotion.

'But you've been avenged all right,' he went on in a moment, 'The thought of your unhappiness has ruined what might, in other circumstances, have been perfect happiness for me.'

Robert held his pipe with one hand and stroked the cat with the other. An odd expression was puckering his face. For one awful moment John wondered if Robert was going to break down.

On the contrary, it was laughter Robert suddenly gave way to. Very briefly. He quickly suppressed it.

'I say, old man,' he said, almost sucking in his cheeks. 'You shouldn't have distressed yourself like that. As a matter of fact, I didn't at all mind your taking Phyllis off my hands.'

John gaped in amazed silence. It was the most outrageous statement he had ever heard in his life.

'You didn't mind?' he repeated at last in what was no more than a whisper.

'No,' said Robert, shuffling down more comfortably in his chair and changing the position of his feet against the mantelpiece.

John stared, and as he stared a dark suspicion began to push its way through the turmoil of his feelings.

'Perhaps you wanted to get rid of your wife?' he said. 'Perhaps you brought me into your house with that end in view?'

'Don't be an ass,' said Robert calmly. 'You know very well, I was never a calculating sort of chap.'

He puffed at his pipe, while John digested the truth of this statement.

'But when it did happen,' said Robert. 'I must admit it was a considerable relief.'

John fell back in his chair.

'What I've gone through on your account,' he said with feeling. 'All unnecessary . . .'

'Quite,' agreed Robert. 'But there you are. You were always like that. Always putting yourself in the other fellow's place. It doesn't do, you know.'

Mrs Dobbs came in with the coffee.

'Shall I pour out or not, sir?' she asked.

'Yes, you do it, Mrs Dobbs,' said Robert comfortably and John had to wait with what patience he could.

When she was gone, he burst out again:

'I don't understand you. You and Phyllis always seemed to get on together.'

'Oh, we got on,' admitted Robert, stirring his coffee carefully so as not to disturb the cat. 'We had to. There was nothing else for it. But I was worried to death for years. I couldn't keep up with Phyllis's expensive tastes. I never had a penny for myself. Perhaps you've more money than I had.'

'You know I haven't,' said John bitterly.

Robert shrugged his shoulders as if to say that was John's affair now.

'You're not implying that Phyllis left you for me because she thought I had more money than you, I suppose?' said John angrily.

'Dear me no,' said Robert, hastening to deny any such idea. 'Phyllis wouldn't think of that. She wouldn't think of anything. She never does.'

John sat in silence.

'Oh, no,' said Robert soothingly in a moment. 'I'm only just explaining that I'm very comfortable, and if you are too, then anything's turned out for the best.'

'I think it's abominable,' said John. 'Most immoral, that's all.'

'Nay, come,' said Robert mildly. 'Who are you to talk about morals? There was no collusion, I assure you. I'd have put up with Phyllis for the rest of my life if I'd had to. But you came and fell in love with her and you went off together without consulting me. If it's turned out that I'm not exactly broken-hearted, you're not going to object to that, are you? Did you want me to be broken-hearted then?'

'No,' said John. 'Of course not.'

'Then what are you complaining about?'

'I'm not complaining,' muttered John. 'I'm surprised, that's all.'

'Life is surprising,' admitted Robert equably. 'Have some more coffee.'

'No, thanks,' said John, feeling strangely depressed.

'Well, I will,' said Robert, helping himself and clapping his feet against the mantelpiece when he had done so.

'I'm just pulling things round,' he said with satisfaction. 'In another twelve months or so, I shall probably be out of debt. For the first time for a good ten years. See,' he leaned sideways and opened the lid of an antique mahogany desk where the pigeon-holes were stuffed with papers. 'Those are just a few of the bills Phyllis left behind her.'

The inside of the desk so strongly resembled his own, though his was of Dutch marquetry, Phyllis's present passion, that John could hardly bear to look at it.

'Don't look so down in the mouth, old chap,' said Robert kindly. 'It's early days yet. You must begin as you mean to go on. Curb Phyllis's mania for spending and you may be all right.'

'But how?' asked John, and then recoiled at the admission this question was.

Robert, however, seemed to find it natural that the second husband should ask advice of the first. After all, who could be in a better position to give it?

'Well, I should put her on an absolutely fixed allowance,' he said judicially. 'And if she buys over and above that, send the things back to where they come from. And if she won't listen to reason, put a notice in the papers to the effect that you won't be responsible for her debts.'

John looked at him.

'This is outrageous,' he said.

Robert laughed. John was deeply affronted. It was all so unseemly.

'I didn't come here to discuss my wife with you,' he said stiffly.

'I'm only trying to give you a few tips,' said Robert genially. 'I want to help you, that's all.'

'I don't want any help, thank you,' said John, forgetting he had asked for it.

'Well, that's all right then. But one last tip I will give you, in spite of yourself. Beware of Arnold.'

'Arnold? D'you mean her brother?'

'Yes, her brother.'

'But I've never seen Arnold. He's in America.'

'At present, yes,' said Robert cryptically.

'Here – what the hell d'you mean, beware of Arnold?'

'What I say. You'll find out. But don't part with a penny either to or for Arnold. He's a bottomless pit, is Arnold, a leaking sieve . . .'

'I think I'll be going,' said John, getting up abruptly.

'Just as you like. I suppose it is getting on to lunch-time. Only, no ill-feelings, old chap,' begged Robert, rising with the cat on his arm.

'Oh, be damned to you,' said John. 'Where did that woman put my hat?'

'In the hall, I should think,' said Robert, going out with him.

'Goodbye,' said John abruptly. 'I wish I hadn't come.'

'I'm sure I don't know why,' said Robert mildly. 'It's been so nice to see you.'

John plunged past the card with the crossed-out 'Mrs', down the three steps and into the street.

He boarded the empty Sunday bus. Since his marriage, he didn't take taxis unless he was with Phyllis. They cost too much. He had a long ride before him. He had tried to get a flat as far away from Robert as possible. He needn't have bothered, he thought bitterly now. Robert wouldn't have minded coming across his ex-wife and friend every day of his life.

John didn't mind how long this ride was. He didn't want to get home before he had somehow sorted things out in his mind. He had always been a stickler for suitability. He liked situations and sentiments to be recognisable, cut and dried – but what could he make of Robert this morning? Robert wasn't feeling what he had expected him to feel. As a matter of fact, he himself wasn't feeling as he ought to feel. Had he or had he not felt a pang of envy at seeing Robert so cat-cosy, pipe-smoking-feet-against-the-mantelpiece, carefree, so almost debtless? He didn't answer himself. He daren't.

It was essential that he should get himself round again to what he had been before seeing Robert. Remorse and all, he wished he could get back. Swirling round squares, throbbing to a standstill at traffic lights, breasting the long straight roads, he worked to reassure himself, to remind himself of his happiness, or what would have been happiness if Robert hadn't spoiled it.

Robert! It had been Robert before, it was Robert again now. Was he always going to let Robert ruin everything? No, he vowed. No, he was not.

Robert had been very clever. He had lost Phyllis. He needed to make out that he was better off without her. It was a case of the docked fox all over again. Robert must be absolutely discounted.

'I shall go on as if I had never seen him,' John decided firmly, getting out of the bus. 'This Sunday morning shall be wiped out of my memory.'

He looked at his watch and saw he was late. Phyllis didn't approve of his being late for meals, although, being Sunday, he knew it would be something cold out of a tin. But he was sorry to annoy her, sorry to do anything whatever that she didn't like. In spite of Robert, he was sorry, he told himself, rushing up the stairs.

He rang his own particular ring at the flat bell and waited, contrition on his lips.

But he didn't need it.

Phyllis flung open the door and, kissing him, cried:

'Such a lovely surprise for you, darling. Guess what!'

He gazed at her, mutely.

'Arnold's here!' she said.